River of Perfumes

Michael Stokey

WARRIORS PUBLISHING GROUP
NORTH HILLS, CALIFORNIA

To
My Mother and Father
who survived my being there.
And Joni
who endured my writing about it.

And in Memory

Semper Gus
Semper Top
Semper Fonebone

Part One

UPSIDE

Chapter One

ARTHUR LATIMERE WRITHED on the ground. He clutched a rubber-tipped arrow to his chest as Billy stood over him, gloating. Billy Huff always beat him, he always beat everybody. But Arthur didn't care, they were 11 years old and the bestest of friends.

When Arthur grew up he would work, like his dad, at the Atomic Test Facility in Mercury, Nevada. It would be dangerous as could be, but the radiation wouldn't hurt him because of his superhuman ability to withstand its effects. He would glow in the dark, and his friends would avoid him and retreat in awe and horror.

"Arthur Latimere! Billy Huff!" Mrs. Latimere called. "You boys get in this house for dinner!"

Arthur wedged lower as Billy ducked behind a clump of mesquite in the desert. "I can't, Ma," Arthur shouted, and clasped the arrow to his chest. "I'm dead!"

"You're going to be dead if you two don't get in here and wash up for dinner this minute!"

"Mothers," Arthur groaned as he climbed to his feet and kicked at the dirt.

When Arthur grew up, no one would tell him what to do or when to do it. He would prospect the desert and discover a cave that would take him down into the underworld. There would be caverns underground and great ogres to defy him. He would thwart them one and all and capture the beautiful queen's heart and rule her domain with feats of bravery and kindness. And of course he would save a special place for Billy.

Arthur and Billy were inseparable. It didn't much matter that Billy seemed older and worldlier in his ways. It was the kind of friendship known only to kids, when just sleeping over at each other's house was enough to make the world a holy, joyous place. It was a triumphant glee, supreme in itself, an intensity reached only when the two were together. Why bonds like that couldn't last forever was beyond Arthur, but grownups never seemed to have them. Maybe grownups just got too complicated. But that would never happen to Arthur and Billy.

The school year ended and they had the whole summer ahead of them. The desert bloomed and wildflowers peppered the valley. The mesquite and shrubs had turned a bright green and even the cactus had started to blossom. Arthur knew them one and all and had names for each of them.

"Arthur Latimere! Billy Huff!" Mrs. Latimere repeated, and the boys quickened their pace and hurried home.

If they ate quickly, there was still enough daylight to run to the creek and catch lizards. They raced inside and slammed the screen door behind them.

Mrs. Latimere was crying as Billy's mother held her close in the living room. Arthur's heart sank. His mother broke into tears without warning. *Didn't she know he had his whole life in front of him? That he would grow up to take care of her?*

Gladys Huff flapped her hand to shoo the boys away as Helen Latimere looked up and braved a smile: "You boys wash up. We're having company for dinner. Mr. McDaniels and his daughter are coming."

Arthur raced to the bathroom to scrub his face. *Patty McDaniels was coming to his house!*

"You like her," Billy teased.

"Who?" Arthur asked.

"Patty McDaniels, that's who!"

"Nawww." Arthur waved a dismissive hand. "She's just a girl." *But the most beautifullest girl in the whole wide world. She would tease him, too, and tell him dark secrets!*

Gladys helped Helen with the roast in the kitchen, slicing radishes and pinching parsley to dress the platter.

There was news on the radio about the atom bomb tests in Mercury, Nevada. The 1950s was the black-and-white decade, when radio was more colorful than television. Baby boomers were still babies, Elvis the Pelvis rocked the nation, Rocky Marciano ruled the ring and Mickey Mantle ruled the diamond. And women had that flap covering the crotch on their swimsuits.

"Why do you listen to that tripe?" Gladys marched to the counter and turned off the news.

"Arthur's father loved the news," Helen said. "He thought it was educational for Arthur. Besides," she wrung her hand towel, "it fills up the house a little."

"Then listen to music," Gladys said, switching stations.

"I'm not ready for music yet. If I hear Rosemary Clooney singing *Tenderly* one more time...oh, why am I doing this?"

Gladys wrapped her arms around Helen. "Because you need a break from grieving," Gladys said. "Now quit your worrying, it's all very social. My goodness, do you think I'd wish Ben McDaniels on you?" Gladys clasped Helen's shoulders. "Listen to me. Whatever happens to us, whatever has happened, we'll always have each other. Our sons are best friends. They have each other and so do we."

Gladys Huff looked into Helen's eyes. "You gave me Billy. Oh, his father thought it was all his doing, but it was you Helen, you. Remember how frightened I was? A child was the last thing I wanted. You gave me the strength, and suddenly we were pregnant, and we both had boys." Gladys extended her forefinger as if flicking a baby boy's genitals. "My goodness, did you ever imagine those could come from us?"

Helen blushed and covered her mouth. "Gladys, you say the darndest things!"

Soon, widower Ben McDaniels and his beautiful twelve-year-old daughter, arrived. Helen greeted Ben nervously, making a to-do over Patty, to hide her uneasiness. Gladys cooed appropriately then vanished to put the biscuits in the oven.

During dinner, Arthur was so bewitched by the flirtatious young Patty seated across the table that only snippets of conversation registered with him. Never before had he felt so anxious. Patty merely had to glance at him, and his heart pounded like a jackhammer. Once, Patty caught him ogling her, and she winked at him. *Twelve years old and she actually winked!* Arthur lowered his eyes and nudged his food with his fork. *When Arthur turned fifteen he would be bold and brazen and scarred from many dangers and adventures. Patty would kneel at his feet and implore him to notice her.*

The grownups' talk grew animated. Mr. McDaniels was loud and told coarse jokes. Helen Latimere smiled and even laughed once. Arthur kept a watch on old lecherous McDaniels. He didn't like the way he leered at his mother. Thick matted hair covered Mr. McDaniels' arms, and Arthur turned away from his heavy grownup breath.

When they finished dinner, Arthur began removing the dishes from the table. "Go outside and have fun," his mother said.

"Do you want to see our bomb shelter?" Arthur asked Patty. He quivered in anticipation.

"Yes," Patty sighed, and his skin tingled. The nearest he had been to her before this evening was during one of the "duck-and-cover" drills at school, due to the A-bomb tests and fear of the Russians. During the last drill, something daring came over Arthur. Instead of ducking for cover under his own desk, he dove under Patty's instead. Patty only giggled and brushed his hand, causing the small hairs on his arm to stand up.

In the cellar, Patty's mouth fell open in wonderment. Boxes of canned foods, dehydrated rations and survival supplies were piled against the walls. It was really used as Arthur and Billy's private hideaway. There were throw rugs on the floor and the boys spent hours playing Jim Bowie and Davy Crockett, sliding on the rugs as if gliding on magic carpets.

Billy felt bored and strangely vexed. He felt a sense of trespass with Patty in their midst. "I'm gonna go out and run," he said, hoping Arthur would follow. But Arthur didn't.

In this strange way, intentionally or not, Billy always paved the way for Arthur's great moments. And Billy left to run and chase the stars.

When they were alone, Patty raised her arms and stretched for Arthur. She liked the sensation of his eyes upon her. "I like your bomb shelter," she sighed as she batted her eyes.

Anything Patty said in her breathy Southern purr was enough to daze and bewilder Arthur. "It's just a cellar, not really a bomb shelter. Dad liked to call it that."

Patty pirouetted. "Do you think the end of the world is coming?"

"Do you?"

"I hope not. Not till I grow up, anyway." Patty twirled another pirouette. "Have you ever kissed underwater?"

"Underwater? No!"

"I have," she said, twirling again. "Last weekend. We were in the springs and Greg Wilgar swam up to me underwater and kissed me."

Greg Wilgar? Arthur knew Greg Wilgar, the bully of the schoolyard. He had greasy black hair that was combed in a ducktail, wore jeans with French cuffs and nailed metal wedgies on his shoes. Arthur suddenly disliked him more than ever.

"I didn't like it," Patty shrugged. "Not from Greg Wilgar, anyway."

"Hey, you want to go outside and play with Billy?" Arthur asked.

Something danced in Patty's eyes. "I think everyone should kiss at least once before they die. Don't you?"

"Die? Who's going to die?"

"You're supposed to close your eyes."

"Huh?" Arthur said. And just like that Patty kissed him.

It was just a peck, but it made Arthur wobble.

"You're funny," Patty giggled and spun on her heels. Arthur's throat constricted. Arthur knew Billy wouldn't be so clumsy. He would have stopped her in her tracks or planted a good one on her mouth and scared her half to death.

"Do you like the girls at school?" Patty asked. "I don't. They're just girls, you know."

"I know." Arthur tried to puff himself up. He walked around the room. "I like playing ball and doing things with the guys."

"Me, too," Patty said. "That's why I can talk to you."

Arthur didn't know what to say to this. It was impossible talking to a girl. She kidded Arthur about being so shy, which distressed him even more.

Arthur finally persuaded her to go outside, where Billy was running and throwing rocks in the desert. He stopped here and there to shadowbox the sky, which was ablaze with a zillion stars. Arthur and Patty sat on a log, and Patty talked about being twelve...

Yet, even at twelve, Patty thought of decay. *Atomic decay. She knew things would end and she had to prepare. She decided to wear black, no, not wear black, but hoard black. Black in a wardrobe.* Her father stocked canned goods in the bathroom. That's where they would live. She cringed when she thought of having to live there. *In the bathroom with Father,* she gasped, *and she would never go to the bathroom again.* First, she would mash his eyes. No, she would hide. So she prepared black. A black skirt, blouse, black shoes, socks and hat. Underpants black. No one would know. She dyed them black and with her other clothes she hid them in a closet to wear when *It* happened. I will not live in the bathroom...

Pause.

Arthur inched nearer to comfort her, but her eyes came alive and sparkled again with something wild and private and dangerous. She inched the hem of her skirt above her knee, and then reached for his hand. Just then they heard her father and Arthur's mother come outside. "Time to leave, Patty," Mr. McDaniels called. Arthur jumped up, both apprehension and awkwardness turning to relief.

Later that night, after the McDaniels had gone home, Billy slipped a towel underneath himself in bed, just as he always did. Arthur was sleeping next to him, dreaming of flying. He flew often when he dreamed, and now he swooped and soared and plummeted pell-mell into the sanctuary of childhood intoxicants. And what vagaries he inhaled from his childhood! The times on the desert dodging tumbleweeds, the carousels, the sudden rainfalls in the desert, and when the skies cleared, how the air smelled of dust and vinegar...as if the Gods were dying Easter eggs!

He also dreamed of the times on his father's knee, when he promised Arthur he could be an elf. His father's eyes twinkled as he patiently assured him that the following Christmas they would go to the North Pole. When the spirit grew as Arthur grew, it was postponed another year and still another, until finally there wasn't any Santa with elves—and there wasn't even any father.

Chapter Two

JAKE ROARK AWOKE EACH NEW MORNING and took to pacing. It was always so; stalking, circling...the same thoughts imploring, his tongue too full of tomorrows.

He prepared for this night, *his* night, and strode down the town's main street toward certain death. Lightning flashed, thunder clapped. Umbrellas from the audience shot up like flares.

Thirteen years old this very day, Jake looked up at the sky and let the rain rake and pummel him. He loved the wrath of nature and loved defying it. From the corner of his eye he saw the skittishness of the audiences' discomfort.

Even at 13, Jake had a stride and a swagger to him. He planted his feet, Matt Dillon-style. Sonny Beavers, playing the villain, snarled with disdain.

Jake was the marshal of the small-scale town, built of lumber from a construction site. He was the final hope in a white hat going up against all odds.

Sonny cleared his holster when Jake flashed his gun and shot him dead, ridding the town of his evil.

Applause from the parents and neighbors erupted, as much from wanting to flee the rain as from the climax of Jake Roark's play. Then they quickly rose and funneled inside.

Jake bit his lip at the spectacle of Sonny's overacting. Sonny still flailed like a fish when Jake walked up to him, twirled his Fanner-50 and slipped it smartly back into its holster, a la Shane.

When Sonny finally rose he swiped gobs of mud off his sleeves and britches. "This is the third play we've done. How come I always gotta be the bad guy?"

Jake stepped back and laughed aloud. "Hey, you want to be the hero, you write your own dang play!"

Jake couldn't remember the first time he knew, but he couldn't remember not knowing. He was going to be an actor, to set the world on its ear. Blessed from the beginning, he was the only child of a mother who loved him and a father who worshiped him. His father once told him the happiest moment in his entire life had been when Jake was an infant, dressed in yellow overalls with red suspenders. He tossed his son into the air and caught him in his arms and thought his heart would burst into pieces.

Even as a child, Jake bristled with a sense of hope and expectancy, though it was sheathed in an armor that others saw as unsettling. With riveting blue eyes, red hair and high cheekbones, he was far too intense to be thought of as handsome. He cherished his friends, though the girls his age shied away from him. There was something restless and brooding about him, something they mistook as troubling. Yet Jake simply wanted to rush through childhood.

It was the outcasts at school who sought him out most. Jake's manner attracted or repelled at once. Yet even the two bullies who had once beat him up were discouraged in defeating him. Poised and inaccessible, he made no effort to avoid them when they met again at school.

His early cowardice spread through him like a stain. He had learned to distrust authority. Rex, Jake's collie, followed him to school one day when Jake was in the fifth grade. Jake heard him barking outside the classroom. He asked his teacher to be excused to take Rex home, but the teacher refused. Jake never saw the dog again.

He was a natural athlete and competed with a fury. The lessons came hard, but they lasted. *"Safe!"* the umpire yelled as Jake slid into second base after hitting in the bottom of the ninth to tie the game. He slid high, his cleats clipping the second baseman's thigh. The second baseman cursed, threw off his glove, backed up several feet and egged Jake to come at him. Jake lunged off the base and was tagged out to end the inning. The other team exploded in the top of the tenth. Jake's haste had cost his team the game. He could still hear the second baseman laughing.

His early influences were rarely his peers. He loved playing ball but avoided organized leagues and much preferred the pickup games with ragtag groups. They took place in the summer when Sonny Beavers' older brother returned to Los Angeles. There were few freeways then, and orange groves still scented the San Fernando Valley. Each summer, Sonny's brother would round up his friends, because his friends were still there and because few people left L.A. His friends called him Bumper. Jake didn't know why, but nobody wanted to ride in a car with him. A ne'er-do-well, who was estranged from his family, Bumper drifted between the Beat Generation and the dawning Age of Aquarius.

But Jake Roark liked him. Bumper was a wild, smooth, cool cat who had been here, there, practically everywhere. If someone mentioned a little shanty bar in the middle of nowhere, Bumper described it because he had been there. Bumper was a rambler, what they called hep, with the roguish airs of being one step ahead of the guys with the girls—and one step ahead of the law.

Following Bumper's lead, everybody climbed the fence at North Hollywood High School. It was an odd collection of guys and saucy girls, and Jake and Sonny always tagged along. The game was slow-pitch softball and there were plenty of extra mitts. No walks or strikeouts, just stand at the plate until you hit the mother. Bumper's local girl, Deanna, was at his side, with her huge bazooms she aimed at everyone.

It was exhilarating being out in the broiling sun, snatching grounders, dodging tags, turning effortless exercise into spirited feats. Bumper jammed a finger on the second ball hit to him, diving for a ball and skidding on his face, though he could care less about the score. By the third game he was a holy sieve and agreed to catch behind home plate to minimize the damage, or so his team thought. But the first two games he was as feisty as anyone, though everyone saw why. Every time he got a hit and reached a base, if a girl covered it, he made sure he got a handful of tit in the process. That the girls didn't mind wasn't lost on Jake and Sonny.

They took a 20-minute break between games and the older guys and girls gulped down beers.

Paddy was the group's bleeding heart. During a breather someone mentioned the space race with the Russians, and Paddy took the opening to politik. His furtive eyes looked everywhere but straight as he delivered a sermon about all the money being wasted instead of spent on the world's starving multitudes.

Everybody had heard it before, and Bumper asked him why he always reduced things to money. "There's things more important than that," Bumper said. "You want to give something useful, how about your eyes?"

"Huh?" Paddy balked.

"There's all sorts of people blind as bats. You're so concerned about the unfortunate, how about giving up an eye? You don't need two, do you?"

"Don't be stupid," Paddy countered, "you can't do that."

"Can too. Read it in the newspaper."

"Well, I don't know about that, but I got a card here to donate my organs if I die."

"Let me see that." Bumper ripped the card from Paddy's paw. "Dig it, man. Now this is for me!"

"Well, I'm proud of you," Paddy stood. "That's probably the only moral thought you ever had."

"Moral, hell!" Bumper contested. "When I go, I plan to take ten others with me! Can you imagine transplanting my lungs into someone? Christ, he'd be dead of cancer in a year! And pity the poor sucker who ends up with my ticker. Or my balls! Wait'll some bastard needs a genital replacement. Is he ever gonna have to break out the excuses."

After the second game, they started playing something called Windy City ball. Bumper had learned it in Chicago. Played by the same rules as baseball, the ball was twice the size of a regular softball, but no mitts were allowed. The ball was spongy, and to catch it you needed soft hands to reel it in like a football. Everyone was really sloppy from beers and there was practically no defense at all. Bumper played catcher. The score was tight, 15-14 in favor of Bumper's team, bottom of the ninth, and the other team batting. Jake and Sonny were on Bumper's team, with Jake at shortstop. There were two outs and still enough time for Bumper to come through like a charm.

A chunky little thing named Sybil was at the plate. She had a bladder problem and was always wet in the crotch. "No sweat," Bumper grinned, and flashed a bunch of stupid signs that meant nothing to the pitcher. Sybil missed a couple pitches, then popped one up behind home plate. "This is it!" Bumper pantomimed tearing off a catcher's mask and circled wildly under the sun. "I got it!" When the ball hit him on the bean, he crumpled to the ground in a dizzying heap and made broad, flailing movements and Tweety Bird sounds.

Picking his moment, with everyone crowded round, Bumper covered his eyes with one hand and pawed out with the other, until he felt Deanna's knee, then patted his way up to her shorts. Jake and Sonny's eyes bugged. "Oooh!" she squealed, pressing his fist to her crotch.

Bumper yanked his hand free and sprang to his feet. "Hussy! We got no time for that. There's a game on the line, and Bumper means business. Batter-up!" Bumper took his position behind the plate, and sneered. "Play ball!"

On the first pitch, Sybil dinked a squibber with so much English on it that both the pitcher and third base-man flubbed it. There wasn't even a throw to first. Sybil was on base and their best hitter was coming up. He promptly sailed one over the right field fence. That was that. Bumper was the goat, his record intact.

Jake always felt a little sad when he walked home these afternoons. It was a brave new language and a bold new world he glimpsed with this crowd. He didn't resent his childhood. No, he was content. But he ached to grow up, to wrest his future from the Now. He was here and alive. He was going to make a difference.

School started and it bored him more than usual now. To his mother's dismay, his grades declined. *Acting* is what he was interested in. To what end did school or good grades play a part? His parents had instilled in him a love for reading, and his mother's heart lightened when she saw him with a book. He read plays and the normal offerings for his age but discovered other works as well. He read *The Catcher in the Rye* and *On the Road*, and even Albert Camus' *The Stranger*. He had heard of Henry Miller, and wondered what his mother would think of him. But Miller was banned in the U.S., so it didn't matter anyway.

But the passions of his youth were mad and fanatical, flourishing in the hours he spent alone in his room. He shared this tumult with no one, and it was there he held fast to his poses.

One day after school, Jake was at his desk. "What are you writing about?" his mother asked. But it was a different story each week. He continued to write plays to perform for the neighborhood, and of course he was always the hero.

Another day, there was a racket in Jake's bedroom.

"Jake, are you in there?" His mother knocked at his door.

"Wait a minute." Jake hid the sword his father had given him and stood in front of the wall he had thrust full of holes.

"What are you doing?" his mother entered.

"Writing about knights."

His mother looked around and Jake tapped his temple. "In here, Mom, in *here*."

On weekends and summer vacations he walked a mile to the movies and sat in the theater all day. He saw *North by Northwest* 11 times over the stretch of a week, spending hours sitting in the darkness.

One evening as the family sat together eating, Jake's mother asked, "Did you hear about Angela Sedaro?

The newspaper said her father came home and found her dead. She hung herself. You knew her, didn't you?"

Jake's stomach churned. Angela Sedaro was the first girl he ever kissed.

They were in the fourth grade and he and some schoolmates were playing in Angela's backyard. They ran, she tripped, and Jake fell on top of her. It was out of a movie, as seemed much of his life, spinning in slow motion. She calmly looked up at him, inviting him, as no other girl her age had dared. There was something anxious and yet vulnerable about her, and he kissed her. The other kids crowded around and applauded. Angela's girlfriends mocked her afterwards, however, and she never returned Jake's interest again.

Her death puzzled Jake. He didn't understand how someone could not relish the miracle of being alive. He remembered her lips, her panting breath on his cheek and how she smelled of lavender.

Jake continued to spend his free days at the movies. He yearned to act, and he wanted to even more after a local TV channel ran *Rebel Without a Cause* five nights in one week.

James Dean electrified him, and Natalie Wood entranced him. Everything about the dramas and adventures he watched in the dark was locked away in his mind.

Over time, he was drawn less to James Dean and more to Marlon Brando. It wasn't a contest of talent, but style. They each had a presence, but while Dean just wanted to be understood, Brando was a force, he was dangerous. James Dean would come at you from underneath, but Brando stood right in your face.

Jake acted in a play in junior high school and during a pivotal scene, summoned tears beyond his years.

Where did they come from? Jake didn't know. He certainly hadn't any great tragedy to draw upon.

Soon, it was more than the process of performing that seized him. Hungry to taste and ingest these different lives, Jake studied his roles and read extensively. Of the period plays, he wanted to know more than the words on paper. He was curious what they ate and how they lived, how they earned their calluses, how they held the reins.

Still, history was a class that was taught in school, a timeline of events that happened in the past. He accepted it, yet he couldn't comprehend a world without him. What every young man must think, he reflected. But if the world didn't know him before he arrived, it was going to know him soon.

One day, near the start of summer vacation, Jake was walking along a street when Joyce Fite stepped in front of him. She was the hottest girl in school and always unapproachable. Her eyes inquisitive, she tilted her head. "Everybody thinks you're so intense."

"I don't know," Jake said. "What do you think?"

But Joyce only smiled, then laughed and walked away.

A few days later, Jake was waiting for a bus after seeing a movie. A bum staggered towards him. Ragged and unkempt, his breath reeked of alcohol.

It wasn't his uncleanliness that made Jake turn away, but a sickening sense of pity and a fear of contagion.

"Hey!" the bum yelled as Jake boarded the bus and the doors closed. "Don't be so fucking smug, you shit! I was you when I was young."

The other passengers looked at Jake, wondering what he had done to the poor man in the street. As the bus pulled away, the bum pounded on the windows.

Why did Jake hold onto that incident? He didn't know. But he knew there was something important to be grasped.

Chapter Three

THE FOLLOWING SCHOOL YEAR was the most turbulent in young Arthur Latimere's life. Old Mr. McDaniels had packed up his daughter and moved. Arthur still felt a pang when he thought about Patty, but it was only a harbinger of things to come. Now, his only anchor, ever at his side, was his best friend forever, Billy Huff.

October came, and a bright red boil formed on the tip of Arthur's nose. For days that seemed like years he went to school with a hand covering the angry red swelling, and hoped none of the girls noticed it, but everybody did. Every passing day it grew bigger and redder. He squeezed it every morning and after school.

Once, his mother caught him in front of the mirror. "Arty, stop it. Squeezing a boil on your face can damage your brain!" But at 11 years old, nobody has the patience to let a thing like that take its own sweet time.

Winter blew in cold and made matters worse. Arthur's nose got redder, and the kids at school called him Rudolph. His only reprieve was Halloween, when everyone wore costumes to school. Arthur dressed as an outlaw and covered his face with a bandanna. Even so, a couple guys held their hands above their heads like reindeer antlers. Greg Wilgar strode over and pulled down the bandanna, but Billy came to the rescue and socked him in the snoot.

Finally, one afternoon Arthur squeezed his nose in front of the mirror, and a big, green pusy core squirted against the glass. It was the most beautiful reflection Arthur ever saw, and the world was new and alive again.

***

"Hey, Artie!" Billy poked his head through Arthur's open bedroom window. "Come on. I got my BB gun!"

A Saturday morning, Arthur's favorite time of day, when the sun came up and the rest of the world hadn't woken and cluttered things. They ran to the creek to shoot crawdads, but the creek was dry, and they spent the morning peppering barrel cactus and anything else that posed a target. Arthur shot well but nobody beat Billy. Billy had seen *Sergeant York* and made a ritual of licking his thumb and rubbing it against the BB gun's sights like Gary Cooper had in the movie. If there was ever another war, Arthur knew Billy would be the greatest soldier ever, even better than Audie Murphy.

***

Billy Huff's father lost his job. Arthur's mother found part-time work at a local diner, where, after school, Arthur and Billy twirled atop the red leather counter stools enjoying a soda or sundae or an occasional banana split. When they had any change, the boys put it in the jukebox and listened to rock 'n' roll and dreamed about the future.

"One day we'll buy a Corvette together and take off on Route 66," Arthur said.

"Naw, but I'll run alongside you."

Billy loved to run, especially when the wind blew the tumbleweeds in the desert. Billy knew they were nothing but old dead sagebrush, but to him they bounced out of the earth and came alive, and flew at him like phantoms. Billy ran and hurdled them for hours, while in his head Gogi Grant sang *The Wayward Wind*.

Arthur liked to be with Billy and worried his time with him was slipping away. Billy was growing older at a faster pace, so Arthur sought other refuges. For a spell, he had a zeal for religion. He was truly inspired! He saw Cecil B. DeMille's *The Ten Commandments* and was awestruck by the feats of Moses. His mother, faintly interested in such matters, exhibited a welcome calm when he announced his new calling. Arthur remembered how relieved she became and how "tranquil" she said he'd become.

As the spirit grew more and more powerful within him, he concocted a master plan. One day he was up eager-beaver at dawn. It was a gray, cranky morning, with rain in the air. He walked a mile and a half to the foot of the mountains, where he began his search for the "burning bush." He combed the hills, but he soon became disheartened, for there was no burning bush or chorus of angels, no sign at all. Then it dawned on him. God wouldn't repeat the same old miracles. Arthur imagined an alternate plan. God would grant him the gift of flight!

He ran home and prepared in earnest for his conversion. He circled a date on his calendar to give God enough time to think about it. He said his prayers. When he grew up, he would swoop down on every nook and cranny, foiling despots in faraway lands.

On the chosen date, a Sunday, Arthur began his trek to the mountains. Once there, he took a deep breath to sear the moment in his mind, his last moment on Earth he would live as other mortals. Then, he mustered all his courage and took off running. He took a great running leap, leaving the ground in total certitude that if only he believed deep and hard enough and was totally faithful and full-believing, God would inflate His Dizzy Gillespie-cheeks and let go with a gale that would send him whooshing through the air in defiance of gravity. Shock-ingly, it was all run, run, run, and leap, leap, leap, and splat, splat, splat. Arthur pushed further and tried to believe deeper. Again and again he dusted himself off, only to leave his feet, but land achingly on the ground. His knees and elbows were bruised and bloodied. His chest sore, his clothes tattered, he finally dragged himself home in shame and disarray.

To his mother's regret, he renounced his new calling. He grew unhappy and miserable, and had never felt such guilt. At last, he decided to correct these misgivings. Brimming with excitement, he knelt down to pray. He divined to meet God, so He could prove His existence. They would talk things over and then make plans. Having promised not to masturbate, he abounded in hope. Arthur bowed and said his most fervent prayer. When he opened his eyes to discover only his own embarrassed reflection in the mirror, he was dumbstruck. Certainly He was jesting! Filled with bitterness, Arthur's eyes welled with tears. And with supreme indignation, he abandoned his belief forever.

But what a funny boy he was! His favorite hero was Adam Strange, the only comic book hero he ever took to. The other superheroes overpowered their enemies, but Adam Strange outthought them. He was a scientist, and every month a Zeta beam zeroed in on him and whisked him away to the distant planet Rann. He was always summoned in the nick of time and waged war against whatever menace threatened the planet. After he outwit-ted the scoundrels, he ran into the arms of the beautiful goddess, Alanna. But just as he tried to kiss her, the effects of the Zeta beam wore off and he was teleported back to Earth.

Arthur decided to make an Adam Strange costume. He had it underneath his clothes, and wore it to school. It was bright, bright scarlet, a splendid suit, and Arthur's head grew light from the powers it gave him. So off he went, supremely content with his secret.

He couldn't say why these things happened to him this day but he supposed he was prancing about so much it was all inevitable. Billy Huff wasn't around this time when he got into trouble with a schoolyard bully, who called him out to fight. They agreed to meet near a cave in the foothills, but when Latimere arrived, the bully was accompanied by two other boys. In no time they confronted each other but as things got heated, Arthur excused himself and ran into the cave. There, he hastily tore off his outer clothing and leaped out of the cave with the most intimidating thud he could muster. What drama! Oh, the gawks on their faces were ludicrous! Naturally, Arthur mistook their reaction for fear, and bristling with the powers within, he walked up to the bully and kicked him hard in the goolies. A masterful piece of dueling! The bully doubled over and started wailing so suddenly it startled Arthur. Arthur was sure they thought he was loony. He had huffed and puffed so convincingly, the other little snots just backed away. Latimere posed majestically, fists on hips, his hair blowing triumphantly in the wind.

Of course, the story got around about how Arthur wore a ridiculous costume under his clothes and how he thought he wasn't to be trifled with. Finally he had to stop wearing the dreadful thing, reddening with shame at every questioning glance.

**

Helen Latimere sobbed last night, and she cried this morning while sharing coffee with Gladys Huff. "Please don't tell Billy," Helen told Gladys. "I don't want my Arthur to know. His father's life insurance policy runs out soon and there isn't enough work here to get by. If we move away, I don't know what he will do without Billy."

But before long Helen had to tell Arthur of her decision. "We have to move," she said. "We just can't make it. I need to find full-time work."

Pangs of dread stabbed Arthur's chest. "When? Where?" Billy was the first one he thought of. Once again, he felt abandoned, much like he had felt when his father died. Even so, Billy's father also needed work, and it seemed Helen and Gladys had been plotting on their own.

***

Summer came, and both families packed up to find a duplex in Las Vegas. Arthur was ecstatic, and without other friends, he and Billy grew even closer. They discovered a new desert with shale cliffs and wild springs at Red Rock Canyon. It was a bigger world, and Arthur's dreams grew bigger.

The very first week, Arthur rushed outside and jumped on his bike. "Let's go, I'll race you!" Billy said, and he ran alongside as Arthur pedaled to Sunrise Mountain.

They spent the summer playing war and exploring, and they snuck into the big pools at the hotels on the Las Vegas Strip. There were all sorts of showgirls in bathing suits, tanned and long-legged, and while Arthur was simply wide-eyed, Billy had a darker desire in his eyes, and had deeper and more grown-up thoughts.

They slept over at each other's houses, just like they had in Mercury. They watched *Have Gun Will Travel* and

Rin Tin Tin, and scores of other westerns on TV. Arthur liked doing everything with Billy. More than a friend, Billy was also a guardian. He had a wild streak in him, that's for sure, but Billy "wasn't afraid of anything or anybody." Arthur knew he seemed like a kid next to Billy, but Billy always stuck with him and always stuck by him. Arthur didn't know why, except maybe because he knew Billy's one big secret.

Saturday night, they watched *Gunsmoke*, and then climbed into bed. Billy put a towel underneath him. He did it free of worry, because it wasn't necessary. Things had changed.

Arthur remembered the first time he asked Mrs. Huff whether Billy could sleep over. Gladys Huff smiled and pulled him aside. "Of course I don't mind, and Billy would love to. But there's something...we don't know why, but Billy still wets the bed."

Her admission surprised Arthur more than her words. *Wets the bed? Nobody wets the bed at his age.* But the very next morning, the bed was wet, and many times thereafter.

September came, and they enrolled in the eighth grade, and for the first time the two were in different classes.

"Hey, Arty!" Billy huffed after the first day of school. Arthur peddled his bike, and Billy ran alongside. "Remember Patty McDaniels?"

"*Patty?* Yeah, why?"

"She's in my class. She's here at school."

Arthur couldn't believe it. He didn't know the McDaniels moved to Las Vegas. "You mean it?"

"And she's got tits, Arty! I ain't kidding. Nice ones. Like this." He cupped his hands.

Billy kept running. Arthur wanted to ask whether Billy told her he was here, but didn't. He didn't like the way Billy talked about her, either. Arthur wondered whether Patty asked about him.

"Did you talk to her?" Arthur peddled.

"Didn't get a chance. But she recognized me and smiled kinda pretty. You know what else? She sits right behind me! And she poked me with her pencil and smiled."

Arthur didn't feel like playing after school. He followed Billy into the desert, but cut it short. He wanted to be alone and think about Patty, think about what to wear and what to say to her tomorrow, because he knew it had to be fate.

 Arthur rushed from class to see Patty McDaniels when the final bell rang the next day. The secrets she once told him made him tremble. Suddenly, there she was, almost floating on air, and Arthur stood his ground for her to notice him. She was with girlfriends and kept on walking. Hesitant to signal her, Arthur let her walk by.

He didn't mention a word about Patty when he and Billy headed home—not one word and he wasn't going to.

"Tell you, Arty," Billy said as he ran. "Patty has changed. She poked me again. She wouldn't let up."

"Just forget about Patty McDaniels!" Arthur said as he peddled.

"I thought you liked her. You used to be gaga."

Later at home, Arthur walked in circles, and when he didn't walk his brain swam in circles. He thought about Patty all night long. The next day, he waited after school again. Billy ran up to him and pointed Patty out, and when Arthur stiffened, Billy called to her. "Hey, Patty, come over and say hello to Arty."

And Patty came over.

"Hi Patty," Arthur beamed and looked for a sign.

"Arty!" Patty sang and pecked him on the cheek. "You're here, too? I'll talk to you, OK?" And she ran off to her friends.

Deflated, Arthur had hoped to talk to her, maybe ask her to a movie, but it was as though she didn't know he existed.

In the days that followed, Arthur refused to wait for her after school again, and he wasn't about to show Billy he even thought about her.

Inevitably, he and Billy separated a little. Not so much after school, but on Friday nights and sometimes Saturday too.

Arthur heard about the make-out parties. Billy went to the gatherings, but didn't invite Arthur because he didn't think Arthur was interested. And he also didn't want to babysit. Arthur heard everyone changed kissing partners, and some even kissed with their tongues, like the French.

Billy didn't gravitate to the worst crowds, or to the really bad guys who formed gangs and smoked cigarettes or sometimes even sniffed gas tanks to get a buzz. He wasn't interested in them. Billy was just interested in girls.

Still, Billy's escalating attraction to girls made Arthur uncomfortable. *Why couldn't Billy just take his time?* Arthur thought about sex, he had stirrings too. But it didn't have to be every minute.

His feelings ran hot and cold about Patty. Mostly, they were hot, but he would never show it. Once, when Patty approached, he actually ignored her.

It rained the next day, and he waited after school, worried he might have offended her. But Patty wasn't there. She was ill and stayed home.

Billy started to smell older to Arthur. Not like Arthur's teacher's breath when he leaned over his desk to check Arthur's notes, and never as bad as old Mr. McDaniels', but there was a musk in Billy's sweat that was not yet in Arthur's.

Then one day, Arthur's life changed. Billy rushed up to him after school and stuck his finger under Arthur's nose. "Do you smell it?"

"What?"

"I told you Patty sits behind me in class, right?" Billy dragged him aside. "Every day, more and more, she keeps poking me in the side and sliding her knees toward the back of my chair. Well, a couple days ago, I finally slid my hand back and touched her knee, under her skirt, and she spread her legs a little. Hey, you listening to me?"

Arthur's head reeled. "Yeah."

"Anyway, today she does the same thing, but when I reach my arm back and under her skirt, she slides up closer, and I reach between her legs, *and she isn't wearing underpants.* So I fingered her. I *fingered* her, Arty! Then she slides up closer, even moves around a little."

Arthur's heart ached as Billy stuck his finger under his nose again. "Can't you smell it?"

"No. I got a cold."

"I'm telling you Arty, everything's different!"

***

For a few in-between days, Arthur withdrew into the comfort of innocence, when he first met Patty, and he and Billy first met and formed the greatest friendship in his life. Arthur held on to the purity of childhood—his first stirrings and awakenings, even his first smells. The smell of ripe pomegranates swiped from a tree, the thick, dank fragrance of newly mown grass, the odor of wet lumber-yards. He retreated under the umbrella of incredible starry nights and walked aimlessly through the desert, which commenced at his backyard. Arthur was always amazed at how clean the desert was, how fresh it smelled in the cool night air.

But things were different and even Arthur felt a changing and churning.

As that wondrous school year ended, he recalled his first night of passion, of bicycling to Sunrise mountain one night and knowing he was on his way to infinite mysteries and the discovery of dark secrets that were locked up inside Patty McDaniels' young body. Billy told him his plan, that they would see her that weekend, and Arthur asked him anxious questions.

On Saturday night, Billy grabbed Arthur and they headed to the house where Patty McDaniels was babysitting. When they arrived, Arthur's heart was thumping. She was babysitting a neighbor's daughter while her parents went out for dinner. Patty had just put the young girl to bed when Billy and Arthur knocked at the door.

It was awkward at first, and Arthur avoided her gaze. Billy and Patty sat on the floor before Arthur finally joined them. He watched her every movement, wondering what he would find beneath the sheer white cloth. Arthur's eyes were wide, and they joked for a spell and she teased him with her eyes. Soon, Billy was so bold as to kiss Patty, and Arthur watched him put his hands on her breasts and squeeze them. He felt weak. When finally Billy moved away from her, she looked at Arthur and smiled at his innocence. He was certain his body was reeling! But she laughed at his turmoil and extended her breasts for his touch. He cautiously placed his hand on her breast, and his fingers trembled. He was feverish at the touch of this flesh which was at once both soft and firm. He sat there, holding onto her, and would have remained there forever had Billy not laughed at him and guided her to her feet.

Arthur followed them outside. Billy hooked one of her belt loops and she pretended to flee from him. Arthur grabbed another belt loop and they ran and pulled, and were pulled by her, until they reached a clump of mesquite trees in the desert. They knelt and caught their breaths. In a moment, Billy cupped his hand between Patty's legs. Immediately, she removed it, and Arthur was terrified and yet happy the evening was lost! But Patty just giggled, and Billy touched her again. He kept it there, massaging his fingers. Then he unbuttoned her Levis and Patty grabbed his arm. "What do I get?" she said.

"Come on!" Billy protested.

"What?" she insisted.

"We'll give you some money!"

"How much," she said, and thinking this to be the issue, Arthur dug frantically into his pockets. They had $1.28 between them. She took it and said, "OK." Just "OK," so indifferently, and Arthur's whole life hinged on this moment! Patty pulled down her Levis and then her underpants and Arthur was sure Patty thought he would faint. She laughed, and unbuttoned her blouse and lifted her bra and her breasts fell out and shined in the moonlight. Her nipples were hard and pink and bounced with the most incredible energy. Billy put his finger between Patty's legs, and she lifted. It took Arthur's breath away. Arthur's throat was so knotted he gasped for air and Patty giggled at his astonishment. When Billy took his finger out, it shimmered with wetness. Then he asked Arthur. He could not move. He wasn't sure where to put it. What if he missed the "place?" "No, no...you once more," Arthur hesitated. When Arthur's turn came again, he could only fumble between her legs. Her hair seemed to splash and entangle his fingers and he was certain her folds were thwarting him. When finally his finger slipped up inside her he thought his entire soul would burst into pieces! He was sure his eyes rolled ridiculously! His brain was teeming, but it was only a moment before he became absolutely giddy from his accomplishment. His chest swelled with pride and gratitude. What mastery, he thought to himself, and was truly proud of his new authority. He could not stop. He went on and on and on and on and when finally he had to trade turns with Billy, he gleefully washed and rubbed his hands with the goo. *Ah, life was miraculous and women unfathomable in their greatness!* Arthur wished to remain there forever...

When they finally headed home, Arthur's heart quivered. The heat of the hour had consumed him, and he plotted his nights for his entire future. The night air was cool and damp and Arthur kept his hand inside his jacket as if it held a jewel. He took it out every few seconds to smell it, and he cursed the wind for drying the juice, and swiping its sweet scent.

Chapter Four

TIME PASSED, though never fast enough for Jake.

Jake Roark won every audition and earned every lead in every play in his sophomore year in high school. He inhabited his characters in ways that devoured him, and it estranged him even further from his friends. His best friends, forgivingly, simply looked at him askance. Well, Jake's in another play, they said.

The things Jake learned from acting he integrated into his life. He knew the effect he had on others, was acutely aware of his *difference*. For a long time, he thought it was normal, and wondered why nobody else seemed to have *it*, whatever *it* was that made him self-contained.

He still attracted the outcasts, the misfits, the rebels. Jake liked a ruffian in high school named Tony Gibbons. He reminded him of Dick Tiger, the world middleweight boxing champion. Jake liked to watch him because Tony had power and natural grace. But Tony Gibbons didn't like Jake, and was determined to make a point.

More than once, Tony bumped Jake's shoulder in the school corridors, going out of his way as Jake saw it. It was a tedious rite of passage, and one day Jake grew tired of it.

Even though Tony was bigger, all muscle and sinew, when Jake saw Tony coming down the hall, a resolve welled up in him. Jake cut diagonally across the corridor and locked Tony's eyes. His body bristled, not knowing what to expect. Ten feet before Jake reached him, Tony extended his arms to stop Jake's punches, though Jake hadn't even raised a hand.

"How you doing, Tony?" Jake asked, face to face.

"Good," Tony faltered. "And you?" But Tony was genuinely pleased Jake knew his name.

In his junior year in high school, Jake Roark took a shortcut across a field and saw a girl in a hot pink dress. It was spring, the sun was setting, and a golden ribbon of light laced the mountains behind her. The sun bled orange, then red on the horizon, as if fleeing from her beauty. Jake felt himself waver, he didn't know why, but he felt the marvel only a confident girl could exude, the greatest of all life's wonders.

"I've seen you," she said, approaching. "You're Jake Roark."

She said something else but Jake didn't hear. He only saw her lips move. "Excuse me?" His temples throbbed.

"I saw you in a play once. You mesmerized everyone. Even me."

What could Jake say to such an admission?

"Better go," she said, and Jake let her walk away.

For a month, he hoped to see her, and crossed that same field again and again. It annoyed him that she was on his mind, and for the first time he went to parties and gatherings, *forced* himself to go, hoping to see her again.

Jake's passion for drama class abated his frustration. While other high schools in the early '60s did musicals or comedies like *The Mouse That Roared*, Jake's drama teacher staged plays by Tennessee Williams, John Osborne and William Inge. They earned controversial reviews, and Jake was written up. Yet the girl in the pink dress still haunted him. Another month passed without seeing her.

Summer vacation came, and Jake began attending movies again. One day, Sonny Beavers, his good friend, grabbed him for a ball game. His older brother, Bumper, was back.

Bumper's latest travels had changed him. A dark scar ran down one cheek, and the roguish airs Jake once admired had hardened. Yet that wasn't what riveted Jake's attention. Among Bumper's troupe of guys and girls, was the girl in the pink dress. She wasn't in pink, but Jake knew it was her. She wore short white shorts and had her hair in a ponytail.

Jake caught her eye, and she stutter-stopped and brightened. He recalled the smile, her bounce and openness, and approached her as Bumper hit the cooler for a beer.

All Jake's rehearsed lines deserted him again, but this time he didn't care. To his surprise, the words rushed out of him: "I looked for you, but I didn't know your name. Do you remember that day in the field when we talked, I tried to find you. How are you? Do you go with anyone?"

"Wait a minute," she gasped, as Bumper sauntered over and wrapped an arm around her waist. He pulled her hip against his and gave her a squeeze. She pulled away a little, but not so much that Bumper noticed. But Jake did.

They played ball. Intent on making an impression, Jake ran everywhere, dove for grounders and shagged fly balls in everyone's territory.

He hit a home run his first time at the plate. In his second at bat, he missed the meat but stretched a single into a double. His dream girl was playing second base, so that made it even better.

"I don't know your name," he huffed and stood up.

"Nice slide. It's Cherie, and I like you, too."

She said it so openly that it stunned him, causing her to double over in laughter.

Everyone took a break when the game ended and Bumper corralled Cherie to give her a kiss. Bumper saw her glance at Jake, and saw that Jake was watching. Bumper then pounded down beers though it was barely noon.

Later, Bumper brought out a football. "A little pigskin, whadya think?"

Everybody wanted to play.

"Here's the rules," Bumper said. "Touch football, two hands below the waist, nothing rough with the girlies, no stealing a feel. Me and Jake will pick the teams."

Jake was surprised Bumper called his name. Jake picked Sonny, and Sonny pulled him aside after everyone was chosen. "I think my brother's mad at you," Sonny said. "Be careful."

"Mad at what?"

"I don't know, I'm just telling you."

The game started out fun enough. Bumper expounded on the rules. The defensive line had to count three seconds before they charged the quarterback, and only rush with open hands, no elbows or shoulders. Every 10 yard gain, the offense had to switch positions. On the second series, Jake made Sonny the quarterback and put himself at tight end. He caught a seven-yard pass and Bumper tackled him hard.

"Damn! Sorry, kid." Bumper helped Jake up. "Got my feet tangled."

"Bumper, what're you doing?" Cherie stalked up to him. "You said it wasn't tackle."

"It was only a slip." Bumper blew his snot out.

Jake went into the huddle and told Sonny to throw him a square-out. Sonny did, and Bumper charged him but caught nothing but air as Jake scrambled past for a touchdown.

During a break, Bumper hit the cooler again and downed another beer in one long pull. His Adam's apple bobbed up and down as he glugged it, and Jake noticed he had a scar there, too.

"Bump, take it easy." Sonny cautioned his brother.

"Shut up, you dipshit, or you'll end up on the ground like your uppity friend."

Everyone switched positions. Jake's team was on defense, and Bumper moved to right guard. Bumper put Cherie at quarterback.

"Wanna rush the little filly?" Bumper challenged Jake.

The ball was hiked. Jake shuffled his feet and counted to three before he made a rush. Bumper caught him with a forearm and knocked him to the ground.

Bumper extended a hand again. Jake ignored it. "I guess we are playing tackle," Jake said.

"A little wake-up call, sport. Get into it."

Jake knew what was happening. Cherie knew what was happening. Sonny and everybody else did, too. Jake's stomach muscles tightened.

Bumper's team punted and turned over the ball. Jake's team ran a running play that netted five yards. Bumper threw an elbow, which Jake warded off.

"That's more like it," Bumper snorted. "Now you're getting it." When Jake didn't respond, Bumper taunted him. "Not afraid of a little contact, are you?"

"Just wondering about your rules."

"Rules! You simple fuck." Bumper threw his cap off, and Jake braced as Bumper charged. He breathed in Jake's face. "Let me tell you something, sport, I'll fuck with you or anyone else I fucking well want to fuck with!" Jake delivered a right cross with the speed of thought, though there wasn't any thinking, only self-preservation. Jake put his weight into it and caught him flush. Bumper crumpled to the grass in front of him. Jake braced, waiting. He knew Bumper would go berserk when he got up, but Bumper didn't move. The crowd circled and hovered over him while Jake stalked, knowing it wasn't over.

Five minutes later, Bumper stirred, and everybody gave ground around him. As he rose, they chuckled and fawned over him, not knowing what he would do or at which one he would flail. "You OK, champ?" someone asked.

"Bump, how you doing?" Sonny said as he helped him up.

Everybody waited for Bumper's assault. Jake waited too, right along with them. Bumper went to the ice chest. Later, Jake learned that he broke Bumper's jaw.

"I need a beer," Bumper snorted, and splashed it over himself. "Time for beer! I mean *everyone*!" They all joined in.

"Fuck, fucking damn! What the hell am I doing here?" Bumper tried to clear his head. His conversation rambled. As he built up steam, his talk darted from wanderlust to existentialism and to the horrible deadness that lay ahead for all of them. "Dumb, wimpy maggots," he spat. "You punks are so lame. You never been anywhere. I *been* somewhere. Hell, I even saw Elvis Presley at a diner in Texas once. He wadn't no big deal, but I seen him, 'cause I traveled. I got outta this shithole. I kicked a bull rider's ass in Casper, Wyoming. A champion bull rider! I smashed his face against a bar rail. You ever been to Wyoming? Any of you? None of you been to Wyoming? Jesus!"

Bumper never came after Jake again, but 10 minutes later, he was bullying someone else, bone-hurt and broken jaw and all. He shoved the guy who had been fawning and stroking him. Bumper just needed to hit somebody.

The guy backed down, but looked to Jake, wondering why he didn't defend him.

Jake had had enough. "See you, Sonny."

"Hey!" Cherie called as he walked away. Jake had actually forgotten about her. "Do you want to see me, or not?"

"I thought you were with Bumper."

"Proud, proud boy. You don't know anything."

Annoyed, Jake turned, and walked away again.

"Hey," she called, "doesn't anybody ever connect with you?"

Jake couldn't believe her arrogance.

"Do you want to call me or not?" she followed. "If you don't, just say so." Then, she stopped, and turned away.

Jake looked at her, at her all-seething sex and righteous aggression.

"Hey," he called.

She strode up to him. "You're strange." She took the band off her pony tail and shook her head. Good God, Jake thought, as her hair fell down.

"Can you remember my number? STate-40458. OK?"

What the hell was *she* so hot about, anyway? Jake wondered how she was so sure of herself.

He spent the next day at the movies. Jake decided to wait three days before he called her. He didn't know why, but guys were supposed to wait three days. In fact, he got home and called her that night.

He asked to see her Friday night. She couldn't. There was a bon voyage party for her mother. Then, she said she could, even though Jake heard an argument with her mother in the background. Cherie's life was more complicated than he imagined.

They drove to a drive-in movie. Cherie pressed into Jake, kissed him with her tongue and he felt a swirling sensation trickle down his gullet and spin in his stomach. Later, he helped her out of the car to go to the concession stand. It was a chilly night, and Cherie shivered. "My womb is cold." She placed a hand on her abdomen. Jake wasn't sure what a womb was exactly but he knew it was something intimate.

Cherie's home life was indeed complicated. Her mother had left for Seattle to take courses in a new rage called Scientology. Cherie lived with her step-dad. He treated Cherie well, but he was an angry little man who drank at night, yet overlooked Jake's presence because he played chess. Her step-father wasn't very good at it but thought he was, and the competition was enough to keep Jake around.

Jake and Cherie's step-father played chess when he got home from work, after which he got drunk and Jake drove the car around the corner, and climbed in through Cherie's bedroom window.

She was the first girl he ever made love to, but she told him he wasn't her first. Then, she told him something else. She was pregnant.

"Bumper?" Jake asked.

"It has to be, but to Bumper I was only a play thing. Of course, he told me I was special, but Bumper wasn't ever going to stay put."

So she was pregnant and could fuck with abandon. At 16 they could play like adults. Her mother, before she left, had taken care of her daughter's predicament. A Scientologist family in Michigan would house Cherie for three months before the birth. Then, they would adopt the baby and allow her visitation if she wanted it.

Cherie quit school. Jake attended just enough to maintain his grades and star in his senior year plays. He played Hal in *Picnic*, and Starbuck in *The Rainmaker*.

During a school break, Jake auditioned for The American Academy of Dramatic Arts, which was in New York City, and was accepted. His mother and father knew their driven young son was not to be dissuaded and started setting money aside. Jake, for his part, got a job at a local malt shop.

When he told Cherie the news about going to New York, her face went blank. Cherie knew he would leave one day, just like Bumper. Except Jake was more serious and would never be back.

He wanted to take her with him and had it all planned, but Michigan was as far as Cherie wanted to go, and as soon as she could, she wanted to return home. Jake felt the world whoosh out of him.

After Cherie left to have her baby, Jake concentrated on drama and saved his money from work.

Finally, toward the end of the school year, Cherie returned home, trim, tan and full of life. When he tried to undress her the first night they were alone, she stopped him. "We can't go all the way," she said. "I want to go back to school."

"Come with me to New York. You can go to school there."

"You don't understand. I like it here. I want to be home for awhile. Besides, New York scares me."

Jake understood her wanting to go back to school, but didn't understand the rest of it.

Her mother returned with a new lover from Seattle, and Cherie's step-father was summarily ejected from their home.

The following week, Cherie asked Jake to her house. She told him to behave. Immediately, her mother attached him to something called an e-meter, Scientology's crude version of a lie detector and adaptability test. Of course Jake's responses went off the graph, and her mother nodded knowingly. She showed Cherie the results to confirm her suspicions, and kept mentioning the word *clear*, but Cherie didn't care. Cherie only knew that Jake was leaving.

They had a lunch of split pea soup and grilled cheese sandwiches at Cherie's kitchen table. Cherie's mother encouraged Jake's plans to leave. She knew all too well the lessons the two of them had taught each other. She read Jake's confidence as arrogance, even insolence. The conversation sputtered, when suddenly a glass shattered on the table near Cherie's mother. It happened quickly, as if a giant hand swept down and crushed it. Jake looked at the milk seeping into the tablecloth and he felt her mother's breath on him.

Then, she leaned closer across the table. "It was you," she told Jake. "This hostility comes from you."

Jake wanted to challenge this preposterous accusation, but she glared at him so severely there was nothing to add.

Part Two

SOUTH SIDE

Chapter One

THE MEN FIDGET. NOBODY SPEAKS OR JOKES. The CH-46 Sea Knight helicopter sat like a giant praying mantis on the 1st Marine Division recon pad at Danang. All on board sat in stony silence. Private First Class Arthur Latimere was excited however. He had four days in Vietnam and eagerly awaited his first ride in a helicopter.

Fifty miles to the north, the biggest battle of the war raged in Hue City. Private First Class Billy Huff was there, running as always. This time, he ran across the province capitol courtyard, enveloped in clouds of tear gas. He and Arthur Latimere never realized their dreams of cruising Route 66 after high school. Billy's wild nature had produced a string of troubles and misdemeanors and the next thing he knew he was running from the law right into a recruiter's office. Arthur was there beside him, though. If Billy was going, so would he. They joined the U.S. Marine Corps on the buddy system. They went through boot camp together, but immediately after, a bureaucratic error separated them. Billy had been assigned to the infantry, while Arthur was selected to be a Marine correspondent.

Now, like the other Marines raked by fire, Billy zig-zagged across the open pavement. Twenty feet from cover, something punched into his head, and he flopped to the ground as blood and brain matter filled his gas mask.

A moment later, a Marine scrambled over, hoisted him up in a fireman's carry and took him to a casualty collection point. A corpsman took a look at Billy then

moved on to someone who could still be helped. The
Marine who carried him grabbed Billy's bandolier, flung it
over his head and headed back into the fray.

At Danang, sandwiched between Corporals Ehlo
and Bayer, Latimere was an incongruous sight to the
hollow-eyed men crammed into the cabin of the helicopter. They tried not to look at him. There was something
wrong there. Barely 19, he looked 15, and his eyes were as
bright as a kid's on Christmas. Didn't the dumb boot
realize where he was headed? His cheery face an irritant,
the men wondered whether the kid was all together.

On either side of him, Ehlo and Bayer did not look
forward to the flight at all. Ehlo was in a blue funk, having
returned the day before from R&R in Bangkok. Now this
Tet shit. It was all too sudden. Whatever happened to
punji pits and snipers the Crotch had trained them for?
Now, the whole Red Army was sweeping down from the
north—and don't tell Ehlo there weren't any Chinese
mixed in with them. Some of them slopes were six feet tall.
Ain't no Vietnamese gooks that tall, Ehlo thought.

Like Ehlo, Bayer was glum, trapped in the zombie
twilight of where he wanted to be and where he was. It was
OK for civilians, nothing more threatening than day-
dreaming, but in Nam such lapses spelled ruin. Eleven
months in-country, now he was practically a short-timer.
Fifty-two days and a wake-up. He was 21, a California
surfer, and proud he had never let his fears run rampant.
For months, he had buried his fear deep inside him, coiled
snakes in the pit of his gut, with nothing but pangs to feed
upon. During the worst times, he offered only an off-
handed quip or a nervous laugh to break the monotony or
tension around him. Now, in every waking hour, he held

the image of his body lying prostrate in the middle of a nameless road, his hands flailing and his head lopped off, desperately trying to reel it into him.

Bayer forced his thoughts homeward. A joke. Nothing was so great there, either—except maybe for mini-skirts. Bayer's stomach knotted and it unnerved him. He had seen the same fear he now felt in his gut in the eyes of too many grunts during his tour in Nam, and had been mindful, even diligent not to return their glances. Not because he thought their fear contagious, but because he didn't want them to see the fate he saw in store for them. In the rear, he saw them anxious and pathetic-looking, in the PX or at Freedom Hill. Later, he saw them in the field, and helped load their torn bodies onto medevac choppers. Bayer had learned to tell at a glance who would survive and who wouldn't.

Bayer pressed his feet against the floor of the helicopter, as if the mere physical act might marshal his will and give him something concrete to rail against. But now the buried snakes, long neglected in his gut, began to feed and devour one another, emerging as one great serpent, whose venomous fangs injected a stream of fear into every artery and cavity.

Bayer knew it for lunacy. Eleven months he had busted his hump, endured the pettiness of the rear, and in the field fought an enemy he could never get his sights on. All that without any bone-deep belief that Charlie really had his number. Suddenly, he was short, waiting to rotate home, and every little sound was a snigger from Death, a summons from Old Nick for an account overdrawn. Now Hue. *Hue!* The name exploded like an artillery shell inside his head.

More Marines piled noisily into the helicopter. Too many men on board, the pilot ordered them off. The chopper bucked as the troops hopped out. In the cold cabin of the helicopter, Latimere saw smudges of sweat on the grunts' rifle stocks. He caught the eye of a man sitting across from him and smiled, but the man's sullen face was closed. Latimere swallowed and instinctively edged closer to Ehlo. Meanwhile, Ehlo sought refuge in Bangkok again, the five days and nights he spent there in bliss. His heart ached horribly. Bangkok. God, it was heaven! His eyes flickered, but the spark that flared up quickly disappeared. He wished he had never gone. Five days in Bangkok had been like being transported to a different planet. Out of the field and living like a sultan for five days and nights. Women everywhere, fucking, sucking. God, they smelled sweet. Then, on the last morning an alarm goes off, a beautiful girl beside him, more beautiful than any girl who had so much as talked to him back home. He ate breakfast in bed, fumbled for one last piece of ass, and seemingly before he changed his civvies he was back in this hell hole with leeches and jungle rot and Charlie standing by to put a round through his head. Ehlo forced himself to blink.

The pilot flicked the master switch. A high-pitched whine filled the cabin, and the rotors slowly turned, whhopp, whhoppp, whhhoppp, then faster, whacking furiously through the air. The pilot moved the controls, hydraulic pressure surged through the system, and the helicopter shuddered and lifted off.

Latimere had no idea where he was going. The Gunny had told him he wasn't going to the field, not directly, but to a base camp up north called Phu Bai. Jumping beans rattled his stomach, yet the concerns of the grunts, even Ehlo and Bayer, were far removed from the pageantry he envisioned. His mind overflowed with all sorts of things, but that's how poets thought. And Latimere wanted to be a poet.

Incongruously, he thought about Patty McDaniels, the only girl he ever saw naked. Somehow, the thought mixed well with the danger and unknown that awaited him.

The chopper's nose dipped, and it lumbered off the pad and over the rice paddies. The sharp scent of chlorophyll stung his nostrils, and he filled his lungs, awed by the ripe and pungent world he was entering.

The helicopter gained altitude and Latimere again sneaked a glance at the men seated across from him. He fidgeted and gripped his rifle, but no matter how hard he gripped it, he didn't feel any meaner. The men looked older and harder than he, haunted even. Latimere wondered about what had changed them. He wondered what he would do when he came under fire. Naively, he thought about these things and felt a rush of adrenaline and envy.

He had no delusions about his courage. He knew he had to make do, and then his own fear was insulated by a belief that the others, the grunts, were there to fight, while he was there primarily to report, not shoot at people. As a Marine correspondent he would be merely a witness, set apart as it were, like a chronicler, or a God.

Suddenly, the bottom fell out, and the chopper plummeted. Latimere's stomach bucked. An air pocket, only a silly air pocket, but a swarm of bees prickled through his veins, and he stiffened should any nincompoop think he was rattled.

The helicopter climbed until the rice paddies below merged into a patchwork quilt of green and yellow squares, and the mountains and jungles glistened black and purple, beautiful and tranquil from above. Then the rotors screamed as they reached the high, thin air where the first clouds enveloped them.

Chapter Two

TWO MARINE CORRESPONDENTS stood in a misty drizzle at the edge of Highway 1 on the outskirts of Hue. The narrow, muddy road was called the "Street Without Joy" from the days when so many Frenchmen died there in the 1950s. The Marines' teeth chattered, and both men were numb. Their clothes stained with sweat and a festering mildew, they smelled of blood, a sweet, repugnant smell that breathed and incubated inside their clothes, trapped there by a cold, nudging rain.

The second week into the battle of Hue, the fighting raged house-to-house on the south side of the city. The Marines suffered a casualty for every meter taken. The grunts fought savagely to get a foothold, but everyone knew the real battle lay ahead—to the north in the Citadel, beyond the River of Perfumes. Several North Vietnamese battalions awaited them there. Lest the grunts had any doubt, the flag of the Communist National Liberation Front snapped high atop a flagpole above the Citadel's main tower.

The correspondents felt strange to leave the city with the battle so far from over. Usually, they stayed in the field from the day an operation started until terminated. Now however, with no end in sight to the fighting in Hue, they needed to get to the rear to write their stories.

Still, waiting at the edge of Highway 1, the two sergeants were grateful to leave the front, and a spasm of glee whored through them. Jake Roark looked up at the dark sky and chuckled. Tennessee Williams was right, he thought—time was the greatest distance between two places. Willie Grimm eyed him and grunted. The chuckle was typical Roark, wry, sardonic and said he had skated through one week of horror but knew full well the worst was to come. A comforting chuckle, also, because Roark knew for the next two days he could coddle himself in the warm, fat arms of the safety of the rear.

Earlier that morning, less than a kilometer away, the two had narrowly survived a rocket attack, stuffing their heads inside their helmets in a frantic God-save-me embrace. Then, before the flak had settled, they scrambled into the open with the rest of the grunts to drag the latest casualties out of the street. Men they had just coaxed stories from had been suddenly reduced to a mangle of pulp and goo. Roark still had a bandolier of ammunition he'd taken off one of the casualties. Now, barely an hour later, they waited to hitch a lift to the rear to file their copy and enjoy a two day reprieve.

Behind them, a deuce-and-a-half truck swerved up the Street Without Joy toward open terrain and the inevitable sniper fire awaiting it. The truck roared past Roark and Grimm, splaying mud and exhaust fumes. Grimm caught the brunt of the muddy backwash, raised his M-16 as an extended middle finger. Only the rifle's safety prevented him from loosing a burst. Roark doubled over in laughter. God, what a treasure he had in Grimm. What hadn't the two of them shared together? Combat had made them more intimate than lovers. It was a swell of pride and unbridled affection, something to keep a check on. Roark knew it even more than Grimm. Code of the grunt: Don't get too close. To hell with it, Roark thought, they were leaving the front. Just this once he allowed himself a warm glow of devotion and camaraderie.

A long, low rumble of thunder turned into the wop-wop-wopping of Huey rotor blades as two helicopter gunships roared over the city. Rockets whooshed and exploded in the distance. A volley of automatic weapons clattered. Only 25 minutes to safety, Roark thought. He remembered he was 22 years old today and smiled. They were headed to the rear, to warm chow and cold Cokes and a full night's sleep without having to keep an eye cocked open—to where they could finally sleep soundly enough to milk a dream about pussy.

The rain came down harder and their fatigue returned. Grimm opened a four-pack of C-ration smokes and lit one. Twenty-four years old, he was gaunt and wiry with coal-black eyes and a pencil-thin mustache. Roark was shorter, stockier, more intense, his striking features marred by a broken nose he had stubbornly refused to have set. He'd lost his freckles but still had a crop of bright copper hair—a preposterous shock of color against the grays and browns of a monsoon palette.

They waited for the next truck out of the city and a pang set in. Their faces drawn and haggard, beneath the layers of grime and stubble of beard, the hollows of their cheeks were pasty from the cloying pall of winter. Already, the novelty of fighting in a city had lost its appeal. Nothing in the jungles and rice paddies had prepared them for Hue. The first days had been deceiving, disorienting. There was so much confusion about resupply routes that the grunts, depleted of water, greedily scarfed down bottles of Vietnamese beer looted from the shelves of vacated shops. Another oddity: At night, unlike the jungle, they usually had a roof over their heads when they held up in the deserted houses.

Yet, gray mornings turned into sour days. Combat was relentless and during the house-to-house fighting, chards of stucco, bricks and shrapnel flew everywhere. To be wounded in the paddies, you had to get hit outright, ricochets were rare. The city was different. Marines suffered fewer KIAs, but it was hard to find a grunt in Hue without cuts or welts from the searing shrapnel and flying debris. Gore and screams and casualties everywhere, the din of the battle was constant, but the previous day had been the kicker. The day before Grimm and Roark left the U.S. command post in the MACV compound, word came over the net that two Marine correspondents had been felled by a B-40 rocket. Suddenly, the loss of two of their own made it all too personal, and Roark squelched a specter of personal responsibility.

Another truck rumbled over the Phu Cam Canal bridge and clamored up the Street Without Joy. Grimm and Roark charged into the road. The bastards would have to run them over. Incredibly, this truck, too, tried to haul-ass past them, and Grimm thumbed his M-16 to semi-automatic. Another splay of mud followed by the high-pitched squeal of brakes locking, and the two dashed for the truck and pulled themselves aboard. The truck lurched forward as they threw down their helmets and packs and bandoliers, and ceremoniously donned their boonie hats. Then, Roark noticed something sticking out of a pocket of the bandolier he had picked up. A letter addressed to PFC Billy Huff from someone in Las Vegas named Gladys. Roark folded it and put it back in the bandolier.

Two Marine privates rode shotgun in the truck bed. They wore new utilities and shiny black boots, the non-hacker uniforms of rear echelon pogues. Their chinstraps were buckled and each wore a flak jacket buttoned to his throat.

The private with glasses looked at them. "I'd put those helmets back on if I were you. We took sniper fire on our way here."

Grimm spat, uninterested in what a pogue had to say. Neither put his helmet back on. It was foolish and spiteful, but one of the bennies of coming in from the field. After only a short time in Nam, the men in the bush developed more respect for the enemy than for the pogues in the rear. They had something in common, even if it came from opposing sides. The pogues, or REMFS (Rear Echelon Motherfuckers) were held in contempt by the combat Marines. Pogues had little choice about their assignment to garrison but grunts still rubbed their faces into their soft rear-area jobs.

The men rode the rest of the way in silence. Grimm and Roark bounced atop their packs, gazing out at the paddies. Thunder clapped and intermittent squalls and sheets of rain swished over the land. The horizon turned dark and ominous, folding in on itself.

Half an hour later, the truck stopped beside the helo pad at Phu Bai, and the correspondents hopped off. Behind them, Sea Knight helicopters were landing with scores of new replacements from Danang. A gunnery sergeant stood next to the landing pad and barked orders above the din of the spinning rotors.

Roark and Grimm trudged past rows of A-frame wooden hooches covered with olive-drab tarps and spattered red with mud. They shouldered through onrushing troops and scurrying little Vietnamese mamasans. When they reached the hut that served as the ISO office, Roark pulled up short, remembering his .45-caliber pistol. He had taken it off a dead lieutenant, and it had since been a source of agitation between Master Sergeant Grover and himself. Pistols were only issued to Marine Corps officers, machine gunners and bloopermen in the field. Correspondents weren't authorized to wear them. Roark unhooked it from his cartridge belt and Grimm stuffed it in his pack.

They bolted up the three steps and went inside, where Lance Corporal Matheson, a spirited kid full of hot excitability, sat leering at a Playboy magazine. He shot to his feet when he saw them. "Grimm! Roark!"

"Hey, Matty," Roark grinned and gave him a bear hug. Grimm hugged him in turn and acknowledged MSgt. Grover over Matheson's shoulder. "Hey, Top."

"'Lo, men." Grover was 42 years old, a by-the-book lifer with short cropped gray hair and a permanent scowl. The snuffies didn't like him, least of all Roark. Top Grover was like watching a walking time bomb. Roark would walk past him and under his breath whisper, "Tick, tick, tick..." Somebody found out the Top had a son back home who had joined the antiwar movement. There were jokes about that, but Grover didn't smile. Top Grover kept a lid on it until word got out that one of his son's letters had peace symbols on them. That was when Roark said the Top had only a one tick left in him.

Roark and Grimm dropped their gear on the floor. Top Grover hitched up his starched trousers and looked at Roark. "Where's your .45, Roark?"

"You told me not to wear it, Top."

Grover grunted. He didn't care for Roark. The young correspondent's insubordination rankled him. If Roark's bladder was bursting, he'd balk at an order to take a piss. Worse, Roark's attitude made Grover's job more difficult disciplining new arrivals. The Top had also pegged Grimm as a renegade, but Grimm had recently reenlisted, and Grover had leverage to deal with him.

The ISO hooch was cluttered with field desks, filing cabinets and metal folding chairs. There was a mimeograph machine, stacks of purple carbon flimsies, and a half-dozen Remington typewriters on the desks. The aft section of the hooch, obscured by a plywood partition, served as Captain Pell's office.

Roark made a beeline for the refrigerator, grabbed a Coke and tossed one to Grimm. "Ahhh," Grimm belched after taking a swig, "Sweeter than round-eyes."

"You been out in the bush too long," Matheson chuckled.

"There ain't no bush where we been, bro. We're talking city."

Roark looked around. "Where is everybody?"

"In Hue," the Top said. "What are you two doing back?"

"We got twenty-five stories between us, Top," Grimm interceded. "Didn't think you'd want us sitting on 'em."

Roark glanced at Matheson. "You get word about Sully and Wilson?"

"Yeah. What happened?"

"What *did* happen, Roark?" the Top jumped in.

"I don't know, Top. Wilson was with Sully."

"You were assigned to Wilson, Roark. What the hell was he doing with Sully?"

Roark blinked.

"Well?"

"We met the night before at the MACV compound. Sully and Wilson hit it off. They wanted to buddy together, so Grimm and I hooked up."

"Dammit, Roark."

Grimm stepped forward to run interference. "Sully had eight months in country, Top. He knew how to handle himself."

"Apparently he didn't, did he?"

"Wilson's been out on ops before," Roark said.

Top Grover was steaming. "Those were two day-patrols outside An Hoa. This is a goddamn major offensive."

"He wasn't exactly a boot," Roark added.

Capt. Pell called out to the Top from his inner office, but Top Grover didn't hear.

"Jesus Bloody Christ!" Grover seethed. "You tell me how something like this happens. Two correspondents with one unit, and they both get hit?" Grover glared at Roark. "The next time I assign you to watch someone, I expect you to watch him, understand?"

A hot, searing pain coursed between Roark's temples. "I didn't see what difference it would make."

"The difference is I assigned him to you, Roark."

Roark's stomach knotted. He had been in Nam two years and he still had to answer to a lifer like Grover. Roark shifted his weight. "Wilson could have bought it buddying with me, same as Sully. There's enough war out there for everybody."

Grover bared his teeth, his face twitched maniacally, and he swiped spittle from his chin. "Don't get fucking haughty with me, Roark. I know what you're thinking. You go to the bush and swagger back here looking down your nose like some high lama. I know what war is. I did eighteen months in Korea while you were still sucking your mama's teat. Ever heard of Korea?"

"Near Tahiti, isn't it?"

"Let me....oh that's rich, Roark. That's real goddamn typical."

Roark held up his hands in surrender. Grover leaned forward and cleared his throat. "But that's not the point, is it, Roark? The point is I assigned Wilson to you. And that goes for you too, Sergeant Grimm. There's not enough correspondents to go around for you two to be holding hands out there."

Capt. Pell stepped into the room, suspending it in silence. A large, powerfully built mustanger who came up through the ranks, he was a dignified man who was fair to his troops. He took a special liking to Roark, his most dependable and prolific writer. Lots of ink about the 1st Marine Division kept the general and his command staff off Pell's back.

"What's the commotion?"

Grover's face shut down hard. He thought better of a confrontation and reined in his anger.

Pell looked at Roark and Grimm. "Hello, men."

"'Lo Skipper."

"How was it?"

Grimm shrugged. "Not bad. A little hairy."

Pell pondered them a moment. "Well, good to have you back." He turned to Grover: "May I have a word with you, Top?"

Pell headed into his office, and Grover followed. Grover shot Roark a warning glance as he shut the door behind him.

"REMF," Roark spat under his breath.

"Forget it," Grimm told him. "The Skipper's behind you."

"Yeah," Matheson chimed in. "The Top's just a pogue."

"A pogue?" Roark smiled. "You're a goddamn pogue, you pogue."

Grimm and Roark grabbed him and wrestled him into a desk. Grover's voice boomed out from behind the partition. "You men keep it down out there."

Matheson adjusted his uniform. "So tell me, how was it?"

"What?" Grimm asked.

"Hue, dammit."

"It was number ten deep shit."

"Not that. I mean the girls."

"Well, the girls...now that's a different story."

"Yeah?"

"You best believe it. Let me see..." Grimm grabbed another Coke and rhapsodized. "Hue. It's like nothing you ever seen, except maybe in an old World War II movie. It's like Paris must have been in the '40s. No rice paddies, no leeches, nary a mosquito. Just city lights and manicured lawns and women. Women with big plump asses like in Reubens."

Matheson hung on every word. "Damn."

"There ain't any women with big plump asses," Roark said.

"There's women," Grimm said.

"They're skinny as chopsticks, with tits like pimples."

"That's for me," Matty cried.

"You know, Matty," Grimm said, "maybe you should go back there with us."

"Huh?"

Roark joined in. "How about it, Matty? We'll cover you."

"I dunno, guys. I'd like to. You know I would, but somebody's got to make a sacrifice and drive the Jeep back here for Top Grover."

Grover exited the captain's office, his jaw muscles bulging like tumors.

"Sergeant Grimm," Grover snapped. "You and Roark grab a hot meal and a good night's sleep. You got a full day ahead of you. I expect those stories on my desk by 1600 tomorrow."

"Check," Grimm said.

"Top?"

"What is it now, Roark?" he scowled.

"Is Wilson or Sully here at D-Med?"

"Negative," Grover said. "They're both at sea, on the USS Repose." Grover fired up a Lucky Strike. "Sergeant Roark, I expect to see you squared away tomorrow. You're not in the field now. Matheson, you give them a ride to the hooch to store their gear and then take them to the mess hall. No joy rides. I want you back in half an hour. Bayer and Ehlo are due up from Danang with a new arrival. They don't know the lay of the land up here and may need to be picked up."

"Aye-aye, Top."

Grimm and Roark scooped up their gear, and Matheson followed them outside. Roark flung his gear into the Jeep. He wanted to kick something. "Save it for the gooks," Grimm said.

"The gooks are OK; it's the pogues that suck." And to Matheson: "No offense."

Matheson gunned the Jeep, broke into a grin and started singing: "Oh-h-h, we like it here..."

The Jeep lurched forward, and Grimm and Roark joined in.

> ...We like it here...
> You're fucking-A we like it here!
> Although we have malaria,
> We still maintain our area!
> We like it here,
> We like it here,
> You're fucking-A we like it here!

Chapter Three

NIGHT CAME AND WITH IT THE MONSOON. Rain pelted down on the base camp, pummeling the red earth and pinging like bullets off the corrugated tin roofs of the hooches.

Ehlo, Bayer and Arthur Latimere arrived late in the afternoon and followed Matheson into the ISO enlisted man's sleeping hooch after an hour well-spent sipping suds with Top Grover in the office. Shocked, the last thing PFC Latimere expected was to drink beer with a master sergeant. All in all, Latimere thought it pretty neat until an apparent thug named Corporal Hines returned from Hue with a lot of sea stories. Hines didn't have blood dripping from his fangs, but to Latimere he seemed to. For a while, the others got a hoot out of Hines, but Latimere did not. When they left, Latimere was grateful Hines had remained behind with the Top.

The men threw their gear on the empty cots. Old and frayed, Latimere's cot sagged when he sat on it, and the legs creaked. Their sleeping quarters consisted of wood framing constructed atop a raised plywood floor. Topped by a sheet metal roof, wire screening served as the walls, aided by roll down canvas tarps to shield them from the winter wind and rain. Naked light bulbs hung from the ceiling. Some cots had blankets and poncho liners on them, including those of the latest casualties, Wilson and Sullivan. Two pairs of grungy-looking utilities were draped over a makeshift clothesline and Latimere wondered whether the dark splotches were bloodstains.

Cpls. Ehlo and Bayer slumped on their cots and sighed. They had insulated themselves, which was all right with Latimere who didn't have a whole lot to talk about anyway. He sat on his cot, lit a cigarette and listened to the wind smack against the side tarps.

A short distance away in the shower hooch, Grimm and Roark had scrubbed off the stench and filth of a week in Hue. They grabbed their soap and towels, stuffed their bare feet into their boots, and slopped through the mud toward their hooch. As they passed a row of hooches, they heard the sounds of poker games, guitar strumming and raucous laughter. Music blared from tape decks, one song spilling into another. *Proud Mary, Leaving on a Jet Plane*, and almost sadistically, a haunting oriental instrumental. They heard snippets of a radio broadcast from Hanoi Hannah as she implored the U.S. troops to go home. *Hold that thought*, Grimm said to himself.

They raced up the steps and barged into the hooch. Inside with Matty, Ehlo and Bayer, they saw the new arrival, Arthur Latimere. Shivering, Grimm and Roark dashed for their cots and slipped into clean fatigues.

"Hey, dudes," Bayer crowed. Ehlo looked up, but he was still despondent over his return from R&R in Bangkok.

Roark buttoned his fly and smirked. "Bayer, I knew you'd get up here just in time for the mopping-up."

"Shee-it," Bayer said. "Hue, ain't the only battle going on. There's gooks down in Chu Lai, same as here."

"You just thought you'd come up to give us a hand, huh?"

"There it is," Bayer beamed.

"Who's the boot?" Roark asked.

"Arthur Latimere, meet Jake Roark."

Roark walked over and shook the new man's hand. "Good to know you."

Grimm crossed to him. "Latimere? I'm Willie Grimm."

Latimere eyed them both with some awe. The gunny in Danang had called them primadonnas, but the snuffies praised them. He heard each had a Bronze Star and more than one Purple Heart, that both had extended, Roark twice. To Latimere, they now seemed larger than life. He wanted to make a good impression and instinctively stood taller.

Grimm smiled easily. He eyed Latimere's PFC chevrons on his collars and flipped one. "You can shitcan these. Out in the bush you got no rank. If you need to tell 'em anything, tell 'em you're Corporal Latimere. They ain't going to know no difference."

"For real?" Latimere brightened.

"That's affirm." Jesus, Grimm thought, he's a goddamn kid! Were these the kind of replacements they were sending over these days? "Welcome aboard," he nodded. "You're now officially part of a real bastard unit."

Bayer chortled. "Words of wisdom from the company sot."

Bayer jabbed a thumb toward Latimere. "Don't mind him," he snickered. "He's still a little shell-shocked. He ran into Hines at the duty hut."

"Hines?"

"Yeah. Hiney dragged his scraggly ass back from Hue this afternoon with a load of sea stories."

Latimere saw Grimm roll his eyes. Maybe Grimm didn't like Hines, either, he hoped. Still, guys like Hines were one reason he volunteered. To prove to himself he could stand up to them. Latimere wondered whether any of these guys was intimidated by Hines. He knew Billy Huff wouldn't be.

Grimm turned to Bayer. "When did you get in?"

"Couple hours ago." Bayer indicated a case of Black Label beer in the corner.

Grimm lurched for it. "You ain't such a turd after all, Bayer." Grimm punched holes in two cans with his KA-Bar, and the suds flew. He took a healthy swig and held up the can. "Ahh, warm as poontang!"

Bayer groaned. "Grimm, you're the horniest sonovabitch I know."

"It ain't horniness, gookbreath. It's psychology. Something's wrong, you got to tie it in with something right. You'll find that out when you see the light."

"Deep," Bayer mocked. "That's deep. Rhymes, too."

"There it is," Grimm beamed.

Over in the corner, Ehlo sighed. He flung his KA-Bar into the deck, and the steel blade twanged. "Aww, man, this sucks."

"What's eating him?" Roark asked.

"Don't worry 'bout Ehlo," Bayer said. "He's suffering R&R withdrawals. The poor sap fell smack in love!"

"Suck the wart on my ass," Ehlo grumbled.

"No thanks," Bayer chided, "you been sucked enough lately."

The guys hooted. Roark felt an earnest concern. He tossed Ehlo a Pall Mall and Ehlo sighed gratefully. By nature Ehlo was decent and more unassuming than the rest. A homely-looking kid, a purple birthmark smeared his cheek. The men cared for him, too, but damn, so many things would get in their way. All the horrors they had seen had to be released somewhere—on someone. Ehlo was someone. That Ehlo had suffered them also was beside the point. There were just so many things about Ehlo to bait them. Those things took priority. Grimm once noted that Ehlo had lips like Yasser Arafat, protruding, wet, and so reddish as to look obscene—as if they lacked that extra layer of skin which would make them socially presentable. When the men came in from the field, the residue of terror turned to craziness and phony bravado, and needed a release. Naturally, it was unleashed on the people they bunked with. Only with their comrades could they vent their fears, churn them into humor, however sadistic, if only to be outrageous and loud enough to drown out the pain that vomited to the surface.

"Hey, Ehlo," Grimm cracked.

"What?"

"This little chick you fell in love with, was she blonde or brunette?"

"Huh?"

"Was she or wasn't she?"

"Brunette, what do you think? She's goddamn oriental."

Grimm mused. "I was afraid of that. Sounds like the same little piece I shacked up with in Singapore."

Bayer got to his feet and snatched a beer. He turned to Ehlo but he was holding court to all. "Now you mustn't go getting too maudlin, Ehlo. That's what R&R's for. Just a little piece of heaven, if you get my bent. 'Cept you made a big tactical error by going so soon. Bloody suicide taking R&R as soon as you did."

Bayer's brow furrowed. "I warned you, didn't I? I can't tell you how many guys I seen who first chance they get punch their ticket for R&R. They shoot their wad and come back here and for the rest of their tour they got nothing to look forward to. Mental, see?" Bayer tapped his temple. "Next thing you know they're shipped back to the States in body bags."

"Screw you," Ehlo scowled. "I ain't going home in no body bag. I ain't even going home. When I leave here, I'm going back to Bangkok."

Everybody guffawed and gave Ehlo the raspberries. Grimm grabbed more beer and tossed cans to the men. PFC Latimere was thankful to be included. From the hooch next door came strains of The Beatles' singing *With a Little Help from My Friends*.

For a moment they sat in wounded silence. Bayer cursed to break the spell, field-stripped his M-16 and started cleaning it. Ehlo sipped a beer and sat down next to Roark. "Hey, Jake. You went to Bangkok on R&R, didn't you?"

"Yep."

"Did you fall for anyone?"

"Five times."

"What do you mean?"

"Different girl each night."

Suddenly the screen door flew open with a crash and Hines stepped in. Packed to the gills with gear, well beyond the standard accouterments, he had four frag grenades dangling from his web gear. He was drunk but not finished drinking. He teetered for a moment and tried to look menacing.

"Well, if it ain't the Green Weenie," Roark cracked.

Hines blinked, while his eyes adjusted to the light. "I heard you were back, Roark." Hines crossed on wobbly legs. Latimere's shoulders tensed. There was no mistaking the alarm in his eyes. The others restrained their derision. In small doses, Hines humored them. Hines could talk a blue streak and it didn't matter whether what he said was off the top of his head, or even if it contradicted his very last sentence, because to Hines, giving it voice gave it instant credibility. He came at you pell-mell, clackety-

clackety-clack, manipulation in place of logic. With Hines it wasn't language, but a steady stream of noise. Still, they got a kick out of hearing Hines talk, though no one loved it more than Hines. He jawed in "militarese" and had a satchelful of aphorisms. "If you get too close to a prick," he'd say, "you're bound to get pissed on." "There's a whole lot you could say about what could have happened, but for what *did* happen, you best see me." Hines' was always the final shout. Over the long haul the men suspected something tired in Hines, as fatigue turns language to rhetoric. They thought it sad at times. He could bare his soul to a buddy and then repeat the same litany to a stranger. The men put up with it because it was the only time Hines seemed happy.

Hines dropped his gear with a thud at Bayer's feet. His voice was raw and guttural. "What the hell you doing Bayer? That's my rack."

"I don't see your name on it."

Hines grunted and booted his gear under a nearby cot. Then he grabbed a beer, saw Latimere, and his face broke into a grin. "Babysan!" Arthur Latimere winced. It was the second time Hines had called him that. The first was in the duty hut with Top Grover. Right then, Latimere knew Hines was everything he hated, every schoolyard bully who ever taunted him or anyone else for as far back as he could remember.

"Well...?" Hines said, "Lookit him, for Chrissakes. He ain't even got any peach fuzz."

"Cut him a huss," Roark said. "Another week he'll have seen everything you have and more."

"Shee-it." The beer made Hines reckless. Normally, he gave Roark a wide berth, but tonight Hines felt cocky. Tonight, he had a brand new pigeon. "Roark, you ain't showed nobody zip. You take a round in the leg and think you're a goddamn hero."

"You might get yours one day if you ever break away from the CP."

"Hell, I can't think of nothing sweeter than a little million-dollar wound like you got. 'Cept maybe I'd want mine to be enough to get me medevacked out of here. Like a nice little round in the cheek of my ass."

"Ain't much chance of that. You're always sitting on the mother."

The men chortled, and Hines plopped down beside Latimere, patted his knee and leaned into his face. "Pay attention, Babysan. You want to come out of Hue alive, you best get yourself assigned to me. Roark's developing a bad track record."

Roark's eyes flared and bored into Hines. Latimere waited for something to happen.

"Screw it," Hines flipped his hand.

"Gee, Sarge," Matheson deadpanned, "the Beaver is just being a creep tonight."

Hines grunted and dug into his breast pocket for a joint. "Here," he cozied even closer to Latimere. "This is so you can be broke-in proper."

"You got a real stroke of dumb," Grimm said.

Hines lit the reefer ceremoniously and held it out to Grimm. "Want a hit?"

"Negative."

Hines snorted and bucked his head in Grimm's direction. "One of the Old Guard," he informed Latimere. "Grimm's a juice freak." He held out the joint for Latimere. "Go on, take it, Babysan."

Latimere looked to the others for help.

"What's the matter," Hines razzed. "You ain't going to tell Hines you never tried this shit?"

"Once, I did."

"Hell, I thought that's all you guys did back home."

"A lot do. Mostly they say that's what you do over here."

"Whaddya talkin'?" Hines riled.

Latimere fidgeted. "They say there's a lot of dopers here."

"Hippie goddamn bullshit, goddamn bullshit!" Hines passed the joint to Bayer and whirled back to Latimere. "What? We had it, four, maybe five times since we been in country? I been here eight months." Hines spat. "Dopers? Sheeit. You know where that comes from? From pogues in the rear. Let me clue you in, Babysan. Seventy percent of the dudes over here are pogues. Rear echelon, desk monkey file clerks. But they get home and talk shit about all the drugs they did and all the action they saw and everyone believes 'em. I'm here to tell you, anyone talks about all the dope he did, never saw shit. He sure and hell wasn't in the field toking up. Maybe out on patrol or a lousy night ambush, but not on no goddamn operation. Christ, who the hell's gonna be out on an op and fuck with his mind like that? Hollywood goddamn bullshit. Your ass is on the line, and you're going to toke up? If Charlie didn't waste you, your goddamn buddies'd blow your ass away. And I'd have a fucking .45 to your head."

Roark slapped his knee and laughed. "Damn, I thought that man's lips would never stop flapping."

Laughter.

"Hey, Hiney." Bayer sipped his beer. "We never knew you were such a philosopher."

"Yeah," Roark spat out a fleck of tobacco. "Testic-lees."

"Fuck!" Hines, losing interest, slugged down his beer and belched. Already shit-faced, he went for another beer. He snatched the joint from Ehlo, took a final hit, knocked off the ash and put the roach in his pocket. Then, he sat beside Latimere again and placed an arm around him. "It's like this, Babysan. First thing you gotta do when you get to the bush is get the grunts' respect."

"Hines, you're so full of shit," Bayer sniggered.

"Clean your goddamn rifle, Bayer. Not that you ever used it."

"I ain't paid to use it, I'm paid to get stories. Speaking of stories, how many did you come back with?"

"Five. What's it to you?"

"You been out all this time and come back with only five stories?"

"Getting back to the subject, Bayer, in case you lost a marble, you weren't issued that rifle to write with."

"Which is why I'm cleaning it."

"You better clean it nicey-dicey. Oh, you're going to like Hue, Bayer. For once, you're going to be able to see Charlie. Not like in the bush. He'll be squatting on rooftops and peeking out windows and popping up out of sewers. He's going to whisper in your ear and be right up your ass."

Latimere tried to picture it, but Bayer had to laugh. "Hey, Hiney. How come you don't write like you talk?"

"Fuck you," Hines spat.

"Seriously. You're a regular poet. All that angry eloquence."

"Fuck you."

"Then again, maybe you do write like you talk. So I guess there's some consistency."

"Fuck you!" Bayer and Hines blurted together.

Suddenly, two outgoing 81mm mortars *THWUMPED*. The men raised their heads. Then a volley of M-16 fire on the perimeter was followed by several short bursts. Latimere's eyes went wide. He looked at the others, waiting to seek cover—like the old duck-and-cover drills in elementary school—but the men were oblivious. A pop from an illumination round rang out.

"Out-going," Hines said. "Relax, you'll get used to it. You're a lucky boot, Babysan. At least you ain't going to get initiated in the paddies, cock-deep in mud and animal dung. You ain't going to get your hands all cut up and infected with elephant grass, so's you gotta make a fist in the morning just to squeeze the pus out."

Hines pantomimed the process and the men shook their heads.

Roark looked at Bayer. "Don't he talk pretty." Everyone guffawed, except Latimere. To Latimere it all seemed surreal.

"Har! Har! Har!" Hines' mind drifted, and his eyes hooded. He blinked several times and patted Latimere on the back. "Don't you worry, Babysan. Ol' Hines will teach you the skinny."

The others stared as this fell flat. Hines started to stand, but the hooch began to whirl and he slunk back down. He grimaced and doubled over. Then it came to him. He sided up to Latimere one last time, and his eyes turned naturally maniacal.

"See these eyes, Babysan? They looked just like yours when I got in country. In a few months you're going to catch your reflection in a mirror and wonder who the hell's looking back at you."

Latimere's throat closed, and hiccupped. Hines pitched forward but reached out a hand and braced himself. Then, he staggered to his feet, uttered a senseless snigger and collapsed in a heap on his cot. The cot gave way, but Hines only muttered a low, drunken moan.

Exhausted, Grimm rose to his feet. "Well, that's enough entertainment for me tonight, gents."

They downed the last of their beers and ground their cigarette stubs into the deck. Latimere's morale sank. He expected the hazing, but he always believed that some bold act on his part would instantly bridge the gap between boot and veteran. There in the hooch he now felt impotent, tiny. An infantile vengeance blazed up inside him, and his fantasies took on childish forms. He thought about Billy Huff. He wanted to grab Hines and shake him. He sensed the others' eyes zeroing in on him, but in fact, nobody paid the least attention.

Roark placed a hand on Latimere's shoulder. He was smirking as usual, but his smirk was benevolent. "We used to have a guy in the unit named Heckler who did the same thing to the boots when they got in country. I guess ol' Hines never got over it. Welcome to Nam, Babysan."

Bayer slapped his rifle back together and Matheson turned out the lights. With the darkness came groans and yawns, then silence, save for the faint call of crickets.

After a moment, Grimm hollered from the blackness. "Hey, Matty."

"What?"

"Don't make a racket tonight, eh? I got some saltpeter in my pack there."

"Fuck you."

Laughter.

Chapter Four

THE MONSOON RAGED. The summer months had been brutal and unrepentant, and everybody prayed for the monsoon to come early. When the monsoon arrived, the deluge turned the red clay into a quagmire and the mud snapped at their boots like rabid dogs, tugged at them like shackles on the legs of prisoners. There were two seasons in Nam and both were merciless.

Captain Mordecai "Mawk" Pell arose at 0500 as he had each and every morning of his 24 years in the Marine Corps. He finished his isometrics, showered and shaved, and headed for the ISO office. There, he started a pot of coffee and sat behind his desk and peeled an orange.

He was annoyed by MSgt. Grover's blow-up with Roark, and he was doubly vexed that he had to call him on it in front of the troops. *Critique in private, praise in public*, Pell believed, but with Grover it became problematic. He didn't like that. There was enough ill will between Roark and Grover not to add any fuel to it.

Still, there were more important things to think about, like writing letters to the parents of Sullivan and Wilson. Military protocol called for the commanding officer to write the parents of the dead, but Pell's was a small, tight-knit unit and unlike most company commanders, he knew each of his boys well. If one was wounded, a letter to the parents was the least he could do.

More than anything, Pell was frustrated, as was everyone in high command at Phu Bai. A week into the fiercest fighting of the war, cooperation between the South Vietnamese Army and American forces had degenerated into a full-scale goat screw. The small, initial victories the

Marines had managed had been fraught with politics and achieved in spite of it. The high command could crow about one thing only. Captured documents and prisoner interrogations revealed North Vietnamese troops had undergone months of indoctrination meant to instill in them the belief that the South Vietnamese peasants would rise up and join them in their struggle to overthrow the "American imperialists." That the peasants gave little or no support at all must have been a serious blow to the enemy's morale.

Pell poured coffee and thought about Hue. The breaking of the annual Tet truce was one thing, but that the offensive raged even in the sacred city of Hue, saddened him. Hue had been the ancient seat of the Annamese Emperors, once the Imperial City of all Vietnam. Pell had seen her beauty first hand on many of his visits to the MACV compound, which housed a small contingent of U.S. soldiers and advisors and overlooked the south bank of the River of Perfumes. He remembered the beautiful residential streets, the rolling, manicured lawns and the delicate French-Vietnamese architecture of Hue's famed university, revered for its teachings and traditions of the past. Buddhist bells gonged faithfully, and winsome Vietnamese girls with shiny blue-black hair, dressed in billowing *ao dais*, strolled the streets in an affirmation of the Buddhist myth that proclaimed Hue to be the lotus flower growing from the slime.

Since he had been dispatched from Danang to Task Force X-Ray at Phu Bai, Pell had learned a great deal about the city and its history. He had seen firsthand its famous Citadel, a monster city-fortress looming like a great, stone sentinel on the north side of Hue. Replete with ramparts and towers and surrounded by moats, its massive outer wall stood 20 feet high and nearly 30 feet thick and encompassed a three-square-kilometer perimeter. The interior boasted a labyrinth of smaller, inner walls, protecting pockets of small cities and marketplaces. In the heart of the labyrinth, sacred temples stood by palaces with exotic-sounding names like the Forbidden City, the Imperial Palace and the Palace of Perfect Peace.

Pell reflected on what he had read about the Citadel. In 1687, long before the erection of the fortress, the Nguyen war lords established Hue as their capital, while the Trinh war lords held domain over the North. More than a century passed before both rivals' armies were defeated by Quang Trung who drove the Chinese from Hanoi in the bloody Tet attack of 1789. Quang Trung then unified the country and proclaimed himself emperor.

Gia Long, the 16-year-old nephew of the deposed Nguyen rulers, had escaped the slaughter of his family and sought revenge. A decade later, with the aid of French weapons and strategists, Gia Long marshaled his armies and swept through the country from Saigon to Hue to Hanoi, ravaging his enemies and re-establishing the Nguyen Dynasty. Avenging the deaths of his family, Gia Long executed the surviving members of the defeated royal family. The fallen ruler, Quang Toan, was made to watch while the conquerors dug up the bones of his father, Quang Trung, and urinated on them. Quang Toan's arms and legs were then tied to four elephants. The beasts were then driven in all directions, and he was ripped apart.

In 1802, Gia Long quickly consolidated power and ordered a Citadel built to impress his enemies. Erected with the help of French advisers, it was modeled after the Imperial City at Peking. Upon its completion, the French were expelled.

Modern Hue, January, 1968, the Vietnamese prepared for the annual, week-long celebration of Tet to usher in the Lunar New Year. To the Vietnamese, Tet was the equivalent of Christmas, Thanksgiving and the Fourth of July combined. The peasants baked traditional cakes of sticky rice wrapped in sweet-scented *dong* leaves. Houses were decorated, and tea and candies and rice wines were purchased. Children eagerly anticipated gifts and *piastre* notes from relatives who traveled to worship at the family altar. January 30 would commence the Year of the Monkey. Tet was holy, sacred. Regardless of the war, as Tet approached each year, both North and South Vietnams agreed to a truce.

During the night of January 29, massive enemy forces from the North attacked every major city and military installation throughout South Vietnam. In Hue alone, eight North Vietnamese battalions swept into the city and quickly gained control of the Citadel. On the south side, everything was overrun except MACV. The North Vietnamese had cut off all electric and communication lines.

Since Hue was considered the cultural center of Vietnam, the enemy correctly assessed they would only encounter token resistance. They easily secured the city and pulled most of their forces inside the impregnable walls of the Citadel. Then, Viet Cong insurgents were sent out with orders to eliminate those targeted as potential enemies.

They rounded up government officials, city administrators, businessmen, teachers and college students, and a list of "questionable" VC sympathizers who could now identify their infrastructure. Their hands were bound and they were herded to the outskirts of the city and executed.

The next morning at Task Force X-ray headquarters in Phu Bai, all hell broke loose. Lulled into complacency by the upcoming Tet holidays, the military command had taken little stock of intelligence reports that indicated a massive enemy buildup. The response was panic and denial.

"What the hell do you mean Hue's under attack?!" fumed one of the command staff. "It's their goddamn Holy New Year. We had a bloody fucking truce!"

Capt. Pell smiled thinly and felt his mouth go dry. He checked his watch: 0650. He slipped on his poncho and trudged through the swamp that was Phu Bai base camp. The rain had subsided, but the wind gusted and bit into his cheeks. He pulled his poncho hood over him and bulled his way to the large base administration building and ran up the steps. He walked down a narrow corridor to a door marked G-2.

Inside, several Marine officers in starched utilities milled about a table with a large pot of coffee and piles of Styrofoam cups on it. Pell poured a cup and took a seat. Half a dozen aides sat at the ready with pens and notepads. A cloud of cigarette smoke had formed at the ceiling.

Major Grotto, the G-2 intelligence briefing officer, walked to the lectern. Brisk, rigid, somewhere in his mid-thirties, horn-rimmed glasses perched above his Dick Tracy jaw. A large tactical map of Hue was on the wall behind him. Arrows designated the location of various Marine units on the south side of the city. On the north side, inside the Citadel, markers denoted specific enemy battalions and troop strength.

Maj. Grotto cleared his throat. "Morning, gentlemen. It's been pretty much the same. House-to-house fighting with damn little ground taken. Fire support for clearing operations is largely limited to recoilless rifles and tank or Ontos guns. It's obvious to the enemy by now that we're not at liberty to blast them out of there. Battalion still can't get permission from the ARVN command to use air strikes or put artillery into the city. They want their precious city taken back, but they don't want it damaged. There may be a light at the end of the tunnel though, which I'll come back to in a moment."

Grotto took a sip of coffee. He picked up his pointer and struck the map. "Latest intelligence reports enemy troop strength at approximately 7,500 men. As of yesterday, on the south side, we've retaken the ARVN armory, the university and *Cercle Sportif.* Hotel Company 2/5 has secured the hospital. Word from the Vietnamese translators is the NVA took the hospital the first day they entered the city. The civilian patients who were able to walk were tossed out bodily; those too far gone were 'eliminated.' The hospital's medical staff was forced to treat the NVA and VC wounded. In case there should be any grumblings on that score, the NVA executed one of the doctors in front of the rest of the staff to get their point across. Ugly business."

The men shifted in their seats. Grotto lit a cigarette then continued. "At this time, Second Battalion, Fifth Marines, is marshaling for an all-out assault on the sports stadium. We expect heavy resistance there. One side faces the Perfume River, which means casualties could be ferried across to a regimental aid station. So the stadium's the key to any success on the North side. Only trouble now is there's a lot of flak about a North Vietnamese flag flying over the Citadel, in full view of the city and the press corps. ARVN officials are screaming they want the Citadel taken ASAP before the NVA turn it into a propaganda weapon. They're hollering about pressing the attack, but clam up when the subject of shelling the Citadel arises. Seems it's one of the few cultural shrines the Vietnamese have."

An officer raised his hand. "Excuse me, Major."

"Yes, Captain."

"Is it true a new company of ARVN is being moved back into the city?"

"That's right."

"Well, that's encouraging, isn't it?"

"Exactly. A light at the end of the tunnel. Maybe when they take a few casualties themselves, they won't be so stubborn about letting us use artillery. Right now, it's a standoff. Meanwhile, the ARVN are sitting cozy while our Marines are getting their asses shot off. But the ARVN are the ones who will have to shake loose. No way can we cross the Perfume and launch an assault on the Citadel so long as we're restricted to using small arms fire. Some of those walls are 30 feet thick. Might as well use bows and arrows. We have to soften those walls up with something. In fact, we expect to get the go-ahead any time now. So that's the plus side. Still, if it isn't one thing, it's another. We'll get clearance for arty, all right, but with the inclement weather, there's no chance of mounting air strikes whether we get the go-ahead or not." The major paused and stubbed out his cigarette. "Any questions? Very well, we'll brief you men again at 1700."

The officers rose to leave, and Grotto looked for Pell. "Captain Pell, may I have a word with you?"

Pell crossed to Grotto and the major shook his hand. "How are you, Mawk? Heard you took a couple of casualties. They all right?"

"One's fine, that we know of. The other was chewed up pretty bad."

Maj. Grotto lit another smoke, inhaled deeply and forced smoke out his nostrils. "Odd thing about correspondents. They get it into their heads they're somehow removed from the battle. They're out there with notepads and cameras like they're watching a movie. Next thing you know, they're being medevacked. Perhaps you can make it clear to them that if we wanted them to be grunts we would have made them 0311s. We want their stories. Probably the only coverage we can count on."

"Yes sir."

"By the way, Mawk, word from MACV is they've bunkered up a house not far from the compound, right across from the ARVN armory. It can be used as a base of operations for your men and any civilian correspondents they escort. Incidentally, do you have any replacements to send into Hue?"

"Three men came up yesterday from Danang. One's new, fresh from the States."

"Well, it'll be a hell of an initiation. I don't envy him. Had you planned on sending anyone in today?"

"Yes, sir."

"Good. I suggest when they get there they contact a Major Rae at MACV. Also, three new civilian reporters have arrived. We've got them over at the officer's mess. A couple wire-service types and a Limey from some British rag. May need to be watched when they get to Hue. There's been too much press about the looting going on there. The goddamn ARVN have been loading up trucks with everything they can scarf from the vacated houses. Not much we can do about that, but I don't want any stories about how it's the Marines who are pilfering the city."

"I understand."

Grotto shook his head. "Damn! I wish we could throw a net over the whole goddamn thing. Even Cronkite's trying to get in on it. Fortunately, the Army's wining and dining him in Saigon. No telling how long they can contain him though. Just tell your men to make sure these civilians get their facts straight."

"Yes, sir."

"I'll tell you something, Mawk. The way I look at it, Uncle Ho has to be desperate to pull off an offensive like this. We give him a major setback here, we may just end this bloody war."

Chapter Five

> *"HUE – LCpl. Steve Berntson, Echo Co., 2nd*
> *Bn., 5th Marines, single-handedly*
> *destroyed an enemy machine gun*
> *position during the initial assault across*
> *the Phu Cam Canal on Feb. 2.*
> *While walking point, Berntson led his*
> *Company across the canal when*
> *automatic weapons fire began*
> *strafing..."*

Inside the ISO office, Roark and Grimm pounded out stories about the first week's battles in Hue. Mostly small potatoes, the stories were bare-boned action pieces for the Marine Corps rag, the *Sea Tiger*. Sometimes, the stories were picked up by *Stars & Stripes* or a small stateside newspaper wanting to publicize a hometown hero, but that was about as far as the stories got. The civilian reporters working in Danang and Saigon wrote the fat stuff—the big picture—peppered with the predictable slant that went with an unpopular war. The Marine Combat Correspondents (CCs) held them in contempt, and there were more than a few snide and envious remarks about how the "Saigon Warriors" popped in after a particularly vicious firefight, shot their film and bugged out on the next available chopper.

If civilian journalists spent relatively little time in the field, there were times when a CC spent more time in the bush than the grunts. When an operation was terminated, the grunts were choppered back to their base camp, usually rating a few days' reprieve. CCs, on the other hand, might only return long enough to write their stories then be sent back out to cover another operation.

For Roark and Grimm, this hop-scotching to the field was a mixed bag. In the rear, they were sure to be jerked with. A truism of war is that the brass in the rear will run the garrison like a recruit depot. It didn't matter if the rear was one mile or 50 from the "front," their compulsion to keep discipline was paramount. The lifers in the rear were pogues, and they knew it. They held sway over the troops with the only power they had: rank, which meant harassment and "spitshine-and-brass." In the bush, Marines fought the gooks. In the rear, they battled the lifers. Malcontents like Roark and Grimm could suffer anything but pettiness. At least in the bush, no one said boo to them.

Not all CCs endorsed this line of reasoning. Most, like Hines, had the good sense to opt for pettiness over combat, harassment instead of danger. When Hines was sent to the field, he went grudgingly and prayed for a "walk in the sun." When it was a walk in the sun, he feigned indignation and bitched to the Top how his valuable time had been wasted. When contact was made, he took a minimal degree of risk, then returned to the rear with a hard-ass swagger and a thousand-yard stare, letting everybody know he had "been there and beyond."

But for Grimm and Roark and a handful of others, the field was a pardon. The grunts might have to take orders, but not a correspondent. A symbiotic relationship, it was the grunts' job to fight, the CCs' job to glorify it. In the heat of battle, the distinction often blurred, but only on the surface. A correspondent might rush toward the fire, but whatever he did, he did by choice. Volunteering made all the difference. It relieved a CC of the fatalism of an order. With an order, a voice flared up inside, wanting to know why the bastard giving the order wasn't risking his ass alongside.

Of course, no CC wanted to be a grunt. It was one thing to visit the asylum, quite another to be an inmate. The guilt of the liberal versus the reality of the convict. Capote vs. Kafka.

In truth, a gung-ho reporter might be treated like royalty. There were tacit understandings. The grunts craved a shot in the spotlight, something to make their miserable existence more tolerable. A little story in the *Sea Tiger* tempered a lot of hostility.

Roark and Grimm hammered at their typewriters. They chain-smoked and gulped strong black coffee, piecing together stories from the scribblings in their notebooks.

Roark typed "-30-" at the end of the story about Berntson and yanked it from the typewriter. He placed it at the bottom of two other pages and handed them to Top Grover.

"Masterpiece number four," he said.

MSgt. Grover was unimpressed. "There's quantity, and then there's quality, Roark."

"One out of two ain't bad."

Grover grunted, and Roark went back to his typewriter. LCpl. Matheson, always an easy target, was slouched in his chair ogling his Playboy magazine. "Lance Corporal Matheson," Grover growled. "You need something to do?"

"Negative, Top," Matheson closed his magazine and sat up in his chair, but there was nothing for him to do.

Ehlo and Bayer huddled beside the coffee pot and muttered to themselves. Their faces drawn and gray, morning brought with it a bleak reality. They hoped to have time to acclimate to the new base camp, but they were being sent to Hue today.

Their edginess was contagious, and made Grover irritable. His eyes shot to Latimere. "Private Latimere."

Latimere jumped to his feet. "Sir."

"There's a stack of Sea Tigers on the desk. Take a look. Get an idea of the kind of stories we want."

"Yes, sir."

Bayer and Ehlo left, and Latimere spoke up. "Captain Pell?"

"Yes, Private."

"Am I going with them, sir?"

"Negative, Private Latimere. Not today. Why don't you and I have a little chat in my office."

"Yes, sir."

Arthur Latimere sat upright in a metal chair in front of Pell's desk. Pell indicated a bowl of candies on his desk. "Mint?"

"No, thank you, sir."

"You eat at the mess hall this morning, Private Latimere?"

"Sort of."

"It's not the best chow in the world."

"No, sir," Latimere smiled, "it isn't."

"Where were you stationed after boot camp, Private Latimere?"

"Camp Pendleton, sir, but only about a month."

"They didn't waste any time sending you over."

"I sort of volunteered."

"Why?"

"I have a buddy over here. And I was curious."

"What do you want to do with yourself, Private Latimere?"

"Here, sir?"

"No. With your life."

"What I really want to do is write. First, I need something to write about, though. Something more to write about, I mean."

Pell paused. Latimere began feeling more at ease. "Do you have a girlfriend back home, Private?"

"No, sir, not really."

"That's good. It's a help sometimes, not to have one. Over here, it's a plus. Helps you keep your mind on things." Then, a smile crept across Pell's face and he raised an eyebrow. "I suppose Hines gave you the treatment."

"Huh?" said Latimere, surprised. "I guess you'd call it that."

"Well, I wouldn't put too much stock in that. Don't let your imagination run wild. Half the men they send over here expect to get shot at getting off the plane. Anyway, save your energy until you get to Hue. Every man here has been through exactly the same thing you're going through now. The not knowing, that's the toughest."

Grateful, Latimere nodded. "Yes, sir, thank you. Sir?"

"Yes, Private."

"I was wondering if you're going to send me out soon."

"Yes. Could be tomorrow." Pell frowned. God, how he hated sending someone out on his first operation.

"One more thing," Pell said. "I don't want you concerned with bringing back stories. This is your first operation, just get acclimated. I'm assigning you to Sergeant Roark. Stick close to him."

"Yes, s..." Latimere stopped himself from saying sir again, since the others all called the captain "Skipper."

"Any questions?"

"No, sir. I mean Captain, Skipper." Latimere wouldn't have known where to start.

Pell leaned forward. "You'll do fine, Private Latimere. You know why? When you come under fire you'll be too ashamed not to. That's pretty much how it works."

Latimere spent the rest of the day new-guy dumb. His day, unproductive and interminably long, was filled with too many questions for which there were really no answers short of being shot at. He did learn something interesting, however. He heard Roark wanted to be an actor. Latimere thought it strange he knew someone who wanted to be an actor. Latimere didn't know whether to believe it, but he wanted to. He felt a kinship with Roark wanting to be an actor, while he wanted to be a poet. But mostly, the day dragged grudgingly, with little to do but watch the guys write.

When night came, the men were tired and sacked-out early. Not much talk in the sleeping hooch, there was no grab-ass or beer or the vitality of any energy. Even Hines barely mustered a half-hearted swagger. Everyone was bent on cocooning, priming himself for the front tomorrow.

Chapter Six

DAWN SNUCK UP like a guerrilla, and it was dingy and gray as the dusk. The wind soughed, sending little ripples down the canvas tarp, and the sidings flapped a reveille. Roark awoke first. It was always so. Regardless of the demons the night delivered him, he awoke with a jolt, percolating inside, ready to face a brand new day. His optimism ebbed quickly this morning however, as the realization of where he was headed hit him. Worst of all was the murky morning, cold and gray and compressing. He hated the monsoon mornings.

Grimm heard Roark's cot creak and sat up, pumping his legs up and down like pistons. He shivered and pulled a blanket around his shoulders. His nose and the tips of his ears were red, and he could see his own breath. He kicked Hines' cot, but Hines only grumbled. Matheson, who wasn't going anywhere, continued to snore, but Arthur Latimere stirred and looked up with bleary eyes.

The men sat silently, shivering in spasms. Latimere thought they were morose this morning, locked in a place that he couldn't reach. Grimm shrugged off his blanket and scratched himself. His gaunt, haggard body looked knobby and disjointed, with bones punching through in all directions. He had the long, thin body of Don Quixote, but he wasn't the slayer of windmills, Latimere knew straight away, because Grimm's eyes were marooned with beware signs in them.

Roark pulled on his utilities and told Latimere to "get a hop on." Latimere thought he seemed in an awfully big hurry just to get to the crummy mess hall.

They got their gear and packs together and headed out. Morning hackings emanated from the hooches as the base camp staggered to life. Grimm noticed a Nikon camera hanging around Latimere's neck and asked, "Where the hell you get that?"

"Brought it from home," Latimere smiled.

"Well, don't get cocky out there. You're a writer, not a photog. We get to Hue, you put that in your pack."

Latimere said nothing but couldn't shake a sinking feeling that the guys were spooked.

Grimm and Roark walked purposefully, while Latimere slogged along behind them, glad the ground was muddy because it hid the shine on his new jungle boots. He tried to keep pace but felt awkward in his gear, and it flapped and made a racket. He was relieved he was heading to a city on his first operation and not into the jungle. He heard all the stories about the "wait-a-minute" boots who couldn't walk down a trail without getting snagged on something. A whole column of men could precede them, slipping through the jungle like oily eels, then comes the boot, noisy as a frat party, and a helmet falls off or his gear gets snagged, and the whole damn company has to stop and wait for him.

They were the first to reach the mess hall, but it filled up quickly. A rash of obscenities greeted the green scrambled eggs and gummy chipped beef on toast. Metal utensils struck the mess trays with obnoxious twangs.

Nobody had much of an appetite, and Roark pushed his gruel around with a piece of burnt toast. Latimere glanced at Grimm and Roark, whom he had liked up to now. Now, however, they made him nervous. Latimere slid his mess tray away. Damn, he thought, a week in country already. Is that all it was? A whole week, and he didn't know a thing. He wondered what he would be thinking tomorrow. By tomorrow, he would probably know plenty. He thought about Hue and pictured a barrage of fire driving him to the dirt and kicking up all around him. He wondered whether he'd have the nerve to raise his head—and more than that, to not only look up but fire back.

Roark sipped his coffee which was weak but hot. Little things gnawed at him. He thought about the influx of ARVN into the city, South Vietnamese soldiers who frequently ran at the first sound of fire. He ground his teeth. What gnawed at him most though was Latimere. "Baby-san," he thought, now there's a name for you. Roark looked at Latimere and took him in full for the first time this morning. Good looking kid, straight off the covers of the *Saturday Evening Post* with those cowlicks and lollipop eyes. Once again miffed that he had been assigned the responsibility for someone else's safety, Roark knew he'd be lucky to make it through Hue on his own without having to nursemaid a cherry. He should have been used to it. He was always getting stuck with a new guy. For some of the CCs, it was the perfect excuse not to take chances. But Roark never liked it. Breaking in a boot was a shit job. He was always looking over his shoulder to see whether the kid had stumbled or bought it. That duty should go to someone more responsible, less impulsive, like Ehlo or Bayer.

It was colder when they went outside and the wind was snapping. They headed for the landing strip, and the clamorous revving of Jeeps and trucks was soon drowned out by the drone of helicopters. Latimere felt a charge riddle through him. Maybe it riddled through Grimm and Roark, too, because Latimere sensed a corner had been turned, and their sullenness gave way to single-mindedness. It was as if they knew where they were heading, and there was no turning back. It was gut-check time.

A flurry of activity at the LZ, Huey gunships and Sea Knight helicopters were lifting off the tarmac. Three trucks idled next to the airstrip, and troops were busy loading C-rations and crates of ammunition into the beds. A ruddy faced staff sergeant swaggered up. "Shag ass! Get a move on! Load 'em up!"

Roark pulled Latimere beneath the overhang of one of the hooches. No point in being mistaken for supply troops. Don't look ambitious, keep out of the way, that sort of thing.

Somebody yelled behind them, and they turned to see Hines double-timing toward them, clutching his gear in one hand and his helmet and rifle in the other. Out of breath when he reached them, he cushioned his M-16 between his knees and slipped on his pack. "Why the hell didn't you wait for me?"

"We wanted to get some chow," Grimm said.

"Shee-it," Hines said, "you eat that slop?"

"We ain't as hard as you are, Hiney. We don't wake up hankering for C-rats."

Hines grinned. He took it as a compliment and looked at Latimere. "I guess everyone deserves one last hot meal."

The staff sergeant in charge of getting the supplies loaded ordered the grunts to board the trucks. He shouted toward the CCs. "You there! You riding?"

"Roger that," Grimm called.

"Then get your ass in gear. Mount up." He pointed to the truck in the middle.

The CCs climbed aboard and stood with the other grunts. "All right, listen up," the staff sergeant bellowed. "You men give me your attention! It's a thirty-minute ride to Hue. There wasn't any sniper fire yesterday, so I suggest you keep those rifles on safety."

"Piss on that," a grunt cracked.

"Knock off the shit! You're gonna be bouncing around in there. Nobody wants a trigger happy fool unloading an accidental burst."

"Fool?" another grunt scoffed. "Ain't no fools up here that I can see, less you know one of us volunteered."

The staff sergeant bristled. "Who the hell's giving all the lip up there?" A chorus of sniggers eddied through the truck beds. "All right," he barked, drowning out the grunts, "Stay alert! Move 'em out!"

This was it, Latimere thought. As the small convoy rumbled toward Hue, he felt his heart booming. Any moment now, he expected to become anxious, but instead he felt composed. Maybe he was so anxious he didn't know he was anxious. However, Roark treated him as if he was shaky, saying he would break him in slow, whatever that meant.

From the moment they left Phu Bai, the salts jawed, brandished their feats and laundered war stories, each man bent on topping the last. The stories were meant to awe the boots, but as always, the real urgency was to blunt the anxiety in the blowhards themselves.

A few men knew each other, but many did not. Before the escalation of the Vietnam War in '65 and '66, units were shipped over en masse. Everybody trained together and bonds were formed. The build-up changed that. Troops were sent over by quotas, some plucked from this unit, others from that, and it was a genuine screw-up when two buddies were lucky enough to draw orders to the same outfit. For the new guys, it was akin to being thrown to the wolves. Beyond an enemy to worry about, there were blustery salts who weren't about to show pity. A boot's education was strictly on-the-job training. Ostracized and alienated, they were granted little slack. Some boots were only good for walking point. It could be a short life span.

The salts in Latimere's truck kept jawing as another new guy listened mesmerized. He wore a dead Marine's helmet that had been issued him that morning. It sported a skull-and-crossbones, and in black letters around the brim was the grunts' holy battle cry, "PAYBACK IS A MOTHERFUCKER!" The new guy didn't understand the purpose of the stories, but he tried to assimilate every word. This was the apocryphal story about the soldier getting captured by the enemy and having his genitals cut off, stuffed in his mouth and then sewed up with barbed wire.

A leathery-faced lance corporal hooted. "That story's been around for years, but it is true the slopes think the way you die is how you're gonna go through all eternity. Here's one I seen for myself. We come across one of our guys who got separated from our company, found him tied to a tree, decapitated, and his head stuffed inside his stomach."

The trucks swiveled through the mud bed that was Highway 1. It was layered with dead leaves and strewn with splintered branches from the skeletal trees that lined the road. They drove past dilapidated thatched huts and hundreds of Vietnamese refugees streaming away from the city. They wore their belongings in layers. Some balanced straw baskets on their heads, while others carried wire-mesh baskets hanging from bamboo rods on their shoulders, holding all the possessions they could carry. Some women carried squealing baby pigs and squawking chickens. As the convoy motored past them, the children cheered and waved, while the older Vietnamese looked on with deep-set misery and undisguised scorn born of too many generations of war. A hundred meters off the road to either side were clumps of trees and hedgerows that offered good protection for an ambush or snipers. But there were miles to go and the men in the trucks were unconcerned.

Hines, however, began to feel jumpy. He needed to rattle something, a bark to keep the world from bucking him off. Incredibly, he sang, *Everybody Must Get Stoned*.

The bemused grunts shook their heads, and a few joined in.

The sky rumbled and grew darker, and the weather turned nasty. The rains came again, and the troops cupped their cigarettes and sat on the hard wooden crates facing outboard. Some pulled ponchos over their heads.

Near the midway point, the men grew insular, burrowing inside themselves. They had little time left, four kilometers of dismal damp terrain before the shock of the offensive would hit them. Time turned precious before a battle, especially a battle they knew was inevitable. They plied deep into themselves in a desperate need for faith and optimism, good thoughts to rejuvenate them, like a fresh gust of wind sweeping through their system cleansing them of fear and dread. Too soon, their metabolism would be riddled with speed. They'd be a jangle of nerves, all ears and eyeballs, until they were nothing but organisms of sight and sound.

None of this seemed so bleak for Arthur Latimere, and despite Grimm's warnings, he began snapping pictures. The misty fields inspired a sense of beauty and awe. His senses overloaded and rushed and sputtered. Dumb, but Latimere remembered when he was a kid, crammed in a room, a school or a movie house, and always wondered what it would be like if the bomb went off, the big one, the A-bomb. He always looked around to count the girls and imagined what it would be like after they survived. Now, he was here and as close as he would ever come to a bomb or death, and he was stuck in the back of a truck with a bunch of grungy grunts.

Latimere gulped the fresh morning air and the pungent scent of rice paddies and buffalo dung and the refugees they passed saluted his nostrils. He let the light rain tap a dance on his eyelids. The grunts' sudden gloominess did not affect him now, nor did the weather, or even his destination. Latimere's psychic weather was gleaming sunshine.

Nor was Roark thinking about the impending battle. He was lost in the lust of his last 30-day leave and that eventful night when Maggie—Maggie! Queen of Hearts! Lascivious seductress!—his mother's next door neighbor, had taken him in whole with her eyes and loins, and her insatiable body. God, what a worker!

Curiously, before heading into the field, Roark found himself thinking of her—someone wholesome and uninhibited at once. It was so early in the relationship it didn't drain him emotionally, not the way thinking about a wife or loved one would. No pangs, it merely made him smile.

Gunfire brought Roark to his senses. The first man hit didn't hear the shot. The round punched through his cheek and tore into his brain and blew out the back of his skull. His head split open like a ripe tomato and spattered against the crates.

In an instant, there was pandemonium. Roark grabbed Latimere and jerked him down, and Latimere hit his spine hard on a crate. Another Marine doubled over holding his groin with both hands. Rounds snapped over the men's heads and slugged into the truck's slats. The grunts in all three vehicles opened up, pouring automatic fire into the tree lines. Roark and Grimm were on their knees, pumping out rounds, as was Hines near the back of the cab. But there were too many men crammed into the truck bed, too little room between the ammo crates, and they squeezed for position, all joints and elbows. The air was acrid with cordite, and a stream of ejected shell casings pinged hot and steady, bouncing off their helmets and searing their necks. Some men couldn't get low enough and slithered over the crates to the other side.

The trucks speeded up, hurling the men sideways. One grunt was launched upright and clutched the slats as a round smashed into his finger. He reared and tried to yank his hand back, but it was stuck to the slat by the force of the impact. More rounds thwacked into the truck and he panicked and ripped his hand free, but left his forefinger. Blood gushed as he keeled backward on his haunches, squeezing his finger. The young Marine felt the clammy rush of shock then terror and denial. Then, he only felt the pain. His breath constricted in tight, quick gasps and exploded in a bloodcurdling scream. The grunts were firing, but Latimere only heard the screaming. He knew the screams would make him sick, and he slithered over the bodies and smothered the wounded grunt's head into his armpit, as much to muffle his screams as to shield him from the fire. The grunt writhed and twisted, his body racked by tremors. He gaped at the stub of his finger until his face turned yellow, and he started to vomit.

The trucks sped onward. More fire erupted from positions along the opposite side of the road. The fire grew loud and vicious, like the parched crackling sounds of wood burning. The men sunk lower and they tried to return fire. B-40 rockets hit the paddies and whooshed across the road. One smashed into one of the stick-trees near the road, and it exploded in a hail of fire and splinters. Flames leaped like talons out at the trucks. In his struggle to shield the wounded man, Latimere knocked the man's helmet off. His eyes went dumb with fright. "My helmet, my helmet!" he screamed. "You're OK, you're OK!" Latimere shouted into his ear. He whipped his own helmet off and covered the grunt's head.

The truck hit a pothole, and the ammo boxes bounced and went flying. Crates fell on top of the men, and they squirmed in pain. A final volley of automatic fire thudded into the crates above them. Latimere cushioned the grunt's head into his stomach. He glanced at Roark. Roark's head bobbed as the truck bucked, but he caught Latimere's eye and winked. Winked!

The trucks clanged ahead as the enemy fire abated. Then, Huey gunships zoomed in from over the horizon, pissing streams of orange machine gun fire into the tree lines. Rockets *WHOOOOSHED* and *BARROOOOOMED* through the valley as the convoy sped toward the village of An Cuu.

Chapter Seven

THE VILLAGE OF AN CUU was deserted except for an undermanned company of Marines that had set in the night before. The trucks swerved to a halt, and the grunts aboard dropped the tailgates and shouted for corpsmen. Marines rushed up as the grunts on the trucks passed down the dead and wounded. Latimere helped his man down and jumped off after him. As the Marines led him away, Latimere remembered the grunt had his helmet, but he was too embarrassed to ask for it back. He climbed back aboard the truck. The grunt's helmet lolled in a corner, and he grabbed it and hopped down. Hines slapped him on the back. "How you hanging?"

"What?" Latimere was momentarily befuddled.

"You OK?" Hines' eyes were dilated.

"Guess so," Latimere stuttered.

"You done all right, Babysan."

Hines steered him to the camp, but Latimere stopped. "I'd really appreciate it if you didn't call me Babysan."

Grimm caught up with them. "C'mon, let's check the CO." Roark joined them as Grimm snagged a Marine and asked him where the Skipper was.

The lieutenant was with his radioman and a black staff sergeant sipping coffee around an anemic fire. A mass of ticks and twitches, he seemed to wheeze where others might breathe.

"Lieutenant." Grimm said.

"What can we do for you?" He looked over Grimm's shoulder toward the pandemonium near the trucks.

"I'm Sergeant Grimm. We're correspondents from 1st Mar Div."

The lieutenant stuffed gum into his mouth. He seemed unable to stop moving. "Some of your people were here yesterday escorting a couple civilians." He nodded toward the trucks again. "What happened out there?"

"Ambush," Hines said. "Rockets and sniper fire."

The lieutenant turned to his staff sergeant. "Help these men. I'll take a look."

When the lieutenant left, the staff sergeant frowned.

"Something else," he kicked out the fire. "We're getting more reporters out here than reinforcements."

"Yeah, our tough luck." Hines lay in the bushes for this kind of bait. The staff sergeant glared.

Roark interceded. "We noticed the bridge was blown. We need to get across. That possible?"

"In a couple hours. We got engineers working on a footbridge now."

"Right." Roark pulled the CCs aside. "Let's check it. This clown has no authority over us."

They were headed for the canal when Latimere said, "Apparently these guys don't like us much."

"Screw'em." Hines noticed Latimere's helmet and did a double-take. Unbeknownst to Latimere, a skull-and-crossbones was scrawled across the front of it, and the words, "PAYBACK IS A MOTHERFUCKER!" The helmet was too large and looked silly on him. "Where the hell did you get that?"

"What?" Latimere looked at the sky above and behind him.

Roark and Grimm also saw it and smirked. Latimere finally realized Hines was talking about his own helmet and took it off and looked at it. He turned a shade of red.

"Damn," Hines said. "I sure wouldn't wear a pot somebody just got zapped in. Bad fucking karma."

The Phu Cam canal was a dirty, 30-foot-wide drainage ditch that separated An Cuu from the south side of Hue. Engineers were at work on a rickety footbridge, but most sat on their butts smoking. Some 2x4s had been nailed together, bobbing at water level with two rope lines stretched between both banks. Several two-story buildings stood across the canal, and beyond were small plots of rice paddies.

"Can this thing be crossed?" Grimm asked one of the engineers.

"Be my guest."

"You mean take our chances."

"There it is," the engineer said.

Roark looked up and down the banks. "You guys take any fire this morning?"

"Nope."

Hines realized how quiet it was. "Where the hell is everybody?"

"Maybe the gooks took R&R," the engineer said.

Roark looked at Grimm. "What do you think?"

"It sucks, if you ask me," Hines pointed to the structures across the canal. "Charlie could be waiting to pick us off."

Grimm thought a moment. "If he is, he'll wait until the whole company crosses, he won't waste it on us. Hell, he could take us here if he wanted."

The engineer suddenly grew worried. "I don't know what you guys are thinking, but nobody here's got any orders to move out."

"We got our own orders," Roark said.

"Suit yourself, but you've been warned. Ain't taking responsibility. It's a free-fire zone out there. The companies that swept through didn't leave anyone in reserve. It's nothing but Indian country until you get deeper into the city."

Roark started across first. His eyes darted from the planks beneath his feet to the buildings across the canal. The footbridge buckled, but he finally reached the cover of an overhanging concrete ramp. Grimm sent Latimere next, and when he was three-quarters of the way across, Hines started over. Grimm started across the planks when Hines reached the other side.

Suddenly, a Huey gunship screamed high overhead, its nose pointed down. Grimm froze as the door gunner cut loose with a burst of machine gun fire. Then he slipped, and one leg went knee-deep in canal water as rounds whacked into the wooden planks and splunked into the water beside him. He yanked on the ropes and pulled himself up and scrambled for the ramp. Tracers beat a path after him as he slammed into the cement wall and more rounds sparked and ricocheted off the concrete embankment. On the other side of the canal, the engineers took cover and frantically waved their arms. Grimm whirled round and snapped his rifle into his shoulder. "Are you crazy?" Roark knocked the muzzle down. "Those fuckers will open up with rockets!"

Grimm's face beat purple with pulsing blood. He jerked free and popped into the open again. The door gunner swung his machine gun toward him and Grimm jerked back under the overhang. They braced for the coming volley, but all they heard was the scream of rotors. They waited when Grimm leaped out again and clenched his fist at the chopper. "We're Marines, goddammit! We're goddamn Marines!"

The chopper held its nose down and jinked menacingly from side to side. A grunt across the canal got on the radio. Other grunts yelled, "Friendlies, friendlies!"

The chopper had a yellow circle on the nose with a black cat painted in the middle. Grimm went ballistic and whipped his rifle up, but Roark slammed it down again. "It's the goddamn Army." Grimm screamed. He cocked his fist at the chopper again. "You goddamn doggie motherfuckers!"

As suddenly as the chopper appeared, it banked and flew away.

Grimm seethed, gasping hard. "I ever see that bastard land I'm gonna blow his doggie head off. Trigger-happy prick."

"You OK?" Roark asked the others.

They leaned back and swallowed in long draughts before their chorus of sighs became nervous titters. An engineer yelled at them from across the bank. "Any of you hit? You need a doc?"

"Negative," Roark called. More grunts ran down the embankment across the canal.

"What the fuck's the Army doing here?" Grimm shouted.

The radioman laughed. "Everyone's here, man! The Army, Air Force, even the Navy wants in. They're dying to lob their arty into the city! Where're you guys heading?"

"MACV."

"You want us to radio ahead?"

"Nah, they can't do nothing. It ain't far. We'll make it—if the stinking Army doesn't blow our asses away."

"You don't want to wait until we cross?"

"We're here now." Hines snapped.

"It's your ass. MACV's half a klick, straight ahead."

Just then, the staff sergeant charged down the bank toward the engineers. "What the hell are you assholes doing?"

"Good question," Roark muttered.

"Goddammit, who gave you men permission to cross?"

Great, Roark thought. *We nearly buy it, and this lifer wants to check our papers.*

"It's all right, staff." Grimm shouted back, "No damage done. We got orders to reach two-five by noon," he lied. He elbowed Roark, "Let's beat feet!"

Latimere tried to fit it into a pattern but couldn't. He remembered from infantry training fire and maneuver, regroup and advance, but none of those tactics applied on the convoy. He thought about the war movies he saw growing up, with their sweeping scale and grand panoramas. Yet all he knew about being under fire was how sudden and shattering everything was, and when it happened, how the whole world was only inches in front of him. Another thing bothered him that he tried not to think about. It had crossed his mind that maybe Hines was a bit steadier than the others. Hines had warned them about crossing the canal, and even though it wasn't the NVA who opened up on them, it was like the engineer said, a free-fire zone. No question he felt more comfortable with Roark or Grimm, but maybe that was because he liked them more.

They huddled in a doorway of a two-story building at the foot of the road, not hiding from the enemy but staying out of sight of the staff sergeant. They could still see him stomping along the far bank flinging his arms in their direction.

They smoked and then moved out. "Not so close," Hines said.

"The area's been swept." Roark replied. "There aren't any gooks here."

"Well, the goddamn Army thought there was."

Roark didn't answer but maintained his smirk of superiority, the one Hines had come to loathe. Just once, Hines wanted to be there when Roark had the piss scared out of him.

The city seemed deserted. Only the distant drone of helicopter rotor blades suggested any military presence. They walked past bunkered store fronts and pock-marked buildings that had been pummeled in the first wave of fighting. Tanks and rockets and LAAWs (anti-tank weapons) had gouged huge holes in the buildings, and their facades had been blackened by smoke and fire. Slabs of concrete cluttered the streets, and in the gutters, every 30 meters or so, lay the bloated carcass of a North Vietnamese soldier frozen in a horrible death pose. The rains had helped blunt the stench of rotting flesh, but bloody wounds and eye sockets had been rooted out by maggots.

Latimere couldn't help but stare. Every new guy stared when he saw his first dead. Latimere thought them funny, the dead—not funny funny, but funny strange. The dead were nothing like he had imagined. He'd seen people die in movies, but he knew they weren't dead, and he watched to see whether their chests moved. The real dead were different. Not because these were slopes, but because he knew they weren't pretending. The real dead didn't move. There was nothing about them that hinted they had ever lived. They were split-open lumps, lifeless and waxy with skin like mannequins. Also, he learned something else. Their eyes were dead, no moisture or reflection like in the movies.

The street dead-ended into a swampy rice paddy shrouded by a low, thick mist. Grimm stopped short and remarked in his best W. C. Fields voice, "Ah, yes—a sparkle of dew, a dainty mist. Soft and fine as Vietnamese cunt hair."

Grimm clutched his heart. "Ah, me pump, me pump."

Latimere was bewildered, but Roark knew Grimm could talk like that.

They stood at a fork in the road. The road to the left curved sharply after a few blocks, while the road on the right ended after a hundred meters and split into another fork. They hunkered near a building for cover.

"Fuck." Hines' irritability mounted. "Straight ahead, my ass. Is that what that turd said?"

"Which way do we go?" Latimere asked after a moment. He wondered why they hadn't waited for the company to cross. Why were they in such a hurry? He heard the Marines had swept the area, but the incident with the chopper had made him superstitious.

Grimm motioned to the rice paddy ahead of them. "MACV has to be across that paddy and up those streets there."

Hines balked. "I ain't walking through an open paddy."

"Come on then," Roark started down the street to his right, and Grimm followed, Latimere a few feet behind.

"Wait one," Hines called. "Look." The guys ambled back to him. "There." Five blocks away, they could barely see it. "That's a tank up there."

"Could be," Grimm nodded.

"Well?"

"For all we know that tank's out of commission." Roark said. "I don't see anyone down there. Maybe it was hit and abandoned. Anyway, that isn't the way to MACV."

Roark started off again, but Hines was adamant. "Roark, you want to go that way, you diddy-bop on. Not me."

"Suit yourself."

Roark kept walking. Grimm and Latimere hesitated, then moved to catch up. "Don't worry," he told Latimere, "Hines'll dick around and end up back at the canal. Probably hitch up with the company when it crosses. We'll wait for him at MACV."

Hines slipped back into the shadows of the building and watched them leave. He wanted to go after them, but his stubbornness prevented it. His stubbornness and his anger. Subconsciously, he fueled the anger. When angry, he didn't have to think of being left alone.

Hines had not always been so bombastic. He had arrived in country as apprehensive as any boot, but as the only college man among them, he privately resented being there. He'd had plans to marry, but three weeks before the wedding he got his "greetings" from Uncle Sam. Hines never seriously considered deserting to Canada, but he wasted little time canceling the wedding, offering a lot of mumbo-jumbo about how going off to war wouldn't be fair to his fiancée.

Like most boots during that phase of the war, Hines spent his first months in country braving *punji* pits and booby traps and the occasional sniper, who was rarely seen but who could pin down a company for an hour. Most battles were waged against the furnace of the day and the shivering cold of night. Disease claimed more casualties than Charlie. It was more "search" than "destroy," and the monotony was as spiteful as a palsy. He'd soon learned there wasn't anything in the whole stinking country that didn't try to bite, sting or kill him. If the leeches, centipedes and snakes were unrepentant, they were not nearly so debilitating as the prickly-heat malaria or bouts of diarrhea from drinking tainted water. He'd drink three or four canteens a day, but in that heat he never pissed because he'd sweat it all out. Firefights were sporadic. Occasionally, he'd sweep a ville anticipating contact but only found a few *mamasans* and young girls. Sometimes, he'd see a pot of boiled rice, enough to feed a dozen guerrillas, and he'd know the VC were near because rice wouldn't keep more than an hour in that climate.

Up to then, Kennedy's splendid little war was still called a "police action." The obscenity of being upgraded to a "cold war" was yet to come. That took place after the North Vietnamese army swept south in early '67, with the shit hitting the fan southwest of Danang during Operations Union I and II.

For Hines the crunch came on Union II, shattering any illusions he had about staying anonymous or trying to bide time until he rotated. He kept the trauma at bay in the daytime, but at night it pounced on him and splurted through his dreams like a burst appendix.

He relived the incident in splices, like a badly cut movie, but the numbness had never left him. A fortnight into the operation, the company to which he had been attached had been decimated and the men who hadn't fallen from enemy fire had collapsed from heat stroke, some so bad the blood in their brains had stewed. One day, after crossing the paddies toward a ville, where they planned to hole up for the night, they called for a resupply drop. Hines had made up his mind to chopper out. Already, he had twice as many stories as he needed, so nobody in the rear would question his return. Before they arrived to where they would settle in for the night, all hell broke loose.

The point man tripped a Bouncing Betty that took out three men. Everyone hated bounding mines, high-explosive projectiles the Viet Cong rigged up a dozen different ways. Conical in shape with a super-fast fuse, they had three prongs jutting out of the ground. When triggered, the mine shot three feet into the air and went off in a flat trajectory aimed at the genitals. It was a psychological tactic, and the troops were rightly paranoid about them.

When the betty blew, the rest of the company was still in the open, and the NVA kicked in with mortars and shredded the men in the fields. Bodies and limbs flew, and the ground belched and roiled like a churning sea. Screams rent the air, and Hines curled up behind a paddy dike. Something struck his leg. He groped frantically for a wound and finally realized it was only a dirt clod.

The grunts laid down fire and Hines heard someone scream in the paddy in front of him. He inched his head up then scrunched back down. Over the din, he heard the sound of his own breathing. Move, he told himself, as he fought the shakes. Suddenly, a corpsman hurdled over him and charged into the open. Hines watched the corpsman run until a mortar hit and decapitated him. The corpsman's legs carried him a few more steps before the body crumpled.

The grunts intensified their fire, and a fireteam broke forward, scrambled into the paddy and fanned out for the wounded. A second fireteam came up and crouched beside Hines. A grunt elbowed him hard in the shoulder. "Move yer ass! You hit, or what?"

"I thought I was, but I guess not."

"Then get your ass in gear and come with us."

Hines, on legs of rubber, followed them into the paddy. His only thought was to reach one of the wounded, not the dead. Trying to move the dead was hell, the dead weighed a ton. Just then, another barrage of mortars shrieked down, and the men scattered in all directions. Hines and the team leader dove beside a grunt. The grunt lay face down and Hines kicked his leg but got no response. The team leader rolled him over. Dead. He grabbed him under the armpits and told Hines to get his feet. "Cover us," he yelled behind him. *"Move!"* he barked at Hines.

Hines grabbed the man's legs and pulled hard. Suddenly, the man's boot and severed foot came away in his hands, and he landed on his back, his insides turned to mush. Blood from the boot dripped into his mouth and he gagged in revulsion. He hurled the boot away, but the team leader yelled for him to grab the grunt's legs again. Hines stiffened in panic. Another mortar blast covered him with dirt. The team leader shouted, and hit him with his rifle butt, but Hines was balled up in waves of nausea. Bile welled in the back of his throat and the next moments were lost to him. The grunt's exhortations were futile now to Hines, garbled as if coming from the bottom of a well. When it was finally over, Hines was helped to safety and placed with the rest of the casualties.

After that, Hines was convinced he had seen it all. Definitely more than the other CCs, even Roark. What the hell had Roark seen anyway? Big fucking hero. What was getting shot compared to having somebody's foot come off in his hands?

Hines remembered the horror, when suddenly he was jolted back to his immediate situation. He heard something scrape along the floor on the second story of the building above him. He backed further inside the doorway and checked the doorknob. Locked. He clutched a grenade with a sweaty palm and reminded himself to bounce it off the walls so no one had time to throw it back. He fingered the pull ring and waited. Again he heard the scraping, this time followed by a sad, forlorn whine. A dog. Hines almost giggled. Only a goddamn dog.

He edged onto the sidewalk and began moving down the street, his back flattened against the building. He ducked inside another doorway and glanced up at the blown-out windows behind him. He tried to whistle but didn't have enough spit. When finally he got it out, there was no response. He was sure it was a dog. The mutt was probably afraid of being eaten. Goddamn gooks will eat anything, he thought.

Hines reached the first intersection where he stopped and glanced down the side streets. He zipped up his flak jacket. Goddamn Roark, Goddamn Grimm. Suddenly, he bolted across the intersection and walked fast toward the carcass of the tank in the distance.

A few streets away, Grimm, Roark and Latimere came to a dead end and stopped before another rice paddy.

"What now, Columbus?" Grimm said.

Roark shrugged. "Beats me."

Latimere barely listened. He was amazed at the city's beauty. More than beautiful, it seemed strangely normal. Except for signs of shelling, the city might have been anywhere, any number of suburbs back home. Palm trees lined the streets, devastated houses stood beside homes left unscathed. Latimere thought it eerie seeing the war-torn and the perfect side by side. He could tell which houses had been used by both armies in making night camps, as they were littered with spent shell casings, bloodied bandages and discarded debris. Many of the houses looked freshly painted, Latimere guessed in anticipation of Tet. Some had quaint front porches with white railings and French doors and shutters. Some yard trees had branches blown away, and some gardens had been battered by the monsoon and the heavy tromp of boots.

Grimm pulled out his flask of Jack Daniels and smiled. A soft mist clung to this paddy, too. "God," he exclaimed, taking a swig, "Damn, this city's beautiful." He turned to Latimere, "First thing I'm doing when we get settled is stake out a skivvy joint. Nothing like a poke to purify the system." He handed the flask to Latimere. "Babysan, you ain't had nothing until you've had a tight-twatted Vietnamese university girl. Sweet-smelling too, kind of curry-like. 'Cept this time I'm gonna need more than a single. Have to line up a double!"

Roark chuckled. "A double dose of the black syph, maybe."

Grimm laughed, remembering when he was first in country a dose of the clap led to two weeks of penicillin shots. The shots bothered him far less than staying off beer and Cokes.

Roark took a slug and passed the flask back to Grimm. They looked past the fallen power lines to the misty paddy in front of them. The road split into another fork.

"More cover if we go left," Roark said.

Grimm stowed the flask, and they started off. Halfway down the block, the road curved sharply, and the houses ended. A row of small rice paddies mirrored those on the right. A built-up area with two-story buildings was several hundred meters in front of them. MACV had to be beyond those buildings. It would be the shortest route, but it meant they would be in the open. Better to double back.

"Screw it," Roark said, and jabbed his rifle at the road ahead.

They started moving, and Grimm turned to Latimere. "I'd thumb that safety off if I were you."

"Huh?"

Fifty meters farther, they grew conscious of the trees lining the road and the cover they afforded. Grimm walked the right side, Roark the left. Latimere picked up the rear a few meters behind them.

The gaps between the trees widened. Only a small lump at first, a knot in the back of their throats, but Grimm and Roark swallowed. Then the lump slipped into their bellies pulling a heavy noxious anchor behind it. They had a bad feeling that they couldn't quash.

Latimere knew straight away something was wrong. He knew by the antennae that went up from the two men in front of him, from the tilt of their heads as they listened all ears, the way a blind man listened. Latimere didn't know it yet, but it was always the ears. The first thing he'd experience was sound. Hearing was all that mattered. If he heard it, he could still be counted among the living.

"Keep it spread," Grimm said. Sweat on the back of his neck thickened into a grimy film. Twenty meters farther, Grimm and Roark stopped and Latimere stutter-stepped to a halt behind them. The buildings ahead seemed an interminable distance.

Grimm cursed himself. Once again they were screwing the pooch in the middle of nowhere. Once again he allowed Roark to put them in the shit. What was it last time? Screw the last time, think about now. Grimm hated this shit. In a battle or firefight he was in his element, he could deal with that, but in these kinds of whack-offs he knew he was asking for it. He could pull off 20 major ops and no sweat, but then do something stupid like this and get his ass handed to him. About as spastic and senseless as stepping in front of a tank.

Grimm dragged a cuff across his forehead and mopped sweat from his brow. "I think it's time we talk"

"You ain't hearing chimes are you, maestro?" Roark asked.

"Don't dick with me."

"Chimes?" Latimere asked.

"Grimm swears he hears chimes whenever something's going to pop."

"I thought you said this area's secured." Latimere took a step toward them.

"Stay there!" Roark snapped. He eased his finger onto the trigger of his M-16 and scanned the paddies. He kept his eyes moving, so anyone watching wouldn't know he had spotted him.

Grimm looked across the opposite paddy but knew he wouldn't see anything. He listened more than looked. All of his senses were centered in his ears, but he only heard the sound of his eardrums pulsing. His muscles went taut and he poised to spring at the first crack of rifle fire.

"Think we're being watched?" Roark whispered.

"Does a nun have a pussy?" Grimm asked.

Latimere's heart jumped. What the hell were they talking about? His eyes moved between Grimm and Roark, and then darted to the paddies. The paddies stretched east to a wall of hedges and trees, and a thick, low mist gathered and obscured everything but the treetops. Dark, angry clouds hung low on the horizon, purple and black like a predatory shroud. Latimere looked at Roark and Grimm and grew more frustrated. "Are you guys going to tell me what's going on?"

Grimm blinked, annoyed that Latimere was talking.

Roark had a thought. He turned around, looked past Latimere and waved his arms in exaggerated arcs as if signaling someone back at the houses they passed. He shook his head "no" and gave a "thumbs-up" sign implying everything was clear. "Think they'll open up?" he asked Grimm.

"Not if they've swallowed your bullshit. Sincerely hate to say it, but it might just work." He knew if the gooks thought they were out there reconnoitering, they wouldn't be so eager to reveal their position. He also knew they had to act now to pull it off. "OK," he said, "let's head back slow. You first, Babysan. Just act like nothing's happening and start heading back."

"What *is* happening?" Latimere stammered.

"Just walk," Grimm barked low.

Latimere moved out. He glanced back to see whether the guys were following. Grimm snapped at him to keep moving. They walked as slowly and calmly as possible. Every ten meters, Roark signaled the houses again, giving "no sweat" signs and shaking his head.

Twenty-five meters from the houses, the blistering pop-pop-poping of automatic fire rang out. All three hit the deck and slithered on their bellies to the edge of the road behind the cover of the paddy dike. It was a moment before they realized the bursts came from several blocks away. Roark jumped up, yelling, *"Let's hit it!"*

They ran for the houses, zigzagging down the road, dodging imaginary rounds until they rounded the corner of the first house and slammed against the wall, gulping down air.

Roark peeked around the corner but saw nothing. He grinned at Grimm's scowl.

Grimm caught his breath. "It's my lead now, unless you got any more bright ideas."

Roark smiled. "What say we turn this operation over to Babysan?"

Grimm eyed him hard but slowly gave ground. He turned to Latimere. "How about it, Babysan?"

"Huh?"

"Where do you say we head?"

"Back to the tank?"

Roark spoke first. "Tank sounds good to me."

Chapter Eight

AN HOUR LATER, they could smell the Perfume River as they walked up Duy Tan Street. They reached the first throng of refugees, looking wary and wretched, uncertain whether to be grateful or fearful and watched the Marines with expressionless faces. Many of the refugees slept in the streets at night. Others had holed up inside the vacated houses behind the MACV compound. One hundred thousand South Vietnamese had already fled the city and the thousands that remained were either too poor, frightened or stubborn to leave. A cyclo-rickshaw driver peddled past, but there was no one to taxi and no safe place to go. Ancient elders with long, wispy beards stood guard over wooden handcarts with rickety wooden wheels, scores of children and orphans among them. Like children everywhere, they played in the street, and a few jumped up and down on top of an old burned out Volkswagen.

Listening to the gay shrieks under their condition astonished as well as saddened Latimere. Some children begged for candy, and he instinctively reached into his cargo pocket.

"Didi mao!" Grimm barked. As the children slinked away, he turned to Latimere. "Don't reach for something unless you have it."

"But I do. I have a candy bar."

"You have one for all of them?"

They rounded the corner to Le Loi Street. Two weeks earlier, Le Loi had been the loveliest avenue in Hue. It ran along the southern bank of the Perfume, past the MACV compound and elegant villas, beyond the university and Circle Sportif with its beautiful verandas and rolling green lawns. The houses and villas had since been blasted to rubble, and now teemed with refugees.

The MACV compound, a large rectangular, two-story building with arched porticoes, was surrounded by what looked like a motor pool, as nearly every Jeep still functional was parked outside its gates. Latimere saw a message scrawled across the side of one of the Jeeps: "Nape a Nguyen for New Years!" He cringed at the words.

A large bombed out area was beyond the rows of Jeeps between MACV and the southern bank of the Perfume. It had been transformed into a makeshift marketplace, where hundreds of peasants cooked food and peddled wares. To Latimere it was eye popping. It didn't matter that the older peasants wore dingy gray and brown pajamas, because the young pretty girls had on colorful silks, and splashes of red and yellow, lime and orange made it wildly exciting and spectacular. The realization astounded Latimere that even in the midst of war, meager livings needed to be earned. The more resilient entrepreneurs squatted beneath thatched umbrellas, selling fruits, boiled chickens and spicy noodle soups. The air was filled with haggling and bartering, and there were cries in pidgin English of "Coka, coka!" and "Maline numbah one!" and "Never hoppen, GI!"

The CCs pushed toward the MACV compound. Soon, they saw Hines near the tall iron gates leaning against a pillar, smoking a cigarette, watching them and smiling. "Nice you guys could make it," he said. "Getting worried about you."

"Yeah," Roark said. "We took a detour. Shame you weren't with us."

"You hear anything," Grimm asked.

"Everybody's holing up, getting ready for a big push. Day after tomorrow, they're crossing the Perfume. Fucking river Styx, you ask me. C'mon." Hines led them toward a house set up for the press.

Halfway down the block, Grimm stopped and filled his nostrils. He hadn't eaten since morning and he knew it wouldn't be long before the only chow they'd get would be C-rats. The steam and spices smelled warm in the damp air, and the others followed as he pushed through the refugees and milling ARVN soldiers. Peddlers beckoned from all directions. They brushed aside dirty faced street urchins that clung to their legs and pawed their gear and weapons.

Grimm stopped near a gaggle of elderly *mamasans* squatted around a huge pot of soup. Their lively talk was in eerie contrast to the devastation around them. The *mamasans* wore conical straw hats, and their teeth were stained black from chewing betel nut.

Steam wafted from the soup, and the *mamasans* thanked them for buying. Latimere, too mesmerized to eat, slid quietly into the crowd. Once again, the blaze of colors jumped out at him, stark and vivid as though the world was younger, more alive and seen for the first time. He snapped a picture of a young Vietnamese girl who shrank from him. A small boy, his scalp shaved and disfigured with sores, clung to her waist. Flies buzzed, and the girl shooed them away and hid him behind her back from Latimere. Two ARVN soldiers smiled at the girl but glared at Latimere.

When they rained down, they came without warning. Sometimes Marines heard the shrill whistle of their flight, and sometimes in the night they heard the distant thumps as enemy mortars left their tubes. Now, swallowed in the din of the marketplace, there were only two white flashes and sudden hot bursts of metal. The crowd gasped as though struck by a blow to its collective solar plexus. Screams rang out as more mortars crumped a path toward MACV. Roark found Latimere and yanked him down behind a wooden ox cart. Panic seized the crowd, and peasants stampeded, bowling over pots and trampling others as they fled into the city and away from the river.

Immediately, the mortar pits at MACV pumped out return fire. Roark waited while the refugees streamed past him. Then, he grabbed Latimere and ran toward the Perfume, certain the enemy wouldn't waste time on them with hordes of Vietnamese heading the other way.

In a moment, they reached a row of dwarf trees at the edge of the beach and dove behind a row of sandbags, Grimm and Hines behind them. Through the trees, they saw the brown and choppy Perfume. A small urban area called the Strawberry Patch was across the river on the northern bank. A grove of trees was beyond the Patch and beyond that the ancient, massive wall of the Citadel. Foreboding and impregnable, the giant stones glistened black and were choked with foliage.

Grimm brought out his flask when a splurt of enemy rounds thwacked into the trees. The men hunkered down, and Grimm took a swig.

Roark cursed, galled that the ARVN fled into the city while some bastards were zeroed in on them.

Grimm read his mind. "Once again, you're the sorry ass who went this way."

The mortar pits at MACV kept up a steady rattle of fire. Roark scanned the area across the Perfume and popped off a few rounds. Another volley of fire shredded the trees above him, and he scrunched back down. Angrily, Roark popped up again and cooked off the rest of his magazine. He watched his orange tracer rounds arc over the Perfume and disappear inside the Citadel. He realized shooting was pointless and sagged back down again. Roark knew they were in no danger if they kept their heads down, but Hines sneered at him, relishing his discomfort. "Shit, it's only a little fire. I thought you Stanislavsky types craved new experiences."

Latimere shifted his legs, still stunned by how fast and indiscriminate the slaughter had been. He wondered whether he would ever be as callous as the men beside him.

Columns of black smoke rose from inside the Citadel where the MACV mortars hit their mark. Roark looked down the bank. The Nguyen Hoang bridge, connecting the south and north sides of the city, was 200 meters to his right. Enemy divers had blown the bridge during the initial assault, and its steel trusses lay twisted like broken bones. A section of its belly had plummeted into the Perfume. A company on foot could traverse the girders but there was no way to move trucks or armored vehicles across. Roark's eyes stopped on a group of ARVN on the bank behind the massive bridge supports. They took turns shoving each other into the open and waving their arms at any snipers across the river. When he saw they drew no enemy fire, Roark felt a surge of revulsion.

Grimm took another slug of Jack Daniels and the liquor warmed his stomach. He handed the flask to Hines, who swallowed more than his share. "Pass it on," Grimm said. "And keep it out of sight. Anyone sees us drinking, our ass is grass."

"Now that's something we could use. How did you like that stuff, Babysan? Pure Laotian Gold."

Latimere adjusted the settings on his camera and inched up to snap a picture.

"Whadya see there, Babysan?" Hines said.

Roark jerked Latimere back. "Stay down." He whirled on Hines. "He gets hit, and it's my ass, not yours."

The men bided their time and passed the flask. Hines took another swallow and nudged Latimere. "Babysan, that walled monstrosity you saw is what the gooks call the Citadel. That's where Uncle Ho plans to choke our chickens."

"Cut the crap," Grimm said.

"I'm only giving Babysan a little history lesson." Hines fussed and looked at each in turn, Grimm, then Latimere and Roark. Then, he downed the flask and shook his head. "Christ. I'm stuck out here with a bush-beast, a cherry and a goddamn starlet, and you suckers wonder why I drink."

The enemy mortars had ceased, but outgoing mortar fire from MACV continued. When they walked back to the marketplace the Vietnamese were returning to collect their wares. Roark thought it incredible there were not more casualties. Except for the first barrage, most of the mortars had landed inside the MACV compound.

Roark spotted a *mamasan* and her baby on the ground when they reached Le Loi street. She squatted in the road, pawing at her baby whose chest was blown open. She sobbed and pounded the ground with her fists. Several ARVN stood to the side, smoking and cajoling in high-pitched giggles. It sickened Roark that no one helped her. The woman rocked back and forth and clutched her baby to her breast as if her heart could beat for both of them.

Roark knelt in front of her, and the *mamasan* clutched her baby and shrieked and rattled off a string of curses in Vietnamese. Roark felt her pain and flinched. Where the hell was a corpsman? Would no one help? He stared at her, numb with anguish and impotence. Maybe a corpsman could "knock her out" if only he could get her to MACV. He bent to her and she rolled over and kicked at him with both feet. She slammed her eyes shut as if only he would vanish if she didn't have to look at him.

Grimm put a hand on Roark's shoulder. "Come on, there's nothing you can do. She don't want your help."

Her wails pursued them as they headed down the street. Hines took the lead. They turned left at the corner, walked two short blocks and crossed a small intersection. A row of concertina wire stretched across the street and three ARVN soldiers manned the wire in front of the armory. The house that had been requisitioned as an informal press center was farther down the block. As they approached, one of the ARVN raised his hand. "No Malines. *Dung lai.* No Malines."

Hines pointed at the camera around Latimere's neck. *"Bao Chi. Bao Chi!"*

The ARVN understood but didn't give ground. He shook his head. "*No com bic. Dung lai.* No Malines!"

It would have been possible to bribe their way through, but something snapped inside Roark. He thrust his rifle into the ARVN's throat. The incident with the *mamasan* ignited him. *"Bao Chi!"* Roark snarled in fanged-out rage, his face flaring crimson.

The ARVN's eyes popped wide. Latimere, almost as stunned, watched the ARVN's Adam's apple rent up and down.

A sudden clamor in the armory's second story windows, and soon more ARVN looked down and poked out their rifles. Grimm and Hines swung their weapons at them. For a terrifying instant, they looked into the void one twitch from annihilation, waiting for the first movement to send them into the abyss. Finally, an ARVN officer in the window called for his men to lower their weapons and ordered the guards in the street to roll back the concertina. As two ARVN drew back the wire, Roark kept his rifle muzzle against the other ARVN's throat. He held it there longer than necessary, and when he pulled the rifle down exposed a nasty red ring on the ARVN's neck.

The correspondents were finally waved through. Grimm let the other CCs go ahead of him as he walked backwards down the street. He smiled at the ARVN but kept his finger near the trigger.

"Shaky bastards, ain't they?" Grimm said over his shoulder.

Hines seethed and lashed out at Roark. "What the hell was that about? You think that was funny? They could have shot our asses!"

Roark ignored him. Latimere tugged Roark's elbow. " *'Bao chi'*, what's *'bao chi'*?"

"Dink-talk for correspondent."

The armory and the houses along the block were pockmarked from small arms fire. There were yawing holes in the walls from rocket and mortar fire as the destruction was worse closer to the Perfume.

Hines turned into a small courtyard. It had been a quaint house with a front porch and green shutters on the windows. Now, the planter boxes were blown off their hinges and lay upended in puddles in the yard. Thousands of spent shell casings and splintered glass and rubble littered the ground. Despite the rains and constant damp, a fine layer of brick powder covered everything.

The CCs spotted Ehlo on the porch wolfing down a loaf of French bread, and he jumped up when he saw his friends. The hurt and scent of Bangkok now seemed faint and fetid, like a sad, wet dream. Ehlo had finally put that behind him. The CCs rarely got to buddy-up in the field, and Ehlo was honestly glad to see them. "Them cheese-dicks actually let you through the wire?

"What's their story?" Grimm asked.

Ehlo snickered. "Last night we got no shut-eye 'cuz them pricks kept talking so loud. Probably scared to close their eyes. Finally, I threw a couple illumination grenades at them. Fuckers went apeshit. Even popped off a couple rounds at us. Assholes."

"That's good PR," Grimm said.

"Screw 'em." Ehlo smiled. "Check out the house."

Ehlo marched them inside. Roark immediately peeled through the kitchen and went out a back door where he could be alone. He still trembled from the close encounter with the South Vietnamese soldiers.

Without electricity, the house was musty from the odor of men. However, a worse stench soon hit them. The civilian reporters who had circulated through had been too lazy or spoiled to dig holes and defecate outside, and the toilet was plugged and piled with waste. The bathroom door was off its hinges, and they tasted the fetid smell as it clung to the roofs of their mouths. Black silks had been draped over the windows, and a murky shaft of light came through a blown out section of one wall. Housing a dozen men, the floor was cluttered with half-eaten C-ration cans, and packs and sleeping bags were stacked in the corners.

"What do you think?" Ehlo grinned. "All the con-veniences of home, eh?"

"Where's the furniture?" Hines asked.

"The ARVN got it across the street. But hell, it beats the paddies."

"Where's Bayer?" Grimm asked.

"With Golf company escorting those hacks we brought with us from Phu Bai. There are more civilian douche-bags out front there and more getting briefed at MACV. Always think they can bullshit the brass for more info."

Roark joined them, and they went out on the porch where the civilian reporters and photographers snapped pictures of each other.

"Pussy flicks," Hines grunted under his breath.

Ehlo arched an eyebrow. "We got a little ghost-time. How about we scope out the area?"

"Fuckin-A," Hines agreed.

"Maybe we should link up with our units," Grimm said.

Hines huffed. "Jesus, don't be so bloody gung-ho. Ain't nothing coming down until day after tomorrow."

"Just speaking for myself, so don't get excited, Hines. I don't mind taking a walk, but I'm tying up with Fox Company before dark."

"Tonight?"

"Grimm's right," Roark said. There were times when slack time seemed worse than a sweep, especially when the sweep was inevitable.

The muscles in Hines' jaw tightened, and his lips quivered as he remembered the convoy to Hue where he toyed with the idea of playing it loose for a couple days, at least until they had to cross the Perfume. Now, there was no way he could let the others join their units while he hung back at the doctor's house. "Fine, that's later then," he said. "We'll link up before dark. Let's *di-di*." He headed for the street and called back to the others. "You coming?"

The CCs followed, except for Roark. "See you guys back here," he said.

"You staying?"

"Just keep an eye on Latimere," Roark called.

"Babysan?" Hines snorted. "Shit. The kid's got a goddamn escort service."

In the street, Latimere asked Hines, "Listen, I know I haven't been here long, but would you mind not calling me 'Babysan'?"

"Relax Babysan, we all got call signs. Grimm's Batman. Roark's the Super Grunt—except some of us call him Nguyen because he's got more time in country than the goddamn zips. Ehlo's Fonebone and they tagged my ass with Urinal Man. That ain't a story you need to hear just yet. Make you a deal. Another month in country when you ain't so cherry, we'll call you Papasan."

Back at the doctor's house, Roark sat on the porch, relieved to be alone. Difficult keeping people at arm's length, there was never any privacy in Nam, and even buddies grew immune to the need for solitude. It was constant companionship seven days a week, even hard to get alone in the crapper.

Roark slipped off his pack and flak jacket. He craved his privacy, needed it like a fix. He lit a smoke, and the smell of dried blood from the *mamasan* and her baby on his fingers repulsed him. His fingers stuck together and he grabbed a handful of dirt and rubbed it into his hands. Getting rid of the smell of blood seemed impossible. It mixed with a man's sweat and grime and insect repellent, and he could smell the sweet, sickening stink of it days later when he wiped his brow or put his hand to his lips to drag from a cigarette.

Roark glanced across the street at the ARVN armory and his insides tightened. The ARVN sneaked glances out the windows, as if playing hide and seek. People rarely got under Roark's skin. He likened anger to any strong emotion and believed it shouldn't be given away lightly. People had to earn it. It bothered him when he let somebody get to him, but the ARVN had a knack for it.

The first time Roark worked with South Vietnamese soldiers, his hand was nearly blown off. The second time, he got shot. He knew perhaps it wasn't their fault, but he didn't like the flinching bastards and considered them bad luck.

Roark remembered an operation in March '67. The ARVN and Marines were to cordon an area so several hundred peasants could harvest their rice and put a stop to roving VC units who infiltrated Dai Loc to exact rice taxes from the farmers. Lima Company moved into position but had to wait until afternoon before the ARVN moved up to join them. By then, the grunts were sitting ducks. The enemy opened up, and Roark was hit first. It happened so fast he didn't even know it until he felt a warm, thick wetness oozing down his leg. He and the other casualties were dragged behind a hedgerow to wait for a medevac. When it landed, several ARVN sprang up and jumped aboard the chopper. They had bandages wrapped around them, which startled the grunts because nobody had seen any ARVN getting hit. The answer came when the chopper touched down in Danang and the ARVN piled out before the wounded Marines were unloaded. They took off running, tearing off their bandages as they ran out the gates. There wasn't jack-shit wrong with them. They had bandaged themselves up to get helo-ed out. Nobody could do anything, but there wasn't one grunt there who didn't want to put them back on the chopper and throw them out at a thousand feet.

Roark stopped thinking about the incident and lit another cigarette. Again, he smelled the blood. He smiled, though. He thought it odd how many important things he was numb to, and how many dumb things he remembered. The dumb things always did him in. He remembered the time he was hauling ass in a Jeep through sniper country, swerved onto a side road and nearly rear-ended a tri-wheel Lambretta. The Lambretta kept moving at a snail's pace in front of him. The driver wore an olive-drab field jacket and he figured him for an ARVN, deliberately putt-putting slow just to get him mad. He honked and shouted, but the Lambretta wouldn't speed up, and he gunned his Jeep and veered to the side. It was a narrow road, and he had to be wary because the paddies on both sides were a swampy quagmire. One wrong move and he'd be wheel-high in mud. He drew his .45 to scare the little shit, but when he pulled up beside him and looked at the driver, he was an old Vietnamese *papasan* who looked so terrified, Roark got sick to his stomach. He'd do something like that and spend the rest of the day smiling like a moron at anybody and everybody just to atone for it.

Chapter Nine

THE STREETS OF HUE were empty and bleak. It would be dusk in an hour, and the refugees gathered their children and whisked them inside the abandoned houses. When barred from entering an already overcrowded house, the families pushed on to the next. An affluent area of Hue, it was the perfect place for squatters, as the well-to-do had fled. Many of the wealthy had been captured by the communists and assassinated, and those who escaped the initial purge piled everything they could into cars and sped south.

Ehlo led Hines, Grimm and Latimere to the same three *mamasans* who had sold him bread earlier. The men bought loaves and wedged them under the straps on their packs. They bought an extra loaf which they broke and shared, and the bread smelled wonderful and tasted delicious.

To Grimm and other veteran grunts, the war seemed on hold during moments like these. They put their fears on standby. The ability to mentally check out during these lulls allowed them to keep their sanity. To cope, the men followed the unwritten code. If they weren't under fire, no fire existed. Nothing mattered if it wasn't crushing down on them directly or invading their small world. Even on a sweep, the code held up. A platoon on the flank could be caught in a firefight, but unless they were being routed no one reinforced them. Fifty meters away, a Marine could squat behind a paddy dike, take a crap and joke about the rounds zinging over his head.

A Marine could be out on a hump with his mind on pussy—a Marine's mind was always on pussy if not on

Charlie—while his buddy in front of him, cautiously soft-foots it because his attitude's different. His attitude has him thinking he's one snap of a twig away from tripping a booby trap and bringing the jungle to life.

In combat, everything was filtered through attitude, but the attitude wasn't constant. It changed, arced through the troops like an electrical charge. Even under fire, two men side by side didn't react to a battle the same way. Anxiety and fear. Primary attitudes. There were others. Anger, duty, even suicidal fits of blind invincibility. There was no way of knowing what someone else went through, because a man couldn't know where another man's head was, or what he had to fight through to survive what was easier for another. At least *that* time.

Everybody's private fear was private. Even if they talked to you about it, it was private. During nighttime bull sessions, men bragged how mean they were, but it was only fear, all of it. Some never mentioned it, and for some, it was all they talked about. They snorted and stomped and took out their fear and played with it. Grimm remembered one grunt's story: "I'm walking point one night when I practically trip over these zips on the trail. They're out there to ambush us, but they're so pumped up on opium they can hardly move—and I'm so jacked up on adrenaline, I'm barely able to waste 'em. But I grease 'em, and then I stand there, flailing my arms like Boris fucking Karloff, so whacked out I drop my load. Oh yes, I was scared all right. I was what you call scared fucking shit-less."

The CCs ambled on and ate bread. Latimere was still thinking about the mortar attack and wondered whether he'd ever get used to it. What Hines had said about Roark was also on his mind. "Is what you said about Roark wanting to be an actor true?" he asked.

"You doubt it?" Hines replied. "You're damn straight he does. God knows he does enough posing over here. Just watch him, for Chrissakes, all enthralled with himself. Acts like everything he does is in close-up, like somebody's always taking his picture.

"Let me tell you something about Roark," Hines said. "Roark thinks he's just passing through, like Nam's got nothing to do with him, which is a dangerous fucking attitude for the rest of us. He can think what he wants, but he ain't getting me killed. Once, we were out on an op and took some fire. I looked over and he's checking his pulse. He's smirking and checking his goddamn pulse. Tell me that's normal." Ehlo exchanged a glance with Grimm and they chuckled. Hines continued, "I'll tell you something else. Roark had a spider monkey he found on an op and took a liking to. He let it live and crap in his fucking utility shirt. One night, we're chowing down, and the monkey peeps out looking for food, and we start getting mortared. Roark dove for cover like the rest of us and fell on the monkey and crushed his skull. That's the only time I ever saw Roark mopey."

They turned a corner and Hines took the lead. In his dim witted way it pleased Hines and made up for the fact they wouldn't follow him earlier. They stopped in front of a battered yellow house where three young girls were cooking in the front yard. One girl plucked a chicken, while the others chopped vegetables into a large black kettle over a fire. The girls, pretty and flirtatious, had obviously "adopted" the house and now used it as their own. Hines' eyebrows pumped as one girl lifted her blouse and flashed her breasts and giggled. "You wike, GI? You want boom-boom?"

Latimere was startled. He hadn't seen a girl's breasts since his eventful night with Patty McDaniels. He wondered whether the girls were prostitutes. Then, he noticed another girl staring at him from hiding behind the porch post. Her huge almond eyes made her look younger, more exotic than the others, and butterflies jumped in his stomach. Latimere edged to the side to see more of her, but she ducked behind the post. He finally caught her eye and smiled, and when she smiled back, a stab of pain shot through him. The exchange was not lost on Hines and he gave Grimm a poke on the arm.

Just then, a fireteam of ARVN sauntered up the block on the far side of the street. The girls' attitudes instantly changed. They rushed to the porch, slinked behind the posts, and hid their faces. Grimm turned toward the ARVN, whose private conversation grew heated. One ARVN jabbed his rifle at the girls. The girl who had flashed the Marines, cocked her elbow and pumped it at the ARVN in the French "fuck off" sign. The ARVN halted momentarily but caught Grimm's glare, and the girls dashed into the house.

The CCs remained until the ARVN had gone. Hines bantered about bartering protection in exchange for freebies, but Grimm nixed it. Latimere wondered why the girls needed protection. He looked back at the ARVN as they continued up the street.

Back at the doctor's house, the CCs split off. Roark grabbed Latimere and set out for Hotel Company. Not much daylight left, and Roark walked down the middle of the street to keep a high profile. Night was falling fast, and he didn't want to be mistaken for the enemy. If they didn't find Hotel Company soon, they'd be forced to spend the night in a house with squatters.

They rounded a corner when Roark heard a bolt slam home and froze. Several Marines poked their heads out of a house. "You guys lost?" one called.

"Hope not. This Hotel Company?"

"That's affirm, who're you?"

"Correspondents."

"Fuck," the Marine emerged from the house. "You know something we don't?"

"What do you mean?"

"Every time one of you dudes shows up, it means we're gonna make a sweep. We ain't crossing the Perfume, are we?"

"Not that I know of. Where's Hotel Six?"

"CO's that way."

They walked down the block until Roark saw a radioman and turned into a courtyard figuring it might be the CP. Grunts were grumbling and chowing down in the yard, getting ready to crap out.

"Look what I got." A grunt brandished a new box of C-rats. "Spaghetti, can you dig it?"

"Yer ass. Let me see."

"No lie. Spaghetti an' goddamn meatballs."

"Wop food."

"Beats ham an' muthus, you greaser."

Roark walked up to the CP. "Skipper?"

An officer looked around. A permanent crease lined his brow, the burden of caring for too many men and grieving for too many casualties. "I'm Captain Felts," he said.

Roark introduced Latimere and himself.

"Good to have you. We had a reporter here a few days ago."

"Probably Grimm."

"That's him. Good man. You staying the night?"

"Yes, sir."

"You men got chow?"

"We're set, thanks."

"Could be a little cramped around here. You can check one of the other houses if you want."

"Thanks."

Latimere followed Roark to a house on the corner. A three-foot-high cement wall hemmed the front yard. Lance Corporal Thurman, the squad leader, was organizing the night's watch. Toting an M3A1 sub-machine gun, he had hair-trigger eyes and was strung tight as a drum. His weapon was unauthorized, but Roark figured he was good with it, and in the field that was all that mattered.

Thurman called to them. "You guys replacements?"

"Nope."

"So who?"

"Correspondents."

"Fuck," Thurman spat. "No offense. Thought maybe I could give one of my guys some rest for tonight." Thurman's utilities were smeared with bloodstains, and the thick powdery chalk of dried sweat caked his eyebrows and temples. "Don't suppose one of you would like to volunteer for watch?"

"I will," Latimere said.

"Yeah? appreciate it. Oh-four-hundred to sun-up OK?"

"Sure."

"Thanks, kid. You two can crap out by that tree. I'll tell the guy you're relieving. Better get a jump-on if you ain't chowed down yet."

Thurman left, and Roark shook his head. "Didn't you ever learn nothing about volunteering?"

Latimere shrugged. They shucked their gear and heated their C-rats, beans and franks for Roark, pork slices in juice for Latimere. Roark took out a bottle of Tabasco sauce and squirted several dollops onto his beans and franks. He tore off a chunk of French bread and tossed the rest of the loaf to a circle of nearby grunts. Latimere hated pork, and so drank coffee and nibbled on bread instead.

Latimere glanced at the men in Hotel Company, aware of how different they looked. They were grunts, not correspondents. A pall of death hung over them. Haunted faces and gutted eyes, to a man they looked ragged and fatigued. The large number of blacks and Chicanos among them was testimony that Vietnam was a class war—the middle class stayed home and the lower classes were sent here. To Latimere, even the white guys looked somehow tainted. He could not believe they volunteered. Of course, it was a moot point. "Volunteering" for the Marine Corps was easier when Uncle Sam would snatch you into the Army anyway.

Of the correspondents he'd met, Latimere thought perhaps only Grimm looked the part of a grunt, with his gaunt, haggard face and fierce black eyes. Roark might be as experienced but he was so aloof and impenetrable, Latimere thought if he had gone through what the grunts went through, it never took bone-deep. Roark had the air of an inheritor about him.

Latimere breathed into his canteen tin and steam from the coffee shot into his face. Warm and invigorated despite the grunts' despair, there was no denying he felt a twinge of camaraderie. He knew it was nuts. He knew it instinctively and from the faces of the men around him who had "been there" and survived.

Roark finished his rations and they laid out their ponchos and poncho liners. Darkness fell, and Roark crawled inside. He lit a cigarette and raised one corner of the poncho to let the smoke out.

"Hey Babysan," he said.

"Yeah?"

"Just one thing. You see anything moving on watch tonight, you best start cranking. Ain't none of that 'halt, who goes there?' shit."

Something stabbed him in the ribs and Latimere started. Cold and hard, and it stabbed him again. Latimere rolled on his side, stared up at a hulking silhouette. No moon out; he couldn't see the man's face.

"You the one supposed to relieve me?"

"Yeah," Latimere shook off the cobwebs and worked off his poncho. He rose quietly as he could. The last thing he wanted was a grunt getting after him for making noise. He groped for his rifle and followed the Marine.

The grunt led him to the low concrete perimeter wall.

Latimere knelt and the grunt wedged himself into a corner. Latimere still couldn't make out the grunt's features, but he stared at the silhouette and awaited orders. The grunt sighed and sat quiet for a moment. He was too tired to sleep. All around him Latimere heard the calls of crickets and the sound of fitful sleep and moans.

"OK now," The grunt whispered. "Keep an eye peeled down that street."

Latimere nodded. "Got it."

"Anybody comes up that street, don't wait till he makes you, OK?"

"Yeah. Thanks."

The grunt sighed. "You're green, ain'cha?"

"Sort of. How'd you know?"

"I know," he chuckled low. "They pointed you out to me last night. Gawd, I needs a smoke."

"I got one."

The grunt snorted. "Best not light up, Greenie."

"Oh, yeah," he caught himself. "I forgot. I got a candy bar. You want half?"

"Thanks."

Latimere unwrapped his candy bar, conscious of the noise. He broke off a hunk and handed it to the grunt. Huddled together in the blackness, two hours before dawn, Latimere felt a growing affinity between them, an intimacy.

"How long you been in-country?" the grunt asked.

"A week."

"A week? Aww, Greenie." The grunt groaned. "I was back in the world not long ago. In Hawaii, for R&R. This girl, young chick, sixteen-like, comes up to me. Think, wow, maybe something nice happening here. Then she asks me, 'How many innocent people you kill?' Plenty, I say. Who you got in mind? I thought it was neat putting her down that way, but later I think, Christ, why'd she have to say a thing like that? Let me tell you. Take your R&R in the Orient. I'm from Illinois and I never seen an ocean. That's why I picked Hawaii. You go to Hong Kong or Kuala Lumpur. There you just get laid and forget everything. Yeah, maybe I'll extend six months just to go on a real R&R."

"Seriously?"

"Naw, but it's no good back home."

"No?"

"They treat you worse'n the gooks do. They don't blow you away, but they kill you just the same. Just the way they look at you." The grunt sighed. After a moment, he said, "A week, huh, that's all? Aw, Greenie. I got thirty-eight days and a wake-up. Right now, all I want is to get my ass out of Hue City. Just get the hell out. Well, think I'll grab some zzzs. G'night, Greenie."

Chapter Ten

AT SUN-UP, WORD SPREAD through the ranks that they would move out by 0800, and it was greeted with the normal expletives as the grunts hacked on cigarettes, drank coffee and drearily checked their gear.

The Marines knew that once again they were headed into the shit. They knew it was a dim hope to cling to, but a few thought it was possible there wouldn't be any contact. It was rumored that most of the NVA had crossed the river to the north, but nobody with more than a month in-country was gullible enough to bite on it.

Latimere, caught up in the nervous tension and orderly chaos, wiped the dew off his rifle and checked his camera as Roark left for the CP.

Briefing his platoon leaders, Capt. Felts nodded at Roark. One of the benefits of being a CC was correspondents were usually able to sit in on briefings. Felts pointed to a map. "Here's our position. Command wants us to sweep up these streets to the railroad station. We'll be in a pincer movement with Fox Company and orders are to rout out any snipers or die-hards that stayed behind. This L-shaped building by the railroad station is where they're reporting enemy sightings. Two tanks will wait at this intersection in the event we draw fire and need something to soften them up. The CP'll move with 2nd Platoon." He folded his map and stuffed it in his cargo pocket. "That's it. Saddle up. We move out in one-five mikes."

Roark rejoined Latimere at the corner house. LCpl. Thurman called to them. "You guys staying with us?"

"If you're part of 3rd Platoon, we are."

"Stick with us you'll get all the stories you need." Thurman smiled at a frowning LCpl. Rodrigo Villegas, his first fireteam leader, who did not share Thurman's bravado.

An hour later, Hotel Company mustered at the small intersection. The L-shaped building was three long blocks ahead of them. On the way, they passed Vietnamese refugees scurrying to vacate the area.

Two M48A3 tanks thundered down the road and screeched to a halt near the intersection. A light drizzle fell and the air turned cold and heavy. Amidst shouted orders and the sounds of rifle bolts slamming home, 3rd Platoon was ordered into position and double-timed across the intersection to the corner houses on both sides of the street. Crashing through doors, they hastily searched the houses, their rifles on full auto. Once secured, they broke back into squads and fireteams and awaited the next order.

Roark and Latimere waited with Thurman in one of the houses. Not at all what Roark had in mind, he prided himself that he never stayed back with the CP, but he wasn't thrilled about being on point with Latimere beside him.

Latimere watched Thurman confer with his men. Standing next to them, he felt puny and insignificant. Each man carried 60 pounds of gear, including extra bandoliers, machine gun ammo, grenades and Claymore mines and LAAWs. This on top of sweat-soaked flak jackets and four canteens of water. The grunts looked grim, and Latimere thought it like watching condemned men on the way to the gallows. The hair on his neck suddenly grew stiff and he was sure something terrible would happen that day.

The cold pressed into him. His fingers stiff, he kept shifting his weight to help the blood flow in his veins.

Forget it, he told himself. This was the moment he had waited for and wondered about, had been curious about to the point of aching, what every young kid grew up thinking about. Despite his efforts to bolster himself, Latimere's eyes shot to Roark. Roark returned a look of understanding. He knew what the kid was thinking, though for the life of him he could hardly remember when he was that green. Latimere cupped his hands and blew to warm them. He fumbled for a cigarette. "Is it OK?"

"You got time," Roark said. "Listen, this may get heavy so don't try to impress anyone. No John Wayne bullshit."

"Not me." Latimere was pleased that Roark could even think of him that way. But Latimere wanted to talk. "So, what's it like in a firefight? Do you mind?"

"It ain't like getting sniped at."

"You think you'll write about it when you get home?"

"I doubt it. You?"

"I don't know. Maybe. I mean I'm definitely going to write, but maybe something sweeter. I got an idea about this poet..." He saw Roark's reaction and swallowed. "Well, maybe not a poet."

Roark took a last drag and ground the cigarette under his boot. "We start moving, you stay right behind me, asshole-to-belly-button. I don't want to have to look for you. When those tanks move up, stay the hell away from them. They're goddamn steel coffins. The gooks'll zero in on them." Roark looked at Latimere's magazine pouches. "Those mags should go in with the rounds pointed down. You're right handed, aren't you?"

Latimere nodded.

"The tips of the rounds should point to the left. That way you can reload in one smooth motion. You won't be fumbling or have to look."

Latimere checked his magazines and felt calmer. Then a concern crossed his face as he remembered something. "Roark? You have a girl back home?"

"No. Why?"

"Just wondering." he said, relieved.

Thurman signaled them to join him on the front porch. "Here it is. We'll advance up the left side of the street while second squad moves up the right. They think Charlie's holed-up in a building up the road there."

They had an unobstructed view leading to the L-shaped building. There was a short residential block lined with houses and trees, and two long blocks bordered by two-story apartment buildings. Not many trees along the last two blocks and not much cover.

"Today it's our turn to be the guinea pigs," Thurman said. "If the zips are there, it's up to us to draw fire."

"Ain't we the fuckin' Chosen Ones," Villegas said.

"Knock it off." Thurman turned to Roark and Latimere. "They want us to load up with tracer mags. Anyone sees movement, he starts popping rounds to give the tanks a target."

"How about our flanks?" Villegas said.

"Second and First Platoons will take them. Everybody keeps his eyes on that building up the street. You take your team out first, Villegas. I'll be behind you, second and third teams follow me." Thurman looked at the correspondents. "You guys can stick with me if you want."

The grunts reloaded with tracer mags. Thurman saw the camera hanging around Latimere's neck. "You gonna take pictures?"

"No, he's not," Roark took the camera and stuffed it in Latimere's pack.

"Shit. Thought at least we'd get our pictures taken."

"Stand by!" the Company Gunny yelled. "All right, move it out. Slow and easy."

Roark and Latimere moved behind Thurman and the first fireteam. "Use the trees," Thurman told them.

The squads moved forward on both sides of the street. There were trees every 15 meters. The fireteams advanced, leapfrogging in front of one another. A third of the way, a burst of M-16 fire popped on their left. More bursts followed, and the men in the streets scrunched down behind trees. "Spread it out!" Thurman yelled, and some men tore over a low cement wall and hurdled into the yards.

"WHAT THE HELL'S GOING ON OVER THERE!" the Gunny screamed from the intersection.

"HOLD YOUR FIRE! CEASE FIRE!" someone on their flank shouted.

"You spot anything?"

"I dunno, I thought something moved in that window."

"Where?"

"Over there."

"OVER WHERE?"

"OVER THERE."

"GET A FRAG IN THERE, GODDAMMIT."

"FIRE IN THE HOLE, FIRE IN THE HOLE!"

In a moment, a loud blast reverberated as a grenade went off inside the house.

"CHECK IT OUT. GET IN THERE."

At the intersection, Capt. Felts grabbed the handset from his radioman. "Zero Two, Zero Two, this is Six Actual. What's happening forward, over?" Static on the net. Another grenade exploded. "Zero Two, this is Six Actual. Be advised to hold what you've got. I say again, hold what you've got. I'm heading for your pos. Six Actual, out."

In the street, Thurman and his men kept down and took defensive positions. Capt. Felts and his CP group moved toward the houses on the left flank.

"WHO THE HELL'S UP THERE?" the gunny demanded.

"Mayberry's squad." someone replied.

"MAYBERRY? NOT FUCKIN' MAYBERRY. WHAT THE HELL'S GOING ON UP THERE, MAYBERRY?"

"All clear, Gunny," Mayberry shouted. "Someone thought he saw something and tossed a frag. Negative contact. All clear."

"DAMMIT, MAYBERRY. All right, let's get moving again. Slow."

Thurman told his squad to fall in. "You heard the Gunny. We're moving again. Easy."

In a crouch, one fireteam hustled behind a tree and waited for the next team to come up. Then they hustled to the next tree. They moved deliberately, and it took a long time to reach the first intersection. When they made the corner they waited for 1st and 2nd Platoons to finish sweeping the houses on their flanks and pull even with them. Then, the tanks rumbled up the street, single file, and stopped halfway.

At the corner, on the right side of the street, PFC Harold Purvis died happy. His turn on point, he leaned against a tree, hopeful, as he waited for the flanks to pull up. Maybe, just maybe, he thought, there weren't any VC around. He hoped the gooks had *di-di'*d north, which meant they'd be waiting in spades inside the Citadel, but things would be slack until they crossed the Perfume. That would be tomorrow. It might not even be tomorrow, Purvis reasoned, but two or three days. In the bush three days was a stay of execution, a lifetime. Purvis chuckled. What bush? This was goddamn Hue City. He could hear the birds chirping. How's that for an omen? Birds weren't stupid. They were back in the trees. They knew when something was about to pop. They could sense it. They were right, Purvis smiled. Today was going to be all right.

PFC Harold Purvis removed his helmet and dragged a sleeve across his forehead. *Damn*, Purvis chuckled, *he was always drenched in Nam.* If it wasn't from rain it was from goddamn sweat. It was going to be some bad-ass shit across the river, but not today. He had his high school sweetheart waiting back home and here the birds were singing, sweet and lazy. Purvis grinned. He wondered if his sweetheart was thinking of him. He wondered if birds were singing in her part of the world.

Purvis started to put his helmet back on as two AK-47 rounds ripped into him. The first round blew a chunk out of his jaw, while the second round bored through his throat and severed his spinal column. His head lolled at a hideous angle, as he stuck to the tree until gravity reached up and dragged him to the sidewalk.

A split-second it was silent, or maybe such a crescendo of noise their ears could not assimilate the racket. Then the world went mad, and a storm of enemy fire raked the street. The grunts tore for cover in the yards, and the birds exploded in flight like an oil gusher.

Latimere's insides imploded. *THIS WAS IT!* he thought. He was afraid he screamed, afraid everyone heard him, but the noise was inside. His mind short-circuited. *OHGOD! JESUS! OH JESUS.* Roark bowled him over a low brick wall as the grunts spewed out lead to gain fire superiority.

AK fire streamed out from a two-story building across the intersection. Rounds smacked into the low wall and snapped over their heads. The platoon on the right flank pulled up on line and laid down cover fire. The lead tank roared forward, its tracks chewing up pavement. It stopped short of the intersection and traversed its turret, elevating its cannon toward the corner building. A flurry of enemy rounds pinged off the armor, ricocheted violently and felled two Marines. As soon as the cannon launched a shell, Thurman yelled to his squad, "WE'RE MOVING. LET'S GO! GET ACROSS."

Thurman's squad poured over the wall and crossed the intersection, firing in brrrrrpps. Roark followed, shoved Latimere in front of him, but shoved too hard and Latimere went splaying onto his stomach in the street. His helmet rolled off, and a passing grunt kicked it forward as he tore across the intersection. Latimere raised his head as a barrage of rounds chinked into the street and chards of pavement pitted his face. Roark crumped down beside him and sprayed fire in a wide arc with one hand. More rounds pinged off the pavement near Latimere's head, PING-PEENG-PEEEYOOOOOOWWWW. Latimere's throat contracted. THE WHOLE WORLD WAS BLOWING UP! The tank's cannon BOOOOMMED and the ground shuddered beneath them. Latimere wrenched his face sideways against the asphalt and scraped the skin off his nose and cheek. Roark burned through another mag and slapped a new one into the well, then yanked Latimere up and shoved him hard as they scrambled across the intersection. When clear, they hurled themselves flat against the building next to Thurman.

Roark checked Latimere. One side of his face was tattooed with tiny scrapes, and bits of grit and gravel were embedded in his cheek. "You're OK," he said and retrieved Latimere's helmet and slapped it on his head.

Behind them, the tank cut loose again and blasted a hole in the building. Then, each successive shell blew out bigger and bigger holes. Diesel fumes chugged from the exhaust and clung to the cupola like paint. Volleys of enemy machine gun fire spewed from the building and brrriitttzed through the street. The tank's turret swiveled toward the street when heavier fire streamed from the building. The turret stopped mid-way, then rotated back to the right and pumped out another shell. A portion of the second story caved in, and a mountain of brick cascaded into the street as three enemy soldiers crashed onto the sidewalk. More bullets riddled their already dead bodies.

The fire subsided momentarily and the Marines on the right flank charged across the street and through the ground door. As grunts swept the building, there were frantic shouts in Vietnamese followed by short bursts of fire.

The lead tank lurched forward, past the intersection as machine gunfire intensified from the building. Thurman's squad leapfrogged through the firestorm up the second block. They ducked into the first doorway, and the CCs moved with them as another squad moved up on the right. Quickly, the squads behind them closed ranks. The windows in the buildings were shattered or blown-out, and Marines on the run hurled frags through the windows then bent low to avoid the flying shrapnel. Enemy mortars pelted down and jagged shards of metal ripped into the men. Several Marines toppled as others bowled head-long through the windows. Screams of "CORPSMAN UP!" pealed through the column. A direct hit from the tank had gouged out a cavernous section near the entrance of the L-shaped building. Thurman's squad reached the last doorway at the end of the block.

They packed inside the doorway, gulping air, near collapse. Worse than the weight on their backs, the mines and LAAWs and belts of linked ammo, yanked them every which way and constantly threw them off balance. The sweet elixir of exhaustion washed over them like a drug—a chorus of Sirens promising release if they gave in. Only fear pushed them on, riddled them with hellish jets of adrenaline.

Just then, a brief lull in the midst of the mortar barrage, and Thurman's squad bolted out the doorway in wide, outbound arcs to cross the intersection out of the line of fire. The first tank passed them again and cranked out two more shells. Thunderous blasts in close quarters resounded off the buildings and rattled their foundations. Enemy machine guns fused into a ferocious, cacophonous drone. The tank pulled up and covered the grunts' advance with machine gun fire. The point squads ducked into narrow, four-foot alleyways, unable to advance. The lead tank rumbled forward again, its .50 caliber machine gun clacking. As the tanks moved up the column, four grunts broke behind them for cover. A splay of red and green tracers crisscrossed the street when suddenly a B-40 rocket skidded off the asphalt and smashed into the underbelly of the tank. The tank BARRROOOOOMED backward. A shower of hot metal crumpled two Marines in Thurman's squad before the tank pitched forward, the right track knocked off, and its cannon cracked and smoking. A brief crackle of electronic transmission from inside the tank, and then another rocket slammed into its hull. The tank commander threw open the hatch and scrambled out. "GET THE HELL OUT OF HERE, GET OFF, GET OUT!"

The remaining crewmen staggered out while the second tank clanged forward. It veered to pass the lead tank, but the two downed Marines from Thurman's squad lay in its path. The commander in the second tank shouted: "Clear those men, dammit. Move 'em out of there!"

Thurman and Villegas rushed into the street. Rounds snapped past them as they dragged one of the wounded back. Roark and Latimere ran out and hauled the other man to cover.

The second tank lurched forward, metal gears grinding. The commander shouted. "Who's got a visual? Anyone see where those rockets came from?"

"Ground level," Thurman yelled. "Third window on the right." Movement at the window; somebody with a rocket. The tank's .50 opened up first and drove him down.

In the doorway, Thurman tried ramming through, then backed everyone off, and loosed a burst at the door-knob and bulled it open. They quickly dragged the two casualties inside. The second tank screamed forward firing its cannon. The concussion shook the building. The man Thurman and Villegas dragged back had a sucking chest wound and died instantly. Latimere eased the other casualty onto the floor as Roark went for a corpsman.

Latimere bent over him, a young black man. He slid his hand under his neck to support the grunt's head, a small blood puddle where his right eye had been. Latimere didn't want to look. "You're OK, you're OK," he repeated.

He slid the grunt's pack underneath his head. The grunt gurgled as he tried to rise and his good eye rolled back grotesquely. "Easy," Latimere begged.

The grunt stared into Latimere's eyes as blood foamed through his teeth. A tortured flicker of remembered kinship; his words were barely audible. "Aww...Greenie," he gasped.

The grunt fell limp and Latimere reeled back on his heels. Blood drained from his face, and his stomach pitched. Another blast from the tank shook the building's foundation. Shards of concrete crashed from the ceiling. Latimere staggered against the wall to brace himself and retched. Roark rushed in with a corpsman who looked briefly at the casualty and ran out.

Thurman yelled to his troops, "Move it." He and Villegas started out the door when a spurt of enemy fire forced them back. They headed out again and zigzagged up the street, pulling their heads low between their shoulders.

Roark grabbed Latimere. "You OK?" Latimere gaped at him, his mouth an open wound. "Let's go, get your head screwed on." Roark dragged him out the door.

Thurman and Villegas caught up to their squad at the end of the block. They crammed inside a doorway near the foot of the last intersection and Thurman and Villegas squeezed in with them. A spate of enemy rounds stitched the building beside them. Villegas spun round to uncork a burst when a bullet caught him flush in the flak jacket, and kicked him against the wall. Three more rounds dug into his groin and buckled him. His trigger finger locked, and rounds from his rifle spattered off the pavement below his feet. Then, the recoil jacked the barrel up and steered the last of his rounds toward the grunts across the street. Thurman slapped his muzzle up, and Villegas keeled forward. Thurman caught him under the arms and lowered him to the ground. The tank unloaded two more blasts at the building. Black smoke billowed out the windows. Thurman was on his knees. "Villegas, damn you." Thurman pawed Villegas' face, plied his lips up and down. "Breathe, come on." Now, Villegas was nothing but dead weight. "Fuck you then, damn you, Goddamn you." Thurman reared to his feet and bolted into the street. Tears streamed down his face.

More squads closed ranks behind them. Capt. Felts radioed the tank commander to hold his fire. The grunts rushed across the intersection, reached the building, cranked hot bursts through the windows and hurled grenades inside. The first Marine through the door was dropped in his tracks. Thurman pushed in behind, firing maniacally, spewing out lead. He jacked a fresh mag into his weapon and vaulted up the stairs, hurdling dead bodies.

The grunts fanned out behind to sweep the building's ground floor. Roark and Latimere rushed inside. An NVA soldier pleaded in a room upstairs, *"Chieu hoi, chieu hoi."* It was followed by a burst from Thurman's grease gun.

Roark ran up the stairs as Latimere followed. Near the top, Roark shouted, "Friendlies coming up, hold your fire." Checking the rooms crushed by tank fire, they found bodies under the rubble. Sporadic M-16 fire continued from rooms downstairs. Roark heard voices next door and another burst from a grease gun, and headed for it. As they crashed through the door, Thurman stood at the window beside three NVA who lay twisted in the debris.

Thurman made sure they were dead, when Roark heard a moan and swiveled. Roark pulled a door back and saw an NVA officer bloodied and half-buried beneath a blown-out section of the wall. Roark trained his rifle as he approached, and removed the rubble on top of the man. The enemy soldier grimaced and braced back against the wall. His hands were clasped in front of him as if praying, but his elbows were wedged against his stomach, holding his innards in.

Thurman crossed to the injured man. "VC?" he smiled savagely.

The soldier shook his head.

"VC? You want help? You *com bic*?" Thurman knelt. "You know what I think? I think you killed Villegas. You know Villegas? I think it was you." He put the muzzle of his grease gun in the middle of the man's forehead, but the NVA soldier's eyes clouded over and his tongue rolled out.

Thurman spat. He nudged the dead man sideways and his guts unraveled and spilled on the floor.

Shaken, Latimere gasped at the dead man. Roark knelt, then took the red and green scarf off the man's neck, and looked up. "Any objections?"

"Negative," Thurman said.

Roark crossed to Latimere and handed it to him. "Souvenir."

Roark walked briskly up the street, as Latimere trailed him. After Hotel Company had secured the building, Roark rounded up stories, getting only as much information as necessary. Not that he needed much. Five or six paragraphs were a much as the *Sea Tiger* was apt to print. The Joe Friday school of journalism, "Just the facts, Marine."

Roark quickened his step. "Get a move on," he barked.

Latimere, still pained and half-dazed, caught up to him. "Why did we leave so soon?"

"They want us with one-five when they cross the Perfume, and that may be tomorrow."

"But we were just getting to know those guys."
"You don't want to get to know anybody."

Chapter Eleven

AN HOUR BEFORE DUSK, two Huey helicopter gunships made strafing runs over the Citadel. Meanwhile, in the courtyard of the doctor's house, the civilian reporters placed their bets. Ehlo held Roark's .45 in hand, collected the money and matched it with his own. In the bleak afternoon light, the birthmark on his cheek looked more like a smear of blood than a pinkish rash.

Ehlo aimed and fired at a can of ham and limas. The round hit dead center. He fired two more rounds, and the can bucked wildly, spun to the ground, and the contents oozed out. "So much for ham an' muthas," he said.

Hines tore out of the house as if shot from a cannon. "Jesus fucking Christ, warn someone, will ya. Ever heard of 'fire in the hole'?"

Ehlo ejected the magazine, cleared the round in the chamber and blew on the barrel. "Your nerves are frayed, Hiney."

"You saw what I saw today and you'd be fried, too."

Roark took his .45 and magazine from Ehlo and sat by Latimere on the porch. "You done good today."

Numb, Latimere kept silent.

"How you doing?"

"OK. I was just thinking. Do you think we'll get a chance to hook up with two-five?"

"I don't know. Why?"

For the first time that day Latimere smiled. "My best friend is with Golf Company. Billy Huff, I grew up with him. I can't wait to see his face when he sees me."

The name registered dimly, and Roark unconsciously touched his bandolier. He squeezed one of the magazine pockets and something sick spiraled down his chest. He still had the folded, bloodied letter.

"Huff?" Roark stalled, but he knew.

"Yeah," Latimere smiled. He saw Roark turn insular again. Roark patted Latimere's knee and tried not to be obvious. He could not say anything to the kid now. Maybe later, in the rear, but not out here, not in the field.

Hines crossed to the civilian photographers in the courtyard. One of them looked familiar, and Hines stared him down. "Well, if it ain't the asses who sway the masses."

Trilling tried to place him. He extended a hand. "I remember you. I've seen your byline in the *Sea Tiger.*"

"Cut the shit. You seen more than that. I was the one who held your hand on Operation Arizona."

Trilling introduced Hemmings for support. "This is Louis Hemmings, from UPI."

Hines kept his eyes on Trilling. "You're Trilling. Tell me if I'm wrong."

"You have a good memory."

Hines looked at Hemmings. "Your pal ever tell you I was the one who nursed him through his first operation?"

"My first op with Marines," Trilling said. "I was in the Delta with the Army before that."

"In Saigon, maybe. Musta seen a lot of shit coming down from them balconies."

Trilling braved a phony smile. "Seen a lot of poontang."

"Right, you guys make love, not war."

"We do what we're good at."

"So tell me," Hines wanted to push his button. "How's your favorite relative?"

"Who?"

"Uncle Ho."

Grimm walked over and drew Hines aside.

"What's with you?" Hines snapped.

"Keep a lid on," Grimm said and led Hines over to Roark on the porch. "What do you say we case the area, take a little look-see?"

"For what?" Roark said.

"Bennies, brother. Babysan looks like he could do with a little. You can bet there won't be any slack after tomorrow."

Bayer and Ehlo joined them. "What's up?" Ehlo asked.

"Shhh," Hines said, not wanting to tip off the civilians. "How about we check out that house with the chicks. Interested?"

"I'll pass," Grimm said. "There'll be time enough later."

"What later?"

"After the goddamn Citadel."

"Shit. Later, sooner, what the hell's the difference? You're lifer-bait, Grimm."

"Just the same, I'm out."

"Me too," Bayer decided. Bayer had 49 days left in county and even a skivvy run seemed precarious. "Think I'll head over to MACV and snoop some scoop. Want to go?" he asked Grimm.

"No, but I would like some goddamn Tiger Piss." Grimm turned to the civilians. "How about you guys?"

"Huh?" Trilling said.

"Tiger Piss! Gook beer."

"Hell yes."

"Let's go then." Trilling and Hemmings joined him. "We'll see if we can cut a deal with the ARVN."

Bayer looked at Ehlo. "You want to poke around MACV, get some word on the crossing?"

"Yeah, I'll tag along." Ehlo called to Grimm as he was walking out of the yard. "Grimm, scarf some suds for us."

Hines smacked his hands together. He was antsy to get going. "C'mon," he prodded Latimere. "Let's go already."

Roark rapped Latimere's knee. He wanted to get his mind off the Huff kid. "Come on. It'll help you get your poop in a group."

"I don't have any money."

"No sweat," Hines said. "We'll pack a case of rations. Dinks go ape over C-rats."

They walked a few blocks then turned down the street toward the yellow house. Hines balanced a case of C-rations on his shoulder. The yellow house looked deserted. Hines cursed, abruptly aware of the falling darkness. He knocked on the door. "Anybody home?" He couldn't force the door and banged louder. "Hey, it's us. Marines."

A rustling inside, then the door opened slightly. A girl peeked through the crack, the same girl they saw the day before plucking the chicken. Now, her eye was swollen shut, and black and blue. Two more girls crowded behind her.

"We come in?" Hines winced, studying the girl's eye.

The girls debated as Hines wedged his foot inside the door. The girl tried to shut it but couldn't. "Marines," Hines said again, "No ARVN. Friends."

The girls tittered back and forth, and then the injured girl glanced over Hines' shoulder up and down the street and hurried them in.

Inside, there was more jockeying as the three girls debated and peeked out the window. Slowly, their nervousness turned to relief. Latimere noticed the young girl he had seen on the porch now standing alone in the corner. He felt torn seeing her, and her beauty pained him. She looked at him openly, but he could not tell if she was happy.

"Why are they afraid?" he whispered to Roark.

"They're afraid of the ARVN."

"They jealous," the girl with the black eye snapped. "ARVN numbah ten. They come back, do this." She pointed to her eye. "No like us talk with Malines."

Latimere's worried eyes moved to the girl in the corner again. Her mouth trembled slightly—a smile? For a split second he brightened, but then suddenly was self-conscious about the ugly scrapes on his face, and he rubbed his forehead trying to cover them.

Hines set the case of Cs on the floor. This house had also been stripped of furniture. Soon, candles were lit and there was the pungent smell of joss sticks.

Hines leered at the girls from tit to twat and pumped his eyebrows. "Well...?"

"You have money? You want boom-boom?" the girl with the black eye asked.

"No," Latimere blurted, surprised at himself.

"No?"

Roark looked at Latimere and then back at the girls. "No boom-boom," he said. "Talk."

"Talk?" repeated the girl with the black eye.

"Talk?" Hines exclaimed. But he read Roark's mind and said, "OK. We talk a little bit. *Ti-ti, ti-ti*. French, you know? *Parlez-Vous Français?"*

The girl with the black eye was adamant. "No French. Vietnamese."

"No sweat. We talk English."

"*Ti-ti* English," another girl said.

"Listen," Hines explained. "We stay here tonight with you."

"You have piasters?"

"No piasters," Roark said. "Stay. Just talk."

"Talk?"

Hines tired of the charade. "Fuck it. Boom-boom."

The girl with the black eye smiled. "Boom-boom."

"No piasters," Hines said, "C-rats. Beaucoup good."

"C-wats numbah one."

She bent and dragged the case of rations against the wall, then took a candle and squatted in the center of the room. She dripped hot wax on the wood floor and planted the candle in the middle. She patted the floor for the others to join her.

Hines and Roark sat on the floor with the girls, forming a circle around the candle. Latimere joined them, his eyes glued to the girl in the corner. At last, she walked over and sat between the other girls, her eyes cast downward.

The girl with the black eye motioned to the C-rats. "You want?"

Hines grimaced but caught himself. He rubbed his stomach. "Number one."

The girls giggled. "C-wats numbah one."

They fidgeted and looked at each other.

Hines grew frustrated and turned to Roark. "How about it? We ain't got all night."

Hines' comment alarmed Latimere. "Do we just choose?" Latimere whispered.

"Don't worry, Babysan, I ain't picking yours."

Roark looked at Hines. "Who takes who?"

"Shit, they don't care who you take. They're just grateful for a little protection."

Hines chose the girl with the black eye. Despite her eye, Hines thought she looked hot and sexy. He pulled her to her feet and headed toward a bedroom.

In the living room, Roark wasn't ready to choose. Not from politeness, he knew the whores were willing, but his thoughts were of Maggie. *Christ*, he suddenly wondered, *whatever happened to his fantasies about Sandra Dee and Haley Mills?* Maggie is what happened. Wanton, debauching and fiendish as a drug.

What the hell was he to do, sit there all night staring at Latimere and his girl? He couldn't believe how google-eyed they'd become. He began to feel like an interloper.

Roark looked at the girl sitting across from him. "We go?" The girl acted pleased to be chosen. "What about you?" he asked the other girl.

Both girls jumped up, put their arms around him and escorted him out of the room.

In the living room, Latimere avoided the girl's eyes across from him. He stared down the hallway long after Roark and the two girls disappeared, seeking courage to look at her again.

"He call you Babysan," she said.

Latimere was startled by her English. "That's just what Hines calls me."

"I like. Vietnamese name."

He met her eyes. When she held his glance, he looked down. "I no Vietnamese," he said.

"I Vietnamese, but I no VC."

"No. There are no VC. People get killed, but there's no VC."

He spoke without thinking and there was a strain between them. Latimere's throat plugged, and he could not seem to get enough oxygen. The girl's face became suddenly hard. She spoke quietly, evenly, with great dignity.

"You know Quang Tri Province?" He shook his head. "Two year ago, my mother and father, they killed by Viet Cong. The VC say they informers. They make me watch while they shoot them. Then, they try to have me, but one, he like me and stop them. He have me for his own. He say he be back, but I no wait. When they leave, I come to Hue for to work. I hate Ho Chi Minh. But, my brother killed by American bombs when VC hide in our village."

Latimere dared not speak, and she was too strong for tears. She drew a deep breath. As if changing a mask, she suddenly exuded a quality of evanescence. He wanted to say something, but she shook her head and placed a finger to his lips, "No talk."

Her face was yearning, smoldering. Latimere wondered briefly whether the girl was drawn to his innocence or whether she was only grateful for protection, as Hines said. Slowly, deliberately, she unbuttoned her blouse and let it slip from her shoulders. The candlelight danced on her breasts. Latimere tried not to, but he stared at the girl's nakedness. Her nipples were brown and taut, and his heart pounded. She noticed the tension weighing on him.

"Maline," she teased. "You like me?" Then she tilted her head. "You no like?"

Finding it difficult to breathe, Latimere thought. He desperately wanted to touch her and cursed his timidity.

She drew his hand toward her, beckoning him to touch her. Then, she arched her back ever so slightly and her breasts heaved. Latimere extended a trembling hand but as he was about to touch her, the candlelight illuminated the dried blood beneath his fingernails. He blanched as it all swarmed back to him, the battle, the screams, the bursts around his head as he lay in the street. Then the black grunt's face reared up inside him, gurgling through blood and gasping, "Aww, Greenie..." Latimere pulled back his hand. "I'm sorry."

The girl didn't understand.

"Maybe later. After..." he wanted to explain, but he couldn't think clearly.

Disoriented, Latimere rose, not understanding his turmoil. If only he could go outside, get some air, but he was afraid to. Would she let him back in?

The girl looked at him and her face changed from confused to startled and finally determined. She gathered her blouse around her shoulders. "You go now?"

"Maybe."

Her reaction punctured him. He knew he had lost her. His head whirled and he wondered what was happening to him. His sudden panic over losing her overpowered his turmoil, yet his young, foolish pride overpowered his hurt. At last, he said, "You be OK?" He chuckled. "Now I talk like you." Then, suddenly terrified she would think he made fun of her, "I joke. I was kidding."

She looked at him icily. "No sweat," she shrugged.

Latimere winced. She was lost to him now. He wanted to erase everything—if only he could hold her—but he turned and went to retrieve his rifle. Once again, dread ravaged him. He didn't want to go, but when he whirled to face her, she was looking at the floor and all the courage drained out of him. Then, he remembered Roark and Hines and started toward the hallway but stopped. He wondered whether he should interrupt them. He heard laughing, and Hines' booming voice, "'At's it, shake them little titties." Latimere felt mangled.

The girl watched Latimere. She was struck by how young he looked, innocent and yet tormented. His apparent suffering summoned something deep within her.

Latimere turned from the hallway and was surprised to find her staring at him. For an instant, his heart leaped, but he merely nodded sheepishly and crossed to the door.

"Maline," she said. "You Babysan."

Latimere stiffened, and when he turned around, she smiled. He was still afraid to hope, but then she slipped off her blouse and patted the floor. For Latimere, too much was happening. But his features went soft and betrayed his want. And she took him.

Chapter Twelve

THE MORNING AIR WAS HEAVY and a steady rumble of thunder broke against Grimm's temples. He sat up and a surge of prickly heat bristled through him. Damned malaria, he thought.

He stepped over several sleeping bodies, opened the poncho covering the hole in the living room wall, poked his head out and listened to the drum roll. It was drizzling outside and the roar he heard wasn't thunder, but the merciful rumble of explosions. The fire was coming from the U.S. Navy ships off the coast. Grimm knew the South Vietnamese government had finally got off the pot and gave the fucking thumbs up to shell the Citadel.

The explosions boomed louder. Grimm cleared his head and went back to his gear. He took his canteen and splashed water on his face. He thought about the souvenirs he would scrounge inside the Imperial Palace. By the time they were through in the Citadel, he'd be set until the end of his tour. He'd get the prime stuff there, not the junk he'd been pawning to the pogues. Up to now he'd made do with fleecing the dead for weapons and gear. But Grimm scavenged other things as well—sandals, rice tubes, even the dull bread knives the peasants used in the villes. In the rear, he carved communist stars on the hilts and painted them red. He'd met pogues in Danang who gave half a month's wages for "enemy daggers" like that.

Grimm thought about his drinking bout with Hemmings the night before. To his astonishment, Louis Hemmings had matched him beer for beer and by the end of a ball busting, three-hour fandango, Hemmings brandished sea stories to shame even Grimm's.

There had always been friction between the Marine CCs and the civilian reporters and what the CCs perceived a biased press. With Tet blowing up, suspicions had been exacerbated when the press pushed the panic button. For civilians, Tet legitimized the worst of their fears—or hopes—as was the case with some. The offensive saw the enemy abandon rural hamlets and bring the war into the cities. Even President Johnson had been stricken by paralysis since promising "a light at the end of the tunnel." Now, the chaos filmed by the civilian media showed the cities under siege, reminiscent of the old newsreel battles in Europe in World War II. However, this time there was no great Satan to rally against, and Americans grew restless and vocal.

Still, Grimm had warmed to Hemmings, who proved a good audience, roistering mountain of jelly that he was. Grimm believed the civilian press were scavengers and the grunts were fodder. He knew the reasons Vietnam was covered differently than other wars, not the least of which was television. The availability of the helicopter was another. The helicopter, in fact, had become a corrupting influence. The civilian press could not film at night, so there was little incentive to spend nights in the field and grunt it out. Instead, they wrote liquid prose on their verandahs in the rear without the scantest understanding of the day-to-day existence the grunt endured. To Grimm, there were two kinds of journalists—those who covered the war, and those who covered the briefings. At least Hemmings tried to split the difference.

Grimm lit a smoke. Cold and clammy inside the house, only the men's body heat and their tobacco-stale breath generated any warmth at all. The walls were filthy and coated with mold from the constant damp of the monsoon. Grimm shivered and looked around. Then he wadded up the wet poncho and hurled it at Hemmings. It hit him flush in the snout, and Hemmings shot up as if he'd been smothered by a sheet of Saran wrap. Grimm laughed aloud as the effects of a hangover doubled Hemmings over. Hemmings staggered to his feet and stumbled to the bathroom, kicking legs and bodies in his way.

Roark and Latimere awoke. The others stirred and grumbled as they wheezed on cigarettes and drank coffee and cocoa. Groaning, sloshing sounds came from the bathroom.

A new barrage of naval gunfire rumbled. "Hey, is that arty?" Hines asked.

"That's affirm," Grimm smiled. "Which means air strikes next if we get a break in the weather."

Hines mumbled hopefully, but turned sour again when he realized clearance for arty meant they'd cross the Perfume today for sure. His sleep had been fitful and his eyes were red and bleary. Most men got quiet before they went into battle. Hines got loud. He needed to snap at something.

Bayer sipped coffee and ran a cleaning rod and patch down his rifle barrel.

"You know," Hines sneered, "anybody ever counted the times you stroke that thing, they'd think you had a case of penis envy."

"At least I'll shoot off more than my mouth."

Too early to get even, even for Hines. More grunts and straining noises emanated from the bathroom. In the small, crowded living room the stench roiled out and gagged them. Hines fired his Zippo and waved it in front of him.

They made it back to the wire without incident, hollering "*bao chí*" in the streets, and the ARVN let them pass. They were thankful the ARVN Roark manhandled had not pulled watch last night.

Latimere huddled with his cocoa. Still faint from the night before, his head swam. In his mind, he saw the girl's eyes bat open and his heart plummeted. Her name was Lan, and it was the first time he had "done it" and as the ecstasy of his conquest reared, so too did the memory of his asinine faux pas. God, what an imbecile. It had been perfect until he forgot what to do. She had been pinned beneath him with her legs together while his own were spread on top of her. Unable to insert himself despite his efforts, she finally had to tell him to put his legs together so she could spread hers. Latimere hid his face in his hands and shuddered. God, what a dope. What an infant.

Hemmings staggered out of the bathroom, seemingly near death, with a fish-belly pallor and clutching his stomach.

Hey, Hemmings," Grimm said. "You pour it down one hole and squirt it out the other, that how it works?"

Hemmings asked pitifully whether they had to cross the Perfume today and everyone guffawed. Gallows humor. They needed it.

Ehlo stood up and slipped on his pack. Think I'll check with MACV."

"Again?" Hines said. "You checked them last night."

"They didn't know nothing last night. They were waiting on clearance for arty."

"So?"

"So it's obvious we got clearance, or can't you hear? We should get briefed and hitch up with our units."

"Yeah, it'd be a shame if they crossed without us."

An hour after Ehlo left, the CCs and Trilling and Hemmings headed toward Le Loi Street. The rain had stopped, but it was overcast, and beyond the Perfume River, plumes of black smoke shot up from the Citadel and soiled the low gray clouds. Two Huey gunships orbited the river, their guns clacking.

When they reached Le Loi Street, the civilians split off with Bayer to find Ehlo at MACV. Latimere wanted to sit in on the briefing, but Roark, bored by briefings, nixed it. They kept pace with Grimm and Hines and continued toward the river.

Platoons of Marines scattered along the river bank, spread out in case of incoming. They reached a bunker manned by four Marines. Now, there was none of the sarcasm or masochistic humor that usually went with pre-battle anxieties. They crouched behind the sand bags, hands on their rifles, glaring sullenly across the Perfume. The top of the massive outer wall of the Citadel beyond the treetops was half-shrouded in mist.

"You guys One-Five?" Roark asked.

"Delta Company. You?"

"Correspondents."

"All of you? Just what we need, a goddamn squad of storytellers."

Hines glowered. "You know how often we hear that crap? Just so you're clued in, when you guys get pulled out of the field, we write our stories and haul-ass out to another unit while you're resting in the rear drawing slack time. We ain't pogues, so you can stow your salty shit."

Grimm sighed. "That's Corporal Hines, our diplomat."

"Where's Delta Six?" Roark asked.

"The CO's over there."

"Much obliged."

As they walked to the CO, Roark chided Hines. "That's telling it like it is. Of course, I wouldn't mention that little skivvy run last night."

Delta Six, Capt. Donlon, was standing beside a gun emplacement, surrounded by his headquarters group. He handed the handset back to his radioman.

"Excuse me, sir," Hines said. "We're ISO. Just wondering what the orders are, and who's going so we can divide up."

Capt. Donlon studied them. "There's enough of you. Well, I'm Captain Donlon, Delta Company. That's Alpha over there and Charlie Company's set-in behind us. We're still waiting on Bravo, but there doesn't seem to be much hurry. The LCIs haven't been able to make it up river to ferry us over. Tried twice this morning, but drew too much fire."

Grimm asked, "Will all the companies cross today?"

"That's the plan. We'll be bringing up the rear. Could be late tonight or possibly tomorrow. Any of you want to come with us, you're welcome."

"Thanks. We'll grab a few stories while you're still on hold. Check back later."

"See you, men."

The correspondents trudged through the sand toward a group of Marines from Charlie Company clustered across the street. They saw Bayer and Ehlo coming toward them, excited. Trilling straggled behind, helping Hemmings.

"What's up?" Roark asked.

Bayer looked ready to bust. "Hurry up and wait, same old shit. Wait'll you hear this. Walter Cronkite is in Hue. He's got this camera crew and he's all decked out in battle fatigues. He did an interview with a captain two days ago, except there was nothing coming down then, no fireworks. But when they play the interview on CBS News the next night, there's automatic weapons-fire dubbed into the background, like old Cronkite's right in the thick of it."

"Fucking civilians," Hines spat. "Don't do shit and get all the praise."

Roark smiled. "Everyone's got a pecking order, Hines."

Grimm wanted to get going. "Think I'll mosey over to Alpha."

"Bayer and I'll stick with Charlie Company," Ehlo said.

"Guess I'll stick with Babysan," Hines said, "seeing as how he's turning into a killer. Lady-killer, I mean."

"Latimere's with me," Roark said.

"To hell with it, I'll buddy with Grimm, then."

"If you're coming with me, let's go."

"I'm coming, already." Hines slung an arm around Latimere's neck. "But first, how about it, Babysan? You gonna tell ol' Hines whether you got nekkid last night?"

There was little troop movement all morning. The grunts shuffled about on the south bank of the Perfume awaiting orders. Each time the LCIs tried to motor up the river they were repulsed by enemy fire. By late morning, the decision was made to hold, at least until nightfall. The grunts liked the delay but nobody wanted to think about crossing the river at night.

Later, the bank was transformed into a massive staging area. Trucks and Jeeps rumbled back and forth from the stadium, bringing munitions and medical supplies, rations and water. Working details off-loaded supplies as men continued to dig in.

Roark was surprised they had not been mortared. No doubt the enemy used the lull to regroup. They'd had enough to contend with from the naval barrages. The south side of Hue was lost for the communists, but the north side would decide the outcome. History bared her fangs gently and gloated. The communists were confident. For centuries, whomever held the fortress in the north emerged victorious. Now, it was America's turn to meet futility.

By noon, the weather lifted and turned mild. For the first time in a week, they could smell the fetid odor of rotting flesh. The CCs and civilian reporters linked up with their units. Roark decided to cross with Delta Company. While they dug in, Roark had time to snoop around. Across Le Loi Street, usually a bustling marketplace, was now a deserted expanse of rubble. Roark led Latimere around the back of the MACV compound. "Take a walk?"

"Where to?"

Roark smiled. "How about the yellow house. To say goodbye."

"You serious?"

"We have time."

They walked a few blocks, spotted the house and went up to the porch. Latimere's heart was beating. Roark knocked. No answer. He tried the door. Locked. "Check around the side," Roark said. Latimere looked through a side window. Empty. He walked round back and went in through the back door. Roark sat down on the porch, his rifle across his knees. He thumbed the safety off and lit a smoke.

Inside, Latimere checked each room. No one and no belongings. He walked to the empty living room. He looked at the candle wax on the floor, all that remained. Roark rapped on the door.

"No one?" Roark asked when Latimere came out.

Latimere shook his head. "You don't think the ARVN have them, do you?"

"Doubt it. They're probably at the canal with everyone else, wanting to get out of the city."

Latimere wasn't sure. Last night Lan told him she would never leave Hue.

It started to drizzle again. "Let's go," Roark said.

Walking back to the Perfume, Roark hoped to skate for the rest of the day, dig up one or two more stories before he chowed down. He hoped to possibly grab a good night's sleep before Delta made its crossing in the morning. For once, he looked forward to the delay.

However, he soon realized that was not to be. The MACV compound was buzzing with activity. Only mid-afternoon, but troops were mustered on the shore, officers pointed in all directions and platoon sergeants shouted orders. Three LCIs were docked at the bank with grunts on board and more grunts boarding, getting ready to cross the Perfume.

Part Three

NORTH SIDE

Chapter One

PLATOONS FROM ALPHA, BRAVO AND CHARLIE Companies, already at half strength, crammed aboard the LCIs. When they rounded the MACV compound, Roark knew what was happening and headed toward Delta Company's CO, standing at the bunker with his command group.

The LCIs resembled big shoe boxes with forward loading ramps. Each craft was armed with twin .30 caliber machine guns. Grimm and Hines boarded an LCI with the grunts from Alpha Company. Hemmings and Trilling trailed after them. No one wanted to be last to board, which meant he would be first to disembark. Bayer and Ehlo squeezed in with Bravo Company, asshole-to-belly button. Two more civilian photo journalists boarded with them and were shoved to the port side. Ehlo didn't care; he didn't much like them, though he liked them more than the civilians that opted to remain at MACV.

A third LCI took on a decimated Charlie Company, along with the overflow of grunts from Alpha and Bravo. Most of the men were already on board, but the platoon sergeants' constant shouting made everything worse.

Hines fidgeted, the faces around him as taut as his, and tried to hide it. He hated being on water, and now he found himself on a naval craft about to make a landing. If he had wanted to be a Swabbie, he would have joined the goddamn Navy, he thought.

For the first time that day, Louis Hemmings felt better. So relieved to be rid of his hangover, Hemmings had discounted the danger of crossing the Perfume and going into the Citadel.

Back on the beach, Latimere tugged Roark's sleeve. "Do we cross with them?"

"The Top wants us separated," Roark said. "If everyone came in with stories from the same unit, he'd shit in his mess kit. Our turn's coming."

Boat ramps raised and locked into place. Platoon sergeants called, "Face outboard. Stay alert. Eyes peeled."

The men grumbled. "Hey, Sarge," someone called. "Suppose I got time to make a piss call? Only be an hour."

"Dribble it down your leg."

"Can't do that, got a snake in here. Sink the boat."

One by one, the LCIs moved, slowly at first, and then gathered speed, but the farther into the river they churned, the slower they seemed to go. In the river, the LCIs seemed vulnerable and puny, and the Marines grew tense.

The men's eyes were fixed on the Citadel. The ridge of its southern wall was visible above the trees, and the utter immensity of the fortress weighed upon them. Grimm felt it, too. He contemplated the battles that had been fought there through the ages, the swarming hordes with bows and arrows attacking through the flak from cannons and ballistas. Now, a new battle beckoned. Six NVA battalions were dug in and waiting within the walls of the fortress. All the bastards needed were vats of boiling oil, Grimm thought. His blood ran cold, and a dark shadow passed through him.

Roark watched the boats depart, disappointed he was not with them—not with Grimm. Latimere was a good kid, but it wasn't the same as buddying with Grimm. He would miss the bond they had and the humor only two salts could share. With Grimm, he could scoff at danger at times, but with Latimere he had to worry. He was green. Roark cursed that he had been paired with him.

Thirty minutes later, the LCIs approached a loop in the river that would take them to the quay above the northern tip of the Citadel. Dark clouds scudded overhead. In the troop well, the men braced against the waves crashing against the bow and hunkered lower as the river narrowed, and the banks closed in on them.

The boats staggered and increased interval as they neared a dog-leg strip of water that provided the best concealment for an ambush. Hines fidgeted again. Christ, they were creeping along slowly. He bucked his pack higher on his shoulders to lighten the weight. Why was it suddenly so heavy? The whole damn boat seemed heavy and overloaded. A trickle of sweat ran down Hines' spine. He envisioned them being mortared and hurled into the river, sinking fast under the weight of their gear. Hines gripped his rifle and waited for the order to commence prep fire. He wondered what they were waiting for. The gooks knew they were coming—hell, they could be heard a mile away. Hines knew no one believed the NVA in the Citadel would dispatch a sizable force to harass their advance, but a handful of snipers and a mortar crew could wreak havoc.

The boats motored on.

Grimm, the closest thing the Marine CCs had to an action junkie, combed the banks with wary black eyes. His throat constricted. He loved the grueling tension, the anticipatory moments before a battle—for so many men worse than the battle itself, because they had time to think about it. Grimm loved the writhing gut-wrenching wait of it, even the smell of his fear.

The river turned choppy, and the boat shuddered but continued upriver. A wave broke against Grimm's face. Stunned by the shock, he let the water drip, bolted ramrod straight and turned his jaw into the wind.

Hines had just stopped worrying about prep fire when enemy automatic weapons opened up from the heavy brush along both banks. Rounds skipped off the water and slammed into the boats, crisscrossing around them from both shores. Grimm returned fire first, and then the grunts loosed salvos toward the muzzle flashes. Mortars pounded the river, missing the boats, but shrapnel and huge waves of water battered the hulls. Hines was rocked up, and a round smacked into the bow an inch above his head. The LCIs' twin .30s hammered the shoreline and chopped the bushes into twigs. The mortars stopped raining as the lead LCI sped around the bend. The grunts in the other boats kept firing, but enemy fire had finally ceased.

"Anyone hit? Any casualties?" the staff sergeant in the lead boat barked.

"Fuck this." Hines' eyes were shut, and he yelled to himself. A string of spittle dangled from his lip.

Grimm's breath came in ragged gasps, and he looked like a man coming down off a high. It startled Hines.

Soon, the boats pulled up to a ramshackle ferry landing at the Bao Vinh Quay, half a klick north of the Citadel. Platoon sergeants yelled for the troops to disembark and establish a perimeter. No sign of the enemy, and Grimm couldn't figure it.

Dusk closed in. The companies quickly regrouped behind Alpha in the lead, trekked up the bank in wedge formation and waded across a lotus-choked moat into the thick brush on the other side. They came to a narrow, muddy path and followed it until the point squad reached a fork and pulled up. Several Vietnamese peasants suddenly appeared from the thicket, and the Marines went flat. Miraculously, they held their fire. The peasants ran toward them, their hands above their heads and gibbered frantically. "*Dung lai. Dung lai.* VC. VC," they pointed. If they meant to keep quiet, they botched it in their panic. Then, more gibberish nobody understood.

Captain Fowler, Alpha Company's CO, left his CP and headed to the front. His radioman hustled behind him, and Grimm and Hines followed.

The grunts on point trained their rifles on the peasants. Wary of booby traps, the men down the file edged off the road and faced outboard. Capt. Fowler tried to quiet the peasants and sent word back for the interpreters.

Grimm understood a fair amount of Vietnamese and stepped forward. He asked the peasants how many VC were there.

Four, five, six, they disagreed, pointing nervously to the path forking left. Grimm asked what kind of weapons they had.

AKs, *beaucoup* ammo, grenades, they replied. "VC numbah ten," a peasant added, which was the only thing most of the grunts understood. "VC numbah ten," the other peasants chorused.

Capt. Fowler wanted to know where the VC were dug in. Grimm interpreted. "They say six VC have an ambush set up 75 meters down the trail."

"How is it these people showed up to warn us about it?"

Grimm pumped the peasants for answers, and this time, there was fear in their voices. He turned to Fowler. "They say the VC didn't see them sneak past."

The ARVN interpreters came up and a harsher interrogation ensued, but the peasants' answers remained the same.

Fowler ground his teeth. He didn't know whether to trust them but decided to take the trail forking right. As a precaution, he ordered the peasants to walk in front of the Marines. At first, the Vietnamese hesitated, but they reluctantly fell in line, and Fowler started down the path somewhat relieved.

A narrow trail overgrown with grass and tangled roots, the trees hung low, and the branches reached down and snagged them. The peasants had told the truth, however, and finally, the trail led to a large clearing, and the Citadel's massive outer wall stood before them. Two huge gates led to 1st ARVN Division headquarters, the only sector of the Citadel that had not been overrun. The huge stone wall was stained black and slimy with moss. Fowler herded the peasants back and ordered his men down. Then, he shouted across the clearing to the compound. A moment passed, he shouted again, and one of the huge gates opened and three ARVN officers came out. The gate was pulled shut behind them, and they rushed across the clearing to the Marines.

The ARVN officer in charge spoke nervously. "No more come. You stay, you *bic*? You come and VC know, they mortar. You *bic?*"

Fowler's rancor mounted as the ARVN went on. "Tomorrow come. Tomowwow. In morning. Come now, VC mortar."

Fowler held his rage. He glanced at the clearing and said, "We have too many men to be stranded all night in the open."

"No more come, you *bic*? You stay! VC, they mortar. No baloney."

Fowler's astonishment at his slang did not blunt his anger. "I *bic*." He looked over the clearing again and back at the ARVN officer. "Now you *bic* this, and this no baloney. Either you let us inside the compound, or my Marines will assault those gates and break in."

The grunts took him at his word, and with a clamor of sharp smacking sounds, they shouldered their rifles. The ARVN officer stepped back and reconsidered. Then, he shouted to the sentries to open the gates.

It was dusk by the time they entered the compound; the men chowed down quickly and doused their small fires. Later, it rained, and they pulled their gear and blanket rolls under the overhanging roofs outside the rows of ARVN billets. The billets were empty, and many grunts wondered bitterly why they weren't allowed inside. A loud peal of thunder was followed by rain that crashed down on an enormous parade deck. Left of the parade deck, a large moat was bordered by palm trees and another row of billets. The scale of the compound awed them, but as immense as it was, it occupied only a small sector of the Citadel.

That night, Capt. Fowler and the Bravo and Charlie Company COs gathered for a briefing with General Lai, the commanding officer of the 1st ARVN Division to get their SitReps. The general told the Americans his troops maintained only a precarious hold on the compound, while another ARVN unit was stalled in their advance along the Citadel's southeast wall. The rest of the fortress—90 percent of it—was firmly under the control of six North Vietnamese battalions. Another NVA battalion occupied a village west of the Citadel, from which they channeled in resupplies. It was up to the Marines to clear a path inside the northeast and northwest walls, each wall 2,500 meters in length. Once secured, the Marines would be joined by a reinforced ARVN unit. Together, they would push inward and close a noose on the NVA trapped within the Citadel's core of sacred grounds and holy palaces. Once they attained a stranglehold, a squadron of helicopters from the Army's Air Cavalry Division would take out the NVA resupply units west of the Citadel.

What made the plan suspect in Fowler's mind was the enemy offensive had hit every major city throughout South Vietnam. Although fighting in most cities had now been reduced to mopping-up operations, American forces were badly overextended. Making matters worse, coverage in the civilian press was reaching hysterical proportions. The press compared Tet to Dien Bien Phu, and the battle for Hue had become their standard bearer. American generals, particularly the hard liners, were backpedaling rapidly and clamored for a swift and decisive victory. Even bleaker on the home front, President Johnson had turned mute and indecisive while mass demonstrations filled the streets of Washington. While the hawks cooed apologetically, the doves were screeching. Air strikes were called for, the Citadel be damned. Behind Washington's closed doors, America's generals pressed their point the only way they knew. Certainly, President Johnson did not want to be remembered as the first American President to lose a war. Simply put, the Citadel had to be taken—and fast.

Chapter Two

"SHAG ASS. PACK YOUR GEAR. WE'RE MOVING."

Staff Sergeant Whalen, a 30 year-old lifer with two gaping nostrils in place of a face, roused the troops at first light. "MOVE IT, PEOPLE. MOVING OUT IN ONE-FIVE."

Extra ammo was distributed. The men had time for coffee but not chow, and the suddenness of the mobilization made the men's stomachs wretch and pitch with noxious dread.

Moments later, Alpha Company filed out the compound's gates into a narrow street inside the Citadel and strung out in a staggered column. One file took position along the base of the northeast wall, while the other moved beside the small, single story masonry huts lining the other side of the street. The narrow road stretched for several short blocks and then dead-ended into a tower. The Marines knew they would be sitting ducks if the NVA sprung an ambush along the way.

Once in position, they were ordered to hold. The grunts were of the same mind: Hurry-up-and-wait; never fucking changed. The pricks wasted no time at all rushing the grunts up on point, while the CO and his command group, safely down the ranks, diddle-farted around doing God knows what.

To the men, everything felt different in the road. The air, stale and fetid, hovered on the road like a fungus. The entire area smelled of death.

They waited, had too much time to think about Charlie and where he would hide, about the battle ahead, and after the battle, who would be missing that night. Some would die. Some would spend their last night on earth inside an ancient, stinking castle thousands of miles from home. The Marines thought about all manner of things—things they shouldn't think about and things they couldn't stop thinking about—and the grunts who thought these things shed another layer of hope, which became diseased and rotted away.

Capt. Fowler finished briefing his platoon sergeants. Hines listened with disbelief. There had been nothing about air support. Any moment now, word would come to move out. Hines wondered why the rush. He knew the NVA weren't going anywhere. Why couldn't they wait for air support?

Bullshit. Hines couldn't believe it. It reminded him of FDR's decision not to drop gas on the Japanese in the Pacific. Better to sacrifice Marines, which Hines knew is exactly what happened, as Marines died by the thousands on volcanic islands and worthless atolls to preserve the Old Fart's comfort and code of ethics.

The briefing ended and Grimm split off toward the platoon on point. He didn't look back, though Hines was on his heels. Hemmings and Trilling straggled cautiously behind them until they reached the 2nd Platoon's CP and held up. When Grimm and Hines reached the point squad, Grimm asked for Cpl. Davis.

A ruddy-faced lance corporal worked a chaw of tobacco. "Who's asking?"

"Correspondents from ISO. We'd like to tag along."

"Do what you like, just don't get in the way."

Hines held up his M-16. "These things ain't Mattels."

Davis shot him a withering glare and spat a stream of brown tobacco juice. Suddenly, a thought struck him. "They tell you what we're after?"

"All we heard is they want you to take that tower up the road," Grimm said.

"Yeah? Us and who else?"

"Just you, I guess. They said the ARVN swept through here a couple days ago, so they're hoping it's still secure."

"That'll be a first. Where are the ARVN now?"

"Choppered 'em back to Saigon once they knew we were coming."

"Figures," Davis spat.

Near the ARVN compound, Capt. Fowler gave the order to move out and SSgt. Whalen shouted, "Start moving. Don't bunch up."

Davis spat out his wad of tobacco, moved his 1st fireteam forward and followed with his machine gun team.

Hines had a nasty feeling and hung back. This was bad shit, and anybody who didn't know it was plumb-ass mental. If NVA soldiers occupied the tower, Hines knew they would have a commanding view of their advance.

Davis and his squad pushed ahead, while Grimm and Hines stood by. More squads filed past. When Grimm spotted Hemmings and Trilling coming toward him, he suddenly shot forward. No way would he stand picking his nose while a couple slimy civilians caught up with him.

Davis' squad advanced on the right. A second squad moved up the left side near the base of the Citadel's wall. The men advanced as if the tromp of their boots and the clanging of their gear might draw some fire, or at the very least muffle the clamor in their chests. If they were to make contact, they wanted it now, while still within reach of the ARVN compound.

Davis' squad hustled across a narrow side street, moved up the block and swept huts, while the grunts across the road hunkered near the wall. Once, several short bursts of M-16 fire rattled inside a hut, but it was only the product of nervous trigger fingers. There was no return fire.

Hines cursed and started forward. It was always a contest with Grimm. What was moving up compared to having someone's foot come away in his hands? But, when the shit hit the fan, he felt it best to be with somebody he trusted.

Hines ignored the grunts he overtook but felt them eye-balling him. His hang-dog demeanor elicited suspicion.   "Hey man, what's the skinny? Where you rushing to?"

"Beats the piss outta me." Hines continued up the line.

Farther up the ranks, the men grew surly. A grunt moaned, "River City, River City."

"What's River City?"

"Trouble."

"Trouble?"

"River City, spells trouble. With a capital T, that rhymes with P and that stands for pool. Trouble. River City."

"You're mush for brains, asshole."

Hines moved, but the men kept talking the usual grunt-speak. For Marines it was better than silence. Jive, bravado, it didn't matter, as long as they made noise. One grunt groaned, "Gawd, I feel rocky."

"What's the matter, Chocolate? You homesick again?"

"I didn't say homesick. I said I felt rocky."

"Tell you something Chocolate, you're better off here than back home."

"What's that supposed to mean?"

"Buddy of mine rotated back to the World. Second night there he goes into a bar and promptly got his ass kicked."

"What?"

"He was the only one there who didn't have hair below his ears and a gang of long-haired pacifists stomped all over him. Called him a baby killer. So he wrote about how he's coming back here where it's safe."

"Naww," Chocolate groaned.

"Just remember, over here you got a rifle. Back home when someone pulls shit, you're standing there with nothing but your crank in your hand."

"'At's OK, I'll just hose 'em down with that."

"Shit! They'll get on their knees and kiss the little pecker. Hippies're AC-DC. Suck anything that wiggles."

Hines passed another squad of Marines.

"Oh man, I ain't ready for this shit, I should have taken a dump this morning."

"Don't, I'm right behind you. You always have to take a dump when you're heading into the shit."

Another private snorted. He felt good, thankful his squad was moving third behind Davis. If his squad had been up front, it was his turn to walk point. "Ever thought about how bad your shit stinks in Nam," he said. "I got a theory about it."

"Eat your theories."

"It's all about what you eat. In Hawaii, kiwis and pineapples, so it smells fruity. In Canada, it's spicy because of all the French cooking. They're French there, you know. In Nam it's just a godawful fishy smell, like the bowels of a bloated, beached whale."

"What the hell do you know about bloated, beached whales?"

"Fishy-smelling?" another grunt feigned bewilderment. "I'm confused. What do you mean by fishy? Are we talking about shit or pussy?"

"You're eighteen-years-old. What the hell do you know about pussy?"

"I'd know it if I saw it."

While talking, the men unconsciously had bunched up. SSgt. Whalen's voice skidded through the ranks. "Keep moving. Ten-meter intervals."

Davis' squad advanced to within 100 meters of the tower. Hines caught up to Grimm but was mildly disheartened by Grimm's indifference. "Got a smoke?"

Grimm dug into his breast pocket and gave Hines a Camel.

Hines forced a smile. "What do you hear? Your chimes talking yet?"

"We ain't talking chimes, we're talking a goddamn orchestra."

Davis' squad moved forward another 25 meters, and Grimm followed.

Suddenly, a barrage of rockets exploded and the street erupted. Nearby huts hemorrhaged from the concussions, but the grunts hurled themselves through the doors and blown out windows and dove to the floors. Chaos in the street, screams reverberated as enemy machine guns kicked in. Grunts in the open flung themselves to the ground and wedged at the base of the wall. The fire from the tower stitched a path up the road, and slaughtered Marines in place. One grunt made a break across the road and was stood-upright by the concussion from an exploding mortar. He tottered in place while smoke wafted from the fragments embedded in his flak jacket. When he tried again to bolt, machine gun fire severed his legs from under him.

Davis and his men cranked out fire from within the huts. His machine gunner triggered off three to five round bursts. Firing in long volleys would pinpoint his position. The NVA would first target the machine guns.

Now, B-40 rockets gouged the wall, and chunks of stone cascaded into the street forming piles of rubble. The grunts at the wall frantically crawled on knees and elbows to take cover behind them. Each time someone rose to fire, machine guns zeroed in on his position.

Desperate cries rent the din. "Corpsman up. Get a doc. Where's a corpsman, goddammit!" If a corpsman tried to move into the road, he was driven back by fire.

Grimm and Hines were in a hut behind Davis' squad. Grunts manned the windows and pumped fire toward the tower. Grimm's turn at the window, and he cranked through a mag. He slammed a second mag into his rifle and wasted that and then cooked through a third mag. Machine gun fire raked the front of the hut, rounds screamed through the window and ricocheted off the walls. Two grunts were hit. The first caught a flesh wound, but the second took a round in the throat, reeled back on his knees, clawed at his gullet and made desperate hacking sounds. Blood gushed through his fingers as he fought to plug the hole. Then, he gave a final convulsion and pitched forward on his face, drowned in his own blood.

When Hines looked back at the window, he saw Grimm on his back, flailing at his bandolier for another magazine. Grimm caught Hines staring at him—saw Hines frozen in a corner—and bared his teeth.

Hines' eyes bulged. Grimm didn't know whether from shame or fear. Hines low-crawled to the window, wheezing hard. Hines thought he was crawling to the window, but he moved in slow motion, as though swimming against a current. His mind speeded, but his body lagged behind.

Finally at the window, he wedged himself beneath the corner of the sill and gulped air. *GOT TO BREATHE, TAKE A BREATH.*

Just then, a round flew through the window above his head, and Hines scrunched down. *DON'T FREEZE,* he beseeched himself. *GET UP. FIRE!* His mind begged him, implored him what to do, SHOWED him what to do, and in his mind he was doing it. In his mind he was...

A mortar round exploded outside the hut, and the blast shook the walls. Hines rocked backwards. The grunts hit the deck, and Hines balled himself into a fetal position. Something burned his face, and there was nothing but blackness, nothing but darkness around him. His stomach muscles cramped. Nothing but blackness, and he couldn't stop the cramps, and he couldn't see. Hines was blind.

For an hallucinatory moment, a vast ooze spread over him as a buffer against shock. Warm and boggy like a womb, it made everything safe and soundproof. Then, all the noise in the world suddenly crashed in on him. The fire and the screams in the street were bloodcurdling. The racket from the grunts was louder still as they scrambled off the floor into firing positions. Someone behind shouted at him, Hines didn't know what, but he knew it was meant for him. He shuddered violently, and his eyes popped open. He could see.

Hines battled to a crouch. DO IT. FIRE AND MOVE AWAY FROM THERE. He flung his rifle muzzle over the window sill. When another mortar exploded, he jerked on the trigger and expended his magazine in a two second burst.

It took him a moment to realize he had fired, but he had. He'd done it. Now, let someone else come to the window and relieve him.

Hines yanked his rifle down and looked at the men behind him, but nobody moved. The grunts stared. Suddenly, Hines' nerves turned to jelly. He wanted to blubber, lash out at them. In his miserable wretchedness he nearly laughed.

Delirious, Hines lurched to his feet. Caught between shame and fury, he jammed a fresh magazine into his rifle and leaned through the window. A round smacked into the window frame, but Hines didn't flinch. He drew a bead on the tower and cranked off several short bursts. He burned through another mag, continuing to expose himself.

The grunts took turns at the windows. The third time Hines was at the window, he was half-crazed but steadier, as good any grunt there. He spent a mag, then another, but when he reached for a third, he felt a sharp pang of dread. Out of ammo. He had refused to take extra mags because of the weight. He glanced at the grenades on his cartridge belt. He had never used grenades, carried them only as a badge, but they were useless to him here.

At the first narrow intersection, Capt. Fowler shouted for the 106mm recoilless rifle team. Four grunts dragged the cannon into the road and turned it toward the tower. The first shell impacted below the rampart. The second strayed high and wide—a miss. The third shell was a bull's-eye, and it blew a slab out of the tower's turret.

A roar went up from the grunts, but it was short-lived as enemy fire intensified from positions atop the wall on both sides of the tower. "THROW SOME FIRE OUT THERE," Fowler shouted. One man beside the 106 went down, and a corpsman rushed out as the grunts dragged the weapon back.

Another hail of mortars crumped down the road working a path to Alpha's CP. The grunts in the road behind the rubble were still pinned down by fire.

Fowler snatched the handset from his radioman and called for artillery. He was given the stall at first—told arty was tied up elsewhere. Fowler wouldn't hear it. He shouted into the handset, and cursed, "Goddamn you. You put arty on this position now."

When artillery was finally granted, Fowler radioed fresh coordinates and passed the word up the column. A willie-peter round hit 50 meters behind the tower, white phosphorous to mark the spot. Fowler radioed adjustments, and then called for high explosive rounds and told them to fire for effect. SSgt. Whalen yelled up the street. "ARTY ON THE WAY. GET DOWN."

Fowler tried to maintain order amidst the chaos. His radioman, however, went berserk and shouted into the street, "Get down, Mrs. Brown. Mrs. Brown, get down."

His mad cries were heard up the street and inside the huts. "Mrs. Brown?" Hines' voice cracked, "Who the hell is that?"

The grunt manning the window changed mags and snorted, "He always does that."

"Who?"

"Skipper's radioman. Crazy Hasford."

Artillery rounds soon whistled overhead and pounded the tower. The explosions rocked the ground and reverberated through the huts. Ceilings creaked and sagged, loosing cloudbursts of masonry and dirt.

SSgt. Whalen shouted from the CP, "Pull back. Start pulling back."

The grunts trapped in the road were the first to retreat, then the men in the huts streamed out. Many rushed for the wounded, but there were too many casualties, and for the first time in Nam, Grimm witnessed Marines leaving their dead behind. The men not carrying casualties pulled back and stopped in spurts, alternately laying down cover fire.

Enemy machine gun fire withered under the artillery bombardment, but the mortars continued unabated. Another grunt fell in the road near Grimm. He caught the grunt's arm, slung it over his shoulder and jerked him to his feet. The grunt's left leg was shattered, but he hopped on one foot.

Hines bolted to Grimm's side. His only thought was keeping next to Grimm. Grimm struggled with the casualty, while Hines grabbed three mags from him and fed one into his rifle. He crouched behind them, using them as a shield, and as they backed down the road, he fired blindly from behind them.

Pandemonium in the CP. Mortars had wiped out half of Alpha's command group. Capt. Fowler and SSgt. Whalen had tried to restore discipline, but the wounded needed tending and there were not enough corpsmen to treat them.

Grimm and Hines lay their wounded Marine behind cover. Then, seemingly out of nowhere, a mechanical mule, a small, open flatbed vehicle used for hauling supplies, approached. A Chicano with a frozen grin and a ruffian mustache was at the wheel. Lance Corporal David Rodrigez Martinez bobbed and weaved as he zigzagged up the road into Alpha's command group.

Martinez shouted at the grunts standing near a group of casualties. "PUT 'EM ON. LOAD 'EM UP." The grunts quickly loaded the wounded but shivered when they got a close look at Martinez. He was grinning. Martinez had an adenoidal condition that prevented his lips from completely closing, and to strangers the shock of his grin was ghastly.

Corpsmen worked on the wounded, injected morphine into some, inserted IVs in others, passing over whose who were too far gone. Their gear was stripped and their weapons and ammo hurled into a pile. Martinez shouted for more casualties to be loaded aboard.

The enemy mortars had let up but then resumed. Now, Fowler was back on the radio calling for an all out bombardment of the tower. SSgt. Whalen made the rounds and issued words of encouragement. In his sarcastic way, he bent over a grunt shredded by shrapnel. The grunt moaned, and Whalen scowled, "Son, you sorry ass, you ain't hurt that bad. You been bawling ever since you got to Hue. And you're bitching now that you're heading home."

Fowler flung the handset back to Hasford, his radioman. Spent and overwrought, the CO suddenly whirled on Hasford. In the six months Fowler had known him, Hasford had served as his comic relief. Now, Fowler was trying to hold onto his nerves. "Anymore crap about your goddamn Mrs. Brown and I'll have your ass on point. You read me, Corporal?"

Hasford winced. "Read you, sir."

Fowler crossed to comfort his 2nd Platoon sergeant, juiced up on morphine, his kneecap blown off. "You there," Fowler shouted. "You on the mule. What's your name?"

"Martinez, sir."

"Run those casualties back to battalion aid, then get back here ASAP, hear me?"

"Yes, sir. Back in a flash." Fowler couldn't conceal the shudder that ran down his spine when Martinez grinned at him.

In the relative quiet except for the constant rattle of artillery shells exploding on the north side of Hue, LCpl. Martinez bobbed his head to The Animals' *We Gotta Get Out of This Place* as he drove a narrow road inside the Citadel.

Martinez never made it back to Alpha's CP. When he reached the battalion aid station, he unloaded the casualties then helped them aboard the medevac choppers. When he finished, he heard Charlie Company was pinned down inside the Citadel's northwest wall. Since Alpha had pulled back to regroup, Martinez made a beeline for Charlie's position. All hell had broken loose with Charlie Company, and in a battle that had lasted less than ten minutes, 18 men went down.

Martinez made two runs ferrying Charlie Company's wounded to the aid station. In the interim, Bravo Company had been ordered to relieve them, and as soon as he could, Martinez loaded his mule with extra ammo crates to take to them.

There was a lull in the fighting when Bravo replaced Charlie Company, and for the moment, the streets were quiet. Martinez rounded a corner and saw Charlie Company's walking wounded hobble toward him. He slowed down his mule. Zombie-like, the grunts straggled, looking more like POWs than men coming back from a ten-minute battle. They carried their dead in ponchos. Martinez's grin repulsed the men who saw it, but most did not bother to look.

Martinez passed the last of the wounded and veered around a corner, bobbing his head and crooning.

Suddenly, a crackle of small arms fire broke out ahead of him. Five short blocks stretched in front of him, but he saw no sign of Marines. Martinez gunned the engine and weaved his mule instinctively. Near the first narrow intersection he slammed on the brakes, then edged the nose of the mule past the intersection. He glanced up and down the side streets, and then gunned it. The fire had momentarily subsided, but now started again, heavier and louder. He braked again at the third intersection and to his right spotted Bravo Company strung out up the road and pinned down by sniper fire. In the claustrophobic maze of the Citadel's narrow streets, a mere handful of NVA could bog down an entire company. Martinez took a breath, pressed his chest into the wheel, floored the pedal and made an S-run up the road. A round snapped past his ear and smacked an ammo crate. Martinez swerved sharply, and the mule careened into a hut, bounded off a wall and flew up on two wheels before it bounced back, and he regained control. Several ammo crates slid off before Martinez made it to the next intersection. He skidded round the corner and men bunched along the street scattered like geese. "GET THIS STUFF OFF HERE," he screamed.

The men looked at him dumbfounded.

"What?"

"Who the hell are you?"

"UNLOAD IT, GODDAMMIT," Martinez raged.

The startled grunts shot forward and offloaded the mule. Martinez didn't wait for them to finish. He threw it into gear and pealed round the corner as the last of the ammo crates slid off the flatbed and crashed to the ground behind him.

Martinez' apparent fearlessness energized the grunts. Like a shot of electricity, the men leapt into the road, shouting, "GET SOME! GET SOME!" and sprayed fire toward the rooftops down the block.

Martinez zigzagged up the road and braked in front of a doorway where several Marines hunkered inside with casualties. "Load 'em on."

The men heaved two KIAs aboard the flatbed and three walking wounded climbed on. A Marine photographer snapped pictures from the doorway. At his feet, another Marine lay on the ground with a large purple rash across his cheek. He was quickly losing consciousness as blood spurted from a severed artery in the man's leg.

"GET HIM ON!" Martinez yelled.

"Fuckin' wait one!" Bayer shouted.

Bayer leaned over the man and pleaded. "Ehlo? Ehlo." He tied a tourniquet with a strip of surgical tubing. Ehlo pawed at his thigh, and Bayer knocked his hand away until he knotted the tourniquet. Bayer pulled Ehlo's ashen face into his chest. "DON'T DIE ON ME. FIGHT IT, YOU SONOVABITCH. YOU HEAR ME, EHLO? DIE ON ME, AND I'LL KILL YOU!" Ehlo was rapidly losing strength, and Bayer hugged him. 'HOLD ON, YOU'RE GONNA MAKE IT, I SWEAR. HEY EHLO, REMEMBER BANGKOK? REMEMBER? BANGKOK...'

Ehlo went limp in Bayer's arms. "GET HIM ON HERE!" Martinez screamed. Bayer eased his friend back to the floor and checked his pulse—faint.

Bayer grabbed Ehlo from behind and barked at the photographer to grab Ehlo's legs. As they carried him to the flatbed, machine guns opened up and strafed the mule. They ducked for cover as the walking-wounded clamored off. The last man off took another hit before he made it to the doorway.

Martinez hopped off and crouched behind the mule. A Marine with a LAAW moved to the back of the mule and aimed and fired. His aim perfect, two NVA manning the machine gun on the roof flew into pieces in a burst of screaming metal and shattered bones. The machine gun soared skyward, tumbled end over end and crashed down onto the street.

Martinez took his place behind the wheel and shouted for the wounded. The casualties boarded the mule a second time and once again, the NVA opened up from the rooftops. Again, Martinez and the wounded scrambled off and made it safely to the doorway. They jerked Ehlo back, but the battering was taking a toll. Down the block, the grunts returned fire from both sides of the street, chewing up the rooftops and turning the clay tiles into powder. Soon, the enemy fire ceased and Martinez lurched behind the wheel, but a grunt grasped him by his flak jacket and yanked him down. "Stay the fuck put!" Then he saw Martinez's face and winced at his grin, "You're a crazy sucker, man."

Martinez tried to wrest free, but the grunt held fast and called to his men, "SMOKE, GODDAMMIT. THROW SOME SMOKE OUT THERE."

The men popped smoke grenades and hurled them into the road in front of them. Three twangy "pops," and smoke whooshed out, and clouds of red and yellow and lavender filled the street.

"Cover me." Martinez sprang behind the wheel. The Marines poured out cover fire and with the wounded on board, Martinez flipped a U-turn and sped down the road.

By early afternoon, Alpha Company had been ordered back inside the 1st ARVN Division's compound. Medevacs were called in to evacuate the wounded, but incoming mortars prevented any additional choppers from lifting out the dead.

Martinez returned to the compound before dusk and began ferrying KIAs to a newly established debarkation area at the Bao Vinh Quay. The majority of the dead still remained inside the compound, zipped up in body bags and stacked in rows on the parade deck—a ghoulish reminder to the grunts in the compound. The men couldn't look at the body bags without wondering which one covered a buddy.

Among the survivors, few had not suffered some sort of wound or laceration from the maelstrom of flying shrapnel and debris. Before the medevacs had been waived off, some of the more seriously wounded demanded to stay. In a bizarre scene, some men raged and some cried in their refusal to be medevacked—something that never would have happened on an op in the paddies. If Hue counted for anything, many grunts believed it would be the turning point of the war.

Night fell and the men huddled together in tight groups. Hines sat in one, wedged between Hemmings and Trilling. Some men talked, and a few tried to joke but the humor fell flat. When they talked, they spoke of the World or the Freedom Bird, not about loved ones or family—too raw an emotion—but of simpler things like barbecues, homecomings and cheerleaders. The men fantasized about cheerleaders. They were distant, unapproachable, safe.

They did not talk about the dead. Everyone had lost buddies that day. No one in particular was entitled to sympathy.

Most men were battered and resigned, their dull eyes lost in miserable, blank stares. Too exhausted to sleep, it became a joke when so many volunteered for watch. At least standing watch, they might focus on something besides what fate held in store for them.

To Hines' right, Wicker Trilling sat shaking and numb. No moon out, this night was cold and very dark. Trilling was grateful it hid his shuddering.

Wicker Trilling would die here. He sensed it. He crossed his arms, balled his fists and stuffed them under his armpits. He felt tears welling and he bent over and groaned. He felt sick. He was sure he would die in Hue.

The grunts talked again about cheerleaders. Relieved for the moment, Trilling knew no one watched him. He tried to think, to think about anything at all to suppress his dark feelings. Trilling was seized with uncontrollable fear, and he remembered only the battle that morning. He replayed the onslaught of mortars and flinched, saw them burst in front of him and heard the grunts wail. If only he had been wounded, he could have been medevacked out a hero—something to show up the press who'd stayed behind.

All around him the grunts remained mute. They tolerated the civilians, but it was a tolerance borne of exhaustion. Some grunts were sadistic enough to relish their presence, exacting pleasure from the fact they were stuck there with them. None doubted Hemmings and Trilling would *di-di* first thing in the morning.

Hines sat with his back to the parade deck facing the compound wall. The huge stones glistened and annoyed him. The wall seemed to breathe and salivate like a prehistoric beast that had cornered its prey. Hines felt the heavy dampness seep into his lungs and his breath tasted foul, like the air in a dungeon.

Hines had asked Grimm after the day's battle whether he could get the men's stories, and Grimm, far more interested in Martinez's story, readily agreed. Grimm had cornered Martinez once between runs, but Martinez had been in a rush.

When Hines told the grunts he would write their stories, his standing was solidified. However, the grunts were not yet ready to talk and Hines knew it. He had passed the word, even to the grunts he had no intention of writing about, to come to him when they were ready.

Grimm was away attending a briefing, and while grunts sat silent, Hines was desperate to talk. "Hey, what was that weird 'Mrs. Brown' stuff today?"

"It was Hasford, the Skipper's radioman."

"What's he, *dinky-dao*?"

The Marine laughed. "Story goes he had a live-in maid once, a Mrs. Brown. She sort of raised him because his mother was always out with the guys. One day, she bought the farm in a car wreck—Mrs. Brown, I mean. So now, when Hasford's in the shit, he calls her name. Gets his rocks off but keeps him sane."

Grimm came back and sat down beside Hines.

"What's the word, turd?" Hines asked.

"Samey-same. More hassle in the castle. They're hoping for a break in the weather so they can call for air support."

"That's it?"

"They said Charlie Company got beat to shit today, too, and Bravo but not as bad. Bravo's still out there. I just hope Bayer and Ehlo made it out."

Hines shrugged. "Bayer's OK, he's too short to take chances. Ehlo's rammy over his Bangkok puta, no way he'd do anything rash."

Grimm wanted to believe him. He suddenly looked warmly at Hines and rapped his knee. "I owe you."

"For what?"

"You covered me out there today. I appreciate it."

Grimm was serious. He knew one thing for sure. Without fear there's no courage, and judging by that, Hines was the bravest man there.

Hines cherished the unfamiliar glow of respect. He had covered Grimm, hadn't he? It had been smart not to expose himself in the open. If he had caught a round and wasn't able to keep up cover fire, they might all have bought it. But Hines didn't want to think about it much and dropped the subject. "Hear any info about Delta?" he asked.

"Supposed to be crossing tonight, sometime later. Bringing reinforcements with them."

Hines snorted. "Babysan's about to get his cherry popped. You can bet he didn't lose it in the skivvy house."

Chapter Three

EARLIER THAT MORNING, on the south side of Hue, Delta Company got word they would not be crossing the Perfume until nightfall. It meant a day long delay, and since the grunts were dug in and already resupplied, there was nothing to do but to bide time. Latimere longed to grab some badly needed sleep. Roark as much as ordered him to, but Latimere didn't sleep. He couldn't. The grunts were resting in shifts, and every time Latimere closed his eyes, he thought of Roark sitting at the edge of the foxhole watching him. He knew it shouldn't have bothered him, but it made him feel cherry because Roark wasn't sleeping. Besides, how could anybody rest with that racket going on across the river? Hardly a second passed that he didn't hear fighting from somewhere inside the Citadel.

However, the salts were able to sleep and when Roark excused himself, saying he was going after stories, Latimere knew he just wanted to be alone.

Once Roark left, Latimere shut his eyes but did not sleep. He did not dread crossing the Perfume, though he was not nearly so curious as before his first firefight. His mind darted fitfully, jumped from the moment to the battle ahead, anything not to think about the thirteen months ahead of him. He thought about his mother and the simple days back home, of Billy Huff and own his youth and his impatience to grow up.

Latimere smiled when he thought about his Adam Strange costume and his religious fervor. How innocent he was then. Now, lying in the cold packed sand along the Perfume, he felt something rip inside him. What was he doing here? A week ago he had been young. The contrast between his boyhood and the young man he was now was brutal, but even that did not seriously disturb him. What bothered him most was he couldn't imagine Roark—and definitely not Grimm—ever harboring such childish fantasies. He doubted they could ever comprehend such silliness.

And yet, could he possibly be wrong? Roark admitted he wanted to be an actor, even brandished it. What kind of crazy notion was that if not lofty? Roark soon returned and jolted him from his reverie.

The day dragged on. Some men brought out cards and played hearts or gin rummy, locked out the din from across the river. The sound of friendly artillery was only mildly comforting. The men, fat with rations, ate long past their hunger, anything to stay busy and keep their minds off the Citadel.

Later that afternoon, Latimere wandered through the camp and snapped pictures of the grunts. He did so from a distance, mindful not to invade their privacy. He still lacked the confidence to approach them for a story.

Latimere picked up snatches of conversations. One boot, who couldn't have been in-country much longer than himself, talked about the head shops popping up back home. He tried to tell a vet what a lava lamp was and what a bitching, groovy thing it was, but it was hopeless.

Farther up the bank, Latimere stopped to snap shots of the Strawberry Patch across the river. Four grunts sat in a foxhole behind him, one trying to make a point. "You expect those things in war. You adjust. You know what nailed me worse than that? Seeing a dude zapped by lightning. One minute he's walking a paddy dike, and the next, he's a crispy critter face down in the mud with one foot sticking up. You expect to get zapped but not by fucking lightning. It ain't enough having the gooks shit all over you, but you find out you gotta deal with nature, too."

Night came and with it a light drizzle. A cold breeze wafted off the river, flapping at them in wavelets. Just then, they heard the two Navy swift boats approaching, PT gunboats with twin .50 caliber machine guns. A ripple of dread spread through the company. Gunnery Sergeant Jerardi suddenly shouted, "SADDLE UP," and herded the men to a jerry-built dock near the Nguyen Hoang bridge.

When they reached the dock, they saw one swift holding steady in the river. The other moved slowly toward them towing three Vietnamese junks. Everybody's worst fears were confirmed when they saw the junks' sails and riggings had been removed to make room for troops.

Fifteen minutes later, the call to "Saddle Up," was repeated, and then men stood around and bitched another fifteen minutes before being told to "stand easy." The next time they heard the order to saddle up, nobody budged.

Roark stretched out on a sandy knoll away from the company, his back propped against his pack. He and Latimere dragged off a smoke that Roark cupped in his hands.

Then, Gunny Jerardi ordered "SADDLE UP" again and this time, the troops moved. Roark noticed the gunny heading his way, snuffed out his butt and climbed to his feet.

"You there," the gunny yelled, stopping 20 meters in front of them. "You two the writers?"

"That's affirm."

"You plan on crossing?"

"That's affirm."

"Then I suggest you ditch that bush hat, Marine. Ain't no one crossing not wearing a helmet."

Roark spat sideways not to appear too insolent, shoved his bush hat into his cargo pocket and put his helmet on. The gunny turned and walked away. "If you're coming, get a move on."

Latimere buckled his chinstrap. Roark started to warn him but resisted. He knew buckling was for the movies. If a Marine got his helmet caught or snagged in the jungle, it might wrench his neck. Roark knew this was different. They were crossing water.

The grunts shuffled toward the dock, but the boarding stalled another ten minutes, and Roark and Latimere hung loose where they were. A huge, burly figure peeled away from the company and stalked toward them. The big, black grunt, toting an M-79 grenade launcher in each hand, said, "Hey, was that you telling the gunny you was writers?"

"That's right."

"Sumbitch," he strode up to them and beamed a broad, gap-toothed grin. "About time I get my name in the papers." He thrust out a thick hand. Glad to know you."

Roark shook his hand. "Name's Roark, and this is Babysan."

"Latimere." Latimere was quick to make the correction.

The hulk chuckled. "Babysan, eh?" He numbed Latimere's hand in his grasp. "Corporal Hamsun." Hamsun lowered his voice. "*Lance* Corporal, actually." His voice shot up again. "My first name's Rollie, but you can call me Ham."

"Ham?" Latimere asked.

"That's me," Ham grinned. He clutched his grenade launchers and raised one in each hand. "And these here be the Muthas."

Roark felt a tug of brotherhood and laughed. Ham sensed Roark's friendliness but didn't attach any significance to it. Ham expected to be liked.

Ham waited for them to get the joke about the muthas, then held up the grenade launchers. "You ever use one of these? Lost our other blooperman a week ago. Figure I'll be on one side of that swift when we cross, sure could use one of you on the other side."

"I'll do it," Latimere said impulsively.

"Better let me," Roark said.

"I can handle it."

Ham grinned and handed Latimere a grenade launcher with a bandolier of M-79 rounds, and Latimere tied it around his chest.

"MOUNT UP. GET ABOARD!" Gunny Jerardi shouted.

The grunts edged down the bank onto the rickety dock. To their dismay, the first in line were ordered into the junks.

Roark, Latimere and Ham started down the shore. Ham gaped at the writers and grew excited all over again. "You guys want a story, it's Delta Company to the rescue."

Roark let Ham walk ahead of them and leaned into Latimere. "You sure you don't want me to carry that blooper?"

"I can handle it."

"You ever fire one?"

"I have once. In training. It was easy."

"God help us."

Everybody was on board, but another 20 minutes passed before the swift moved—just enough time for the men to hope for a change in orders. All day long they'd been glad the move was put off until nightfall, but now aboard, they grew edgy. No one could fathom why they

crossed at night, not even Delta Company's CO, Captain
Donlon. G-2 was gambling the NVA would not expect a
night crossing and that they, along with the Marines,
would use the night to regroup. Captain Donlon had
doubts. If they crossed without incident, fine, but if they
got chewed up out there, his men would be dead in the
water. Literally. Not enough moonlight to call in Hueys for
air cover, half his men would drown before they could
swim to shore.

Roark looked out at the river and turned to
Latimere, anxiously gripping his grenade launcher.
"Latimere," Roark smiled. "Maybe up the road, you and
that almond-eyed beauty can cross this river in a nice little
rowboat on a lazy summer afternoon, her with a parasol
and in a pink *ao dai.*" He smiled at Latimere's
astonishment. "Were only it were true."

The lead swift churned upriver, lights out, the three
junks snapping in tow behind her. The second swift, close
behind the third junk, ran escort. In the middle of the
river, the men stopped talking and made no unnecessary
noise. The throaty roar of the swifts' engines grew omin-
ously louder.

They neared the first loop in the river. The sailor
manning the .50 cal. machine gun signaled to the grunts to
get down. Ham was on the starboard side of the lead swift,
his M-79 at the ready. Roark and Latimere packed in on
the port side. Latimere's knuckles were white on his
weapon. He shouldn't have taken the M79. He had no
confidence he could even work it. He prayed there
wouldn't be an ambush and ran over the mechanics in his
mind. First thumb the safety off, then fire. Then what?
Break open the breech—he fiddled numbly for the latch—
pull the spent shell casing out and load another grenade.
He unsnapped several pouches on his bandolier to give

him easy access to the rounds. The main thing to remember is do it quick, to look like he knew what he was doing.

The swifts rounded the loop. The first barrage of fire came from the starboard shoreline. Then, the opposite bank opened up, and the grunts cut loose in both directions. The twin .50s hosed the shores. Blinding yellow muzzle flashes from the guns in the boats, and red and green tracers flew across the river. Mortars pounded the water and shredded one of the junks. Two grunts fought to plug the holes while others returned fire.

The men squeezed tighter aboard the swifts, leaving welts as they squirmed and thrashed like fish on a hook.

"GET SOME," Ham pumped his blooper. On the port side, Latimere struggled. He had to think before he fired, and his movements were jerky. By the time he got the hang of it, the Skipper hit full throttle. The swift lurched forward, and the men flew backwards, the junks whipping in line behind them.

"CEASE FIRE, HOLD YOUR FIRE," Gunny Jerardi roared. They rounded the bend as the second swift throttled up on their starboard. As quickly as it had started, it was over.

Gunny Jerardi called for a head count. "Everybody all right? Anybody hit?"

"Nobody except them dumb-ass slopes." Ham said.

Chapter 4

THE NEXT MORNING thin, golden sun shafts fanned through the clouds and flickered like gossamer. Warmer out, the men chopped branches or stuck entrenching tools into the sand and hung their uniforms to dry. A few slipped out of their trousers, and a few wore nothing but flak jackets and helmets, skivvies and boots. Most men wore skivvies in the winter monsoons but not in the summer because of the heat. A Marine could sweat so much he couldn't keep them dry, and they wedged inside his buttocks and rubbed and chafed him raw.

Still, the sun was out, but they knew it wouldn't last. After landing, Delta Company dug in and filled in the sparse perimeter manned by two squads from Charlie Company. At least they hadn't been forced to muck through the dark to the Citadel. There had been casualties during the crossing after all—two WIAs aboard the second Swift and one WIA and two KIAs aboard the junks. A detail bagged and tagged the KIAs, carried them down the shore and stacked them in the cadaver pile.

Latimere was surprised Roark had volunteered to stand watch. Ham did, too, then Latimere, who really didn't want to but suddenly felt he had to. Latimere wondered why Roark had done it, but the gratitude on the grunts' faces told him the answer. Leave it to Roark, he thought. He remembered his first night in Hue when he volunteered for watch, and no one appreciated it. Roark had said, don't volunteer, especially don't volunteer unless you have an audience.

The three faced the perimeter, a barren stretch of sand that offered no cover, and they had to dig in. Latimere used his entrenching tool, but neither Roark nor Ham carried E-tools. Instead, they pulled out their helmet liners and used their steel pots to scoop out the sand. When finished, Ham disappeared and came back with a claymore mine, a small, convex-shaped charge containing 150 steel ball bearings with a killing range of 75 meters. Ham tested the magneto and crawled 20 meters outside the lines, where he jammed the mine's prongs into the sand and camouflaged the charge with loose brush. Then, he came back and asked Latimere whether he knew how to fire it.

"Are you serious? I barely got by with the blooper." It felt good to joke about it.

Ham told him to get down if he fired it or the backblast would shred him. Also, let everyone else know he was firing it. It wasn't just the backblast. The NVA, good at night probing, would turn the mines around to face the Marines. "Then what they do is make a racket and BLOOHEY, you fire it and half your platoon is turned into Swiss cheese."

"How do you know when to fire it?"

"Never mind. Keep them peepers open to be sure no one's sneaking around out there."

Lonnie Carson, one of the company's corpsmen, also stood watch, not to replace one of the KIAs, but in place of a grunt who'd lost a buddy. The grunt had also lost his fear, Carson could tell a thing like that, and that made the man dangerous to everyone. Carson took care of his Marines in all sorts of ways.

Wet in the foxhole, it rained through the night. Roark stood first watch. He told Latimere to get some shuteye, but Latimere took the watch with him, and for the most part kept his eyes open. When Latimere's turn came, Roark caught some sleep, and Latimere stayed awake alone. After awhile, the shape of the brush morphed on Latimere, changed in the dark, a phenomenon of night watch. He blinked to regain focus. When his shift was up he felt sheepish about waking Ham and mulled it over for a while. Ham finally woke on his own and Latimere curled up in a corner and pulled his poncho over himself. Soon the rain beat down harder and Latimere woke up to see Ham shivering without a poncho. Ham had only a drenched poncho liner. He had used his other to load the injured blooperman aboard a chopper and forgot to take it back. Latimere wanted to curl up but instead crawled beside Ham and spread his poncho over both of them. They huddled together and eventually their combined body heat gave off enough warmth to stop their shivering. Latimere finally dozed.

In the morning, they heated coffee and rations, and work details were formed. More good news. Delta was on hold, as were the other elements of the 1st Battalion, 5th Marines already inside the Citadel. Two-man teams were sent out 100 meters beyond the lines to set up listening posts. Seeing the beachhead in daylight, the men realized there was no cover from incoming mortar fire, so they dug deeper fighting positions.

Down the beach stood a rickety quay that Vietnamese fishermen used to dry their fishing nets. The three junks had been cut loose and lay beached on the shore. One swift boat backed out and pulled alongside the quay as the other swift chugged to the middle of the river and held. Grunts loaded the body bags from the cadaver pile onto the swift, bandannas over their faces as the mild weather bred a fetid stench into the bloated carcasses. When the swift pulled out, a Chicano raced up on a mule bringing another load of bodies, which he offloaded onto a new pile.

By 0900, artillery began WHUMPING inside the Citadel and continued through the morning. By noon, Delta Company was still on hold. The weather had something to do with it. With so much radio chatter, the men hoped someone was calling for air strikes.

Ham retrieved the claymore, and he and Latimere were laughing on the perimeter. Latimere noted that Roark was unusually sociable. Ham cleaned his grenade launchers and Roark put on his bush hat and told Latimere how Hines got his nickname. "One night we were properly polluted and staggered out of the Thunderbird Club in Danang. Halfway down the hill, Hines stumbled head-first into a foxhole. It was pissing rain and muddy as hell, so naturally Hines slipped every time he tried to climb out. Nobody would help him. For one thing, nobody wanted to end up in the foxhole with him, but because it was Hines, no one wanted to help him anyway. He got mad as hell and threw gobs of mud at us. Since everybody had to take a piss, we started pissing into the hole all over him. Which, as you can guess, is how he got the name Urinal Man."

Latimere held his sides he was laughing so hard. He'd have given anything to have seen that. "So that's why Hines is so ornery."

Gunny Jerardi was checking the perimeter and headed toward them. A sturdy, compact man, he had the gait of a bulldog.

"Lance Corporal Hamsun!" Jerardi halted in front of them and glowered. The men slouched against their packs smoking, not an ounce of military bearing in the lot. Ham, at least, was reliable under fire, but Jerardi wouldn't bet a nickel on the other two.

"Whatcha need, Gunny?" Ham grinned.

"How is it every time I see you, you're not with your squad?"

"It ain't so, Gunny. If you mean right now, it's because I pulled watch last night."

"I thought you'd have noticed the sun up, Hamsun."

"Can see that, Gunny, but since no one came to relieve me, I figured somebody best keep a lookout on the perimeter. I just took it upon myself to see that no gooks slipped through."

Gunny Jerardi didn't smile. "Then how come I been looking over here for the last five minutes and haven't seen you look at the perimeter once?"

"Negative, Gunny. When I wasn't watching it's because one of my dudes here was. And I have the utmost faith in them."

Jerardi squinted at Roark. He recognized the bush hat. "You the reporters?"

Roark nodded.

"You two pull watch?" the Gunny asked.

"All three of us."

"Least that's something," he growled. Jerardi headed off, then turned back to Roark. "One thing about that bush hat. I expect my people to follow orders and it's a breakdown in the system when someone comes in and fucks with the machinery. You want to look like Jungle Jim, go right ahead, but the hotdog shit stops the minute we move out. I'll abide it in the rear, but nobody moves out with us not wearing a helmet."

After the gunny left, Roark looked at Ham. "Is he serious?"

"Serious as jungle rot," Ham snickered. "Actually, Gunny ain't so mean once you get to know him."

"Anyone can tell that," Latimere said.

"Gunny's got something sour inside him. Sour things you just want to let slide."

"If that's what you call sour, what do you call mean?" Latimere asked.

"Mean's another thing," Ham tried to make a point.

"Mean's different. You have to deal with mean, sour things you don't. Sourness ain't something that's worthy."

Roark smiled at Ham's distinction, but curious, Latimere wondered what Ham would call mean. All in all, Latimere was glad to be there with the in-crowd, the big boys. Latimere marveled at Ham, an affable giant who seemed immune to intimidation and perhaps too good natured to think ill of anyone. He found it hard to imagine what Ham perceived as threatening. "Come on," he prodded, "Name something or someone you'd call mean?"

"You're missing what I'm saying, Babysan. Plenty of things I'd call mean, same as you. Evilness, rottenness—those who're mean and like their meanness. Double-vets, for instance, or them who claim to be."

Latimere perked up. "Who?"

"A double-vet is someone who has sex with a girl and then kills her—or brags he does. Never once knew it to happen, though."

Ham grabbed his canteen, took a swig and passed it to Latimere. Latimere took a drink and spit it out. "What is that stuff?"

Ham slapped his knee. "Kool-Aid, and don't say you don't like it. You've got a lot to learn, Babysan. Water in Nam tastes like piss, so my momma sends Kool-Aid in my care packages. I got lime in one canteen and grape in another."

Latimere made a face and worked his tongue against the roof of his mouth.

"Pull yourself together, Babysan, or my momma will think she's not appreciated." Ham took another swig and smacked his stomach. "You know what bugs me?"

"What."

Ham's voice cracked with energy. "It's what we hear more and more from the States. What a man says never used to bug me as long as he says it to my face. Now, they only finger point and protest, and they think they got all the answers. I'll tell you what riles me. When those draft dodgers talk about the war, it's always about how moral and courageous they are. I wish just once one of them protesters would have the guts to say the reason he ain't here is because he's scared to fucking death to get his head blown off.

"What do they really want? They want me out of this country? Be glad to. They want to know what I'm doing here? Well, speaking for myself, I think I'm doing pretty good. They say they know what I'm doing over here, though they don't ask me but tell me instead. They're back there and we're over here, and they tell us what we're doing here. I admit spending eighteen months in a stink hole can blind you, but one thing I know, I know my hole. So don't tell me what goes on and what goes down here."

Latimere's brow creased. Suddenly, Ham laughed. "Can you believe I'm bugged over a pack of peaceniks?" Ham flicked his big paw as if swatting away a fly.

"I don't hate everything about them. Especially them big-titted hippie girls with no bras. If only they'd move their tits and not their mouths. Hey," Ham scratched his iron chin, "you ever notice how much faster you recover after a blowjob than when you come inside a girl?"

Roark smiled at Latimere's reaction. Ham was right, though Roark didn't have an answer.

They chuckled, and Ham's brow furrowed. "It bugs me, yeah. The stories they print and how they look at us when we get home. Like we're holding onto some dark secret and they're letting you know they know it. No friggin' peacenik's got a right to do that, not about the grunts I lived and humped with and slept beside and fought with. Nobody back there has the right to spit on anyone, that's all I'm saying. They might have sit-ins and grass and girls, but ain't one of them will go to the wall for anyone."

"I don't know," Roark snuffed out a cigarette. "Girls sound pretty good to me right now."

Latimere smiled. "You know what they're saying back home now about the draft? Girls only say yes to boys who say no."

Ham hadn't heard that one and chuckled.

The men were quiet for a moment. Roark felt a connection with Ham. Different from the bond he had with Grimm, this was a kinship of spirit more than something arrived at through shared experience. Some friendships were instant, but in war they added up to more, because a man's life was in another's hands. Ham had been right about that, too. Combat vets would go to the wall for each other. Roark knew this was what kept him coming back to Nam, perhaps why any man returned in any war. Not for the misery and fear or even the adrenaline rush. For that, a man would have to be insane. That men in combat had each other's back was an axiom no one ever questioned. Next to that, friendships and bonds formed outside a war zone seemed frivolous.

Roark looked at Ham and shook his head. He couldn't resist.

"What?" Ham returned Roark's scrutiny.

Roark shrugged. "It seems to me we have a problem of some proportion."

"Yeah?" Ham said. "What?"

"I wouldn't want to probe too deep or anything, but getting lathered up over a bunch of peaceniks?"

"Who's lathered? I just said they bug me. They don't bug you?"

"Of course, but you have to know what's worthy and not let trivial things get to you."

"They don't get to you?"

"Sure, a little," Roark said. "Some things bug me, but not peaceniks."

"If peaceniks don't bug you, what does?"

Roark arched his eyebrows and sat forward. "Whining vets."

"What about the vets?"

"Not vets, *whining* vets. Maybe hippies'll bug me once I get back, but I doubt it." Roark had thought about it a lot. "They reflect on us. Hippies don't stand for us, but vets do. Especially those back home who've made careers whining. And don't forget about pussy. Maybe Latimere has it right. Girls only say yes to boys who say no. I think he's half right. They especially say yes to boys who said yes and then come back and say no. There, she's got the best of both worlds."

If Roark loathed whining veterans, it didn't compare to what he thought about his government's cowardice. It put boys in harm's way but lacked the moral imperative to back them up. For Roark, even that wasn't the worst of it. The hypocrisy was worse. Politicians didn't have the guts to say Americans were fighting for freedom—only for democracy—which meant tens of thousands would die for the right for the Vietnamese to vote themselves into communism if they wanted. To Roark, that was the grandest joke.

Roark shuddered. Why was he even thinking about this?

"I dunno," Ham slowly shook his head. "I don't believe a vet's stress is always a cop out, I think some is real. I read that if you took all the Marine battles in the Pacific in World War II and added them all up, the total fighting days would be less than a grunt sees in one tour in Nam."

Roark had never read that, but if true, it pleased him. Now, he could put the vets on par with the grunts and soldiers of any war. If their wars were more glamorous, Roark's was dirtier. He despised whining vets more than ever now—and a disgraceful nation that spat on them at home. Roark never cared a damn about his medals, but what Ham said had pleased him.

Ham wanted to share a moment. He placed the heel of his fist on Roark's knee. "Did you have a good mother and father?"

"The best. I was lucky."

"Yeah, me too, but were they mad when I joined the Corps," Ham chuckled. "My dad was sick. He always wanted me to be smarter."

After a moment, Roark said, "That's good, Ham." Roark patted Ham's fist. "But we're getting off the subject."

"What subject?"

"This phobia of yours."

"What phobia?"

"Your hippie phobia, Ham. What do you think we've been talking about?"

"It ain't no phobia. They bug me, that's all."

"Oh Ham, Ham, Ham, it's truly painful." Roark shook his head. "Poor Ham's immune to turncoat vets, but hippies and peaceniks discombobulate him. Hear me on this, Ham. Forget the crippled vets I was talking about. It's the other whining assholes Ham wants to defend, because nobody's as bad as them awful peaceniks. Poor Ham's in a dither. Big dude like him has come unglued over someone as saintly as a hippie. Unless she's a big-titted hippie, that is. It's a sad and sorry condition," Roark leaned back.

The three laughed. Several grunts on the perimeter glanced back at the gleeful sound, different from the usual barracks humor, and it chipped away at their sense of well being. Deep in their hearts, the men knew at such a moment that one of them might be gone tomorrow.

Ham placed his hand on Roark's shoulder. "I think you and me are alike in one way. I think we're two of the lucky ones."

The day pushed on. Artillery continued intermittently through the afternoon, and smoke and ash hung heavy in the air. More boats arrived and off-loaded ammo, water and C-rations. Martinez made several trips to the quay with body bags and ferried supplies back to the Citadel. Gagging on the stench, nervous sailors loaded the body bags aboard. Many bags leaked blood and gore. Buzzing insects rose in swarms when one was moved, only to descend again on the pile like a black, carnivorous shroud.

There was still no affirmation of air support, but scuttlebutt abounded. Clearance had been granted for III MAF to move an 8-inch howitzer battery from Southern I Corps to Phu Bai, assigned to the 1st Battalion, 5th Marines. Several tanks and Ontos—tank-like vehicles mounted with six 106mm recoilless rifles—had moved north of the Citadel and were expected to reach the ARVN headquarters before dusk.

Delta remained on hold. When Ham saw Gunny Jerardi making his rounds again, he hustled off to rejoin his squad. "See you guys," he said.

Sometime later, Latimere asked Roark what he would most need to know to get him through the upcoming battle. He knew knowledge couldn't entirely replace experience, and he wondered how long it would take to get it.

"You'll get it soon enough," Roark said. "The rest is luck."

"What do you mean?" Latimere thought it strange to hear Roark talk like that.

"It's a crap shoot, that's all." Roark knew his words sounded harsh and remote, but he wanted to shatter false illusions. "Think you're fated?" Roark asked. "Think all you want, it's still a crapshoot."

"This war?"

"All of it. War, life, death, accidents. Some are simply lucky, while others are snake bit. A crap shoot, understand?"

"I guess so."

"Listen," Roark creased his brow. "Twenty mortars fall around you, and it's a roll of the dice who buys it and who doesn't. One grunt I met back when I was cherry was scared of nothing. No gooks would ever get him, you know what did? A goddamn French mine. He stepped on a mine that had been buried in the ground fifteen years."

Latimere looked doubtfully at Roark, but just then Ham scurried back.

"SADDLE UP," Gunny Jerardi bellowed.

Ham spat.

"STAND BY," the gunny roared a moment later.

"Hell," Ham said. "Stand by to stand by for a possible maybe." Ham checked his M-79s. "Babysan, you sure you don't want one of these?"

"No way, not in the city. Probably blow myself up."

"Could happen," Ham chuckled.

Gunny Jerardi ambled toward them, and Roark ditched his bush hat. "COLUMN FORMATION. WE'RE MOVING."

The two correspondents fell in with Ham's squad.

The point moved out, and suddenly two A-4 Skyhawk jets streaked toward the Citadel with the deep BRURP-BRURRRPING of their guns britzing. Returning, they zoomed low, dropping bombs, and the grunts braced for the impact. BOOM! BOOM! BA-BOOM! Then they screamed away, gaining altitude to make another run.

"ROCK 'N' ROLL!" Ham shouted as the war planes made another pass. "GET SOME. What did I tell you guys? Here on in, we're gonna shit all over Charlie's program."

It took an hour to reach the back gates of the ARVN compound. Dusk fell quickly, and it was overcast and drizzling. Delta Company filed inside. The gray and gloomy compound added to the aching cold from the rain. The men lit smokes to keep warm. Captain Donlon peeled off for a briefing as the rest of the company filed past the parade deck and out the inner gates into a street inside the Citadel. They dispersed inside several small, masonry huts to set in for the night.

"Hold up," Ham said. Roark and Latimere hung back under an overhang near a row of ARVN barracks.

Latimere had hoped to catch sight of Grimm or one of the other CCs, but the other units had already moved out. Two tanks and an Ontos were parked on the parade deck and Martinez was unloading his mule from his last run to the Bao Vinh Quay. Groups of ARVN stood outside another row of barracks joking and smoking.

"Do the ARVN do any fighting?" Latimere wondered aloud.

Ham snorted. "Would you if somebody else volunteered to do it for you?"

"It's their country."

"They're waiting for us to get it back for them. Some ARVN do their share. They got a Black Panther company who are mean mutherfuckers. Best be with that name. But you don't want to be around the rest of them."

Ham double-timed across the parade deck toward Martinez and his mule which was piled high with cases of new rations. Latimere slipped off his pack and lit another cigarette. He wanted to pick up the conversation, but Roark had returned to being his standoffish self. Nonetheless, Latimere tried, "Bayer told me you have a Bronze Star. What did you do?"

"Nothing more than the grunts do every day they're out," Roark wiped his brow and turned away. "I guess nobody expected anything from a correspondent so they put me in for a medal."

Latimere thought about it. "There had to be more than that." Latimere sensed Roark didn't want to talk, but asked anyway. "Was it when you were shot?"

"No."

"You don't want to talk?"

"Nothing to say. We were under fire, and I ran out for some casualties. Grunts do it all the time, but we're not expected to, are we? CCs do only what we have to and not get careless."

"You've been here a long time."

"Couple years."

"Why keep extending?"

"*Khoung biet*," Roark shrugged. "I don't know. Don't read too much into it. The simple reason is I enlisted for three years and still have time left to do. Figure it's better over here than all the spitshine and brass in the States."

Latimere pushed back his helmet and scanned the area. "You think we'll run into Grimm and Bayer?"

"Could be."

"What about Golf Two-Five? Maybe I could find Billy Huff."

Hearing Latimere's dead friend's name started a sickening spiral in Roark's stomach.

"Might. Maybe in a few days, but your ass is tied to me. Don't forget it."

"Don't you get careless, either. I don't want the Top on my ass," Latimere smiled.

Ham returned with several boxes of C-rats. "The pricks are being kind to us, like passing out meals to the condemned. C'mon, we better get back to the unit."

That night, the troops packed inside the abandoned huts. Rain poured off the roofs and formed deep ruts in the road outside. As the hours passed, Latimere sensed a change in the men's moods, and he likened it to a coffin closing. Except for those who pulled watch, the men fell asleep early. For once, Latimere slept like a baby.

However, Roark was restless this night, priming himself for tomorrow. He thought about Babysan's engaging innocence. Latimere reminded him of an eager kid with his nose pressed against a window. He thought about the winding down of his final tour and the battle yet to be fought and knew there was one thing to be grateful for—

that he still had too much time left in country to adopt a short-timer's mentality. He wondered whether it would hit him the same way it hit everybody else he had known over here. After the first spasms of joy washed over short-timers it was always surpassed by terrible tension. Short-timers would do anything to keep out of the field, but their anxiety soon collided with survival guilt from leaving their buddies behind. Roark had been short two times before. Waiting for his 30-day leave, he never felt a thing, because he knew he would come back. He doubted whether fear or guilt would hit him this time, even though he would be leaving for good.

Roark's thoughts streaked randomly, smacked like balls on a pool table. Suddenly, he felt a lustful joy course through him, the residue from his night of debauchery during his last 30-day leave in the States. Revolution in the streets and sex in the air, he had found it difficult getting along with people. Now, he had one tour left in Nam and the rest of his life ahead of him, and the promise of his career had always been enough. The long haired hippie girls with love beads and sandals didn't interest him, and even if they had, they would have found Roark alienating. Besides, how could they stack up against Maggie?

Roark sighed and let himself go. He lay in total darkness on the cold, hard floor and listened to his breath quicken. His palms damp, something in his stomach squirmed.

Maggie.

Chapter Five

MORNING BROKE WITH a torrential downpour. Roark tried to clear his head, the dreamlike quality of the night's reminiscences eddied in his brain like a fever. Subtle changes were taking place inside him. Let them. He yearned for the world of adults, a career, and Maggie had been part of that change.

"LET'S GO. ON YOUR FEET!" Gunny Jerardi's cheery morning greeting.

Lance Corporal Jeffery Ault, 1st Platoon machine gunner, pitched his canteen cup against a wall. "What is this shit? We don't even get coffee?"

Jerardi poked his head inside. "You bitching again, Ault?"

Ault shoved his gear into his pack and cursed again.

"Ault," the gunny said. "Look on the bright side. You always bitch about the coffee anyway, so consider it a favor. Wouldn't want you hauling that pig around on an upset stomach."

The pig was Ault's M-60 machine gun.

Before long, artillery pounded the tower up the road, but despite the bombardment, the wall looked as formidable as ever. The slashing rains obscured much of the men's view, and they could not tell whether the damage to the wall was from the current barrage or from Alpha's assault on the tower a few days earlier. Down the road, piles of brick and rubble protruded from the mud. The cover the piles afforded had been rendered useless by the downpour. If anyone had to dive for cover, they would likely drown in knee deep mud.

Gunny Jerardi poked his head in again. "You want to know why we're saddling up, there's your answer, Ault. Music, ain't it? Soon as that arty stops, we move."

Ault gave a dismissive grunt. "They can arty all they want, but the grunts gotta occupy the ground."

The men geared-up and got to their feet. Squad leaders assigned details to haul more ammo from the CP. Beyond their personal arsenals, most grunts carried two 100-round belts of linked ammo for the M-60s. The A-gunners packed double that. Roark crisscrossed two belts over his chest.

The men paced nervously inside the gutted huts as the rain flooded down. They smoked to kill time and stamped their feet. Their mouths were dry, but it was nothing water could cure. Roark grabbed Latimere and headed to the CP.

Capt. Donlon was on the radio, surrounded by his platoon sergeants. Gunny Jerardi was outside and gave Roark the once-over. The gunny tapped his helmet and nodded smartly. Roark tapped his helmet and nodded back. Amazing, Roark thought, the gunny still had time to think about his goddamn bush hat.

A Marine tank rumbled out of the ARVN compound and clanked 20 meters up the road, spewing gobs of red mud in its wake. When it stopped, the tracks buried in the mud.

Capt. Donlon broke contact with the artillery battery and ordered the tank up on line with the CP. The tank advanced, and the grunts on either side turned away and covered their weapons.

"That's it for the prep fire," Donlon said. "Everybody's aware Alpha got chewed up trying to take that tower a couple days ago. Now, it's our turn. Be cautious. First sign of enemy contact, get your men inside and keep them there until we can move the tank into position. Maybe we'll get lucky, but don't count on it. Charlie might have pulled out, but he could just as easily have reinforced his positions along the wall. Either way, I want it understood that we will take that tower. I don't plan to make this run twice. Move out in one-zero mikes."

Roark found Ham in the lead platoon, but at least it wasn't the point squad. Ham's face was taut, lips thin. He slung one M-79 over a shoulder, loaded the other and jerked the breech shut. "Gut check time."

"MOVE OUT," Gunny Jerardi called. "PASS IT ON."

Ham's squad was third in line. Roark and Latimere moved alongside. 2nd Platoon slogged through the mud at the base of the wall.

The lead platoon advanced through the first block and started up the second. The monsoon-whipped rains blinded them. Spider-leg veins of lightning flashed. Some grunts mistook the thunder for mortars and momentarily went slack in the knees.

"Pissin' rain," someone complained, and the banter commenced.

"Everything in Nam pisses or shits on you."

"Charlie's rained on same as us. Maybe he don't like it either, and crawled back into his hole."

"He lives here, asshole. He's used to it."

"Bullshit. If we're wet, so's he. Nobody gets used to it. You gotta be a fuckin' oyster to like this shit."

The men had reached the end of the second block when word came up the ranks for them to hold. Suddenly, the point man near the wall toppled into the mud. For a moment, the others thought he had slipped. Then, another man went down, and the jangled BRRRRRRRRRRRRP of fire reached them through the din of the downpour.

Rockets thudded into the wall, and in 30 seconds, half of the lead squad had been wiped out.

The men crammed into the huts and poured fire at the tower. The sky went suddenly black and CRAAACKED and BOOOOMED as nature's sounds vied with the guns. Wind beat the rain into thousands of tiny pellets and whipped the road into a sea of red foam.

Rounds clinked off the wall. PEE-YIINNNG. PEEOOWWWWWWW. TEEEEEEEEN. The monsoon raged harder, and the men couldn't see five feet in front of them. Then, just as quickly as it had started, the thunder stopped and the fire let up. Thirty seconds passed. More. What the hell was happening? The men froze in the road, and fought waves of retching terror. More time passed. Suddenly, the grunts near the wall arose en masse and charged for the concealment of the huts across the road.

The NVA soldiers were waiting. The instant the grunts ran, they spewed a barrage of automatic weapons fire. Grunts went down, and some drowned in the muck before enemy bullets punched the life from them. BRRRRP-RRRP-RRRRRP! BRRRRRRRRRRRRRRP! Five more grunts lay dead, and the rest burrowed low in the mud. A hail of fire cut a swath above their heads. Buried to their armpits in mud made it impossible to return fire. Rain slashed at their faces. The men wrenched sideways to offer narrower targets and winced as bullets splurted into the mud around them.

The Marines inside kept up a steady stream of fire. Down the block, the tank rumbled forward but then stopped. The tank commander screamed at the men to clear the road, but nobody heard him.

Ault was among those trapped in the road. He had dropped his machine gun when the fire erupted and scrambled behind a pile of rubble. Now, he blubbered as he grappled for his machine gun, trying to pull it out of the mud. His A-gunner came up to help, but when they tried to yank it up, they were driven down by fire.

"PIG UP. PIG UP. WHERE'S THE PIG, GODDAMMIT?" Ault's squad leader screamed from the huts.

"PIG UP," the men shouted.

"AULT, YOU HIT? WHERE THE HELL IS AULT?"

"I'M IN THE ROAD, GODDAMMIT."

Ault staggered to his feet, tugged the pig free and ran for the huts. In the safety of cover, he hastily stripped the gun and cleaned it.

"PIG UP," the squad leader shouted again.

"I'M COMING!"

The belts on Ault's chest covered with mud, he yelled to the men next to him. "Give me your belts." The men were glad to off load the weight and threw them to him.

"PIG UP, AULT, GODDAMMIT."

"On my way." He pulled back the bolt on the machine gun and rammed it home and tore into the street, firing madly as he moved.

The monsoon pummeled them in fits and spurts. Some grunts ran for the huts, while others dashed into the road to help the wounded. Then, the order to keep moving came from down the column. The point squad waited for the other squads to close ranks behind. The tank roared forward, but had to stop again. Still too many men in its path. During each sporadic lull, the men heard the screams of rent iron singing through the air and casualties clamoring for help.

Doc Carson scrambled among the wounded. Out of battle dressings and surgical tubing, he now used the casualties' belts as tourniquets. Despite the rain, sweat through his clothes formed a white, frothy lather on his utilities.

A man ahead of him screamed. "Doc Carson!" It sounded a long way away, but the man was only five yards away.

"Coming," Carson shouted. "Hold on."

"Please, please…"

Carson tightened another tourniquet, and then rushed to the man's side. He recognized him. It was a New Guy, a skinny kid with freckles. Struggling to keep his head up, he suddenly spat blood and sank beneath the mud. Carson pulled him up and checked his vital signs, but the Marine was gone. Another grunt called. "Doc, Doc, help me." Carson looked to see who called, then spun back. More grunts called. Paralyzed with helplessness, anguished tears streamed down Carson's face. He wiped the tears with a bloody hand and ran to the next man.

The grunts advanced, taking one hut at a time. Ham was in the third hut behind the point squad with three grunts and Roark and Latimere.

The storm had broken suddenly and a soft mist was falling.

Ham and Roark were at a window, Latimere squeezed between them. The enemy fire had subsided, and they saw a flurry of movement along the top of the wall. Then, they heard several tinny thunks and scrambled inside the hut. Roark yelled down the row of stone huts. "INCOMING!"

Immediately, mortars rained. The tank churned forward and elevated its cannon. It was as close as it could get and still fire on the tower. The men who had moved up behind the cover of the tank, broke for the huts. The tank opened up, and the first round blew a crater in the wall. The second smashed into the base of the tower and loosed a flood of rubble into the street. The tank's machine gunner cut loose, but a B-40 rocket burst in front of him and showered him with flak. Another rocket missed wide and screamed into the huts felling two more men. Enemy machine guns raked the area. Capt. Donlon ordered the tank back. A sitting duck unable to maneuver, it drew too much fire. Belching plumes of black smoke, it churned into a side street. Donlon ordered his men to put the casualties aboard, so the tank could haul them back to the aid station.

All along the wall, NVA ammo carriers scrambled between positions. Latimere saw them from the window and shouted to Roark and Ham

"Sonovabitch," Ham raised his blooper. Latimere sprayed a burst and the NVA ducked as the rounds flew wild. Roark slapped Latimere's rifle down. "Aim that thing when you fire it, dammit. You want to hotdog, you do it solo."

Out of the corner of his eye, Ham suddenly saw an NVA soldier sighting in a B-40 rocket, aiming right at them. Ham grabbed Roark and Latimere and drove them to the deck.

The rocket scudded first into the mud and then slammed into the hut. The explosion tortured their eardrums. The concussion split the ceiling, and a cascade of masonry and brick fell on them. The hut absorbed most of the flak from the rocket, but splinters of hot metal zinged into the walls behind them. The front wall gave an agonized shudder and collapsed in a heap.

"Fuck." Ham waved his arms to clear the smoke and swirling debris surrounding him.

Roark jumped to his feet. They had little cover left, and Roark had no intention of staying there and letting the enemy zero in on them again. "Let's get out of here." He pulled Latimere up, but the grunts were still waiting for the debris to clear.

"Get going," Ham rallied the grunts. "One more round, we buy it. Get on your feet. There ain't no wall left."

Ham and Latimere crouched with Roark behind the rubble. The Marines were on their feet but remained flattened against the side wall. "You ready?" Roark called.

"Wait one," Ham said. "Maybe if we stay put a minute, Charlie'll think he got us."

"You nuts?" But Ham was right. So far, none had fired back yet. *OK*, Roark thought, *it was worth a chance*, but anything that landed in the road in front of them would scramble them like eggs.

A machine gunner in the hut behind them started burning lead. A burst of enemy fire responded and smacked into the rubble and chinked off the walls behind them. One round ricocheted and kicked Ham in the hip like a horse, but the bullet was already flattened and only bruised him.

Now, they were certain they had to get out of there. Roark peeked over the rubble but instantly whipped his head back, and felt his legs go out from under him. He tried to suck it up, pretended he didn't see, but he saw it, all right. An NVA had a rocket pointed right at them. He yelled to the others and bristled for the impact. A moment passed. The blood in his head boiled. Another moment passed, and Roark suddenly sprang to his feet. He wouldn't wait any longer to be slaughtered. He had to act, even if it was only to lift his head and watch death come at him.

He peered over the rubble. The NVA soldier with the rocket launcher was pinned down by the pig. When the machine gun slacked off, the NVA soldier raised up again. Roark could only see his helmet and part of his cheek below the brim. He raised his rocket, and Roark snapped his rifle into his shoulder and drew a bead on the enemy gunner. Steady. Steady. Roark breathed and squeezed off three rounds. The enemy soldier's head blew apart, and the rocket fell backwards off his shoulder to the ground. "Fuck you, you son of a bitch."

Roark turned to the others. "Let's go. Now." Latimere and Ham crawled from the rubble and flattened against the wall beside him. The other grunts were still talking it over.

"What's it gonna be?" Roark shouted. The men stared at him mutely. "Make up your minds. If you're not coming with us, at least lay down cover fire."

"Wait, we're coming."

"We might as well move up as move back," Roark whispered to Ham. "Either way, the gooks'll have a crack at us."

Ham moved past Roark and looked around the corner of the wall. A round flew off the wall near his head and shredded the right side of his face. He dropped to a knee like a fighter who'd just taken a left hook to the jaw.

"You OK?" Roark asked.

Ham smeared the blood with his left sleeve. "I guess I'm still here."

Commotion from the huts down the road. The grunts were moving up in force, pushing inside the huts until overflowing. They'd had a breakdown of communication as the CP yelled for the point squads to advance.

"Move," Ham urged his squad forward. Cover fire intensified from the huts to their front and rear. They tore around the wall and barreled through the front door ahead of them. Another grunt made a break and spun wildly in the street. *PA-TINNG! PA-TINNNNNNG!* A round crunched through his helmet and rattled around his head.

His hands shot to his face but two grunts grabbed him under the armpits and dragged him through the mud until another rocket exploded and blew them off their feet.

More Marines went after them as the company pushed up behind them. Along the top of the wall, the NVA retreated. "KEEP MOVING, MOVE UP!" Someone screamed, "ROCKETS UP."

A two-man 3.5-inch rocket team scrambled forward and dropped to their knees. The assistant gunner loaded the rocket and smacked the gunner's shoulder. The gunner squeezed the trigger. One corner of the tower erupted in a giant white fireball.

The point squad rushed out of the hut and ran into the road propelled by the wave of troops behind them. The NVA fled over the back of the wall. "GET A FIRETEAM UP THERE!" a squad leader yelled. More Marines swarmed across the road and clawed up the rubble heap at the base of the wall. The grunt nearest the top of the heap suddenly stopped. Noises in the tower. "Gimme a grenade." His buddies tossed up two grenades. From the huts across the road, grunts strafed the top of the wall. Roark expended a mag. Ham wanted to fire, but he was too close to use his blooper, so he cranked away with his .45.

The grunt near the top of the heap pulled the pins and hurled the grenades one at a time into the tower. Black smoke roiled, and the grunts raced up the heap. The first man to the tower craned his M-16 over the low wall and blindly sprayed a burst inside. Then, he looked into the bunker. Six NVA were splayed against the walls, shreds of skin and blood smattered everywhere.

More grunts raced up the rubble heap. The grunts on top of the wall fired demonically and waved their arms and shrieked. "SONOVABITCH! CHECK IT OUT."

Ham, Roark and Latimere reached the bunker. On the other side of the wall, scores of NVA fled across the muddy yard, bored into spider holes and hurled themselves over a maze of low interior walls. A shooting gallery, it was beautiful. The grunts fired and screamed at their sudden new victory.

"PULL BACK, GET BACK," the men in the road yelled at them. "GET OFFA THERE. ARTY'S UP."

But the grunts continued firing.

"PULL BACK. ARTY ON THE WAY!"

The grunts finally pulled back but blew out their mags before the last Marine slid down the scrap heap.

Eerie holing-up in the huts that night. A fortnight ago, they had been filled with families and cooking and the sounds of children and life—peasants and fishermen living the same way their ancestors had for generations.

Delta Company had accomplished its first objective, and five Marines now pulled watch inside the tower on top of the wall. Roark, Ham and Latimere squatted in a tiny living room with several other Marines. They had fastened ponchos over the windows to black out the light so they could heat their rations.

They ate and smoked. The men clustered in small groups and communicated with a sense of communion greater than words. It had been the worst day of fighting any had remembered, and they didn't know how many more battles lay ahead.

Roark peered at Latimere from beneath his brow, while he swallowed a spoonful of greasy C-ration beef.

Latimere had impressed him, and Roark smiled. This was the worst imaginable baptism under fire. Roark's first experience had been nothing more than being pinned down by sniper fire.

"Babysan, what was your story about the poet?"

Surprised, Latimere thought Roark was teasing and waved it off. "Oh, that."

"Tell me about it."

"It's nothing, really, just an idea. I haven't fleshed it out yet." Latimere's eyes retreated inward. "It's about a wanderer, a minstrel. He travels and writes poems, beautiful poems about the places he visits and the people he meets and the girl he hopes to find. One day, he falls in love and can't write anymore." Latimere shrugged. "He's all filled up and overflowing and happy, and he can't be bothered anymore. He doesn't care about writing, because now he has what he always wanted. Suddenly, he becomes useless. Because there's no room for dreaming, he no longer has a reason to fantasize."

"Maybe that's true." Roark said.

Latimere flushed. "I think it is. If you don't lack something, there's no reason to search for it. You have to be missing something. You need that hole to create."

Roark smiled. "What about the little beauty you were with the other night?"

"Lan?"

"Yeah."

"What do you mean?"

"Maybe you could take her back to Danang with you."

"Danang?"

"If you want to."

"How?"

Roark was having fun, but he was also serious. "First we'd have to find her. But if we did, we could tell the guys on the convoy she's a Saigon correspondent we escorted up here. We drape a couple cameras over her, and what can they say?"

"We can do that?"

"Why not?"

Just then, two grunts, LCpls Graham and Yost, barged through the door and shattered the protective shield in which the men had cloaked themselves. Tears streamed down Graham's face and his mouth foamed, tiny beads of spittle at the corners. Yost tried to console him, but Graham had lost control and hurled his helmet against the wall.

"Hey dickhead," someone growled.

"Sorry, man," Yost said.

"Goddamn Smitty," Graham wailed. "WHY'D HE DIE?"

"Shhhhhh," Yost hugged his friend. "I don't know."

Graham kicked his helmet, and it careened off the wall and bounced toward Ham.

Ham jerked to his feet. "Listen motherfucker, we've all lost friends."

"He was my buddy, you asshole."

Graham broke for Ham, but Yost restrained him.

"Go for it," Ham beckoned with his hand.

"Stow it, Ham," Yost said.

"Tell Graham to stow it. Nobody needs his cheap shit."

Yost lowered his voice, "Graham grew up with Smitty. He wasn't just a guy he met in Nam."

"That's crap. What's the difference where he met him? I met dudes in Nam worth twice the dudes I met back home."

"Forget it."

Ham and Yost glared at one another. Ham looked at Graham and spat again.

Graham's veins bulged. His face was blue and twitched between agony and vengeance. Yost pulled him aside. Graham's feet gave out, and he sobbed as his shoulders quaked. Another grunt helped prop him up and together they pulled him into the back room, trying to muffle his sobs.

In the corner, a Marine shuddered. "That dude's bucking for a Section 8." He raised his empty ration can and crumpled it in his fist. For a moment, it looked as though the Marine would lose it too, but he merely dropped the can and stared at the wall in front of him.

That was the last thing any of them had needed. Difficult enough to keep their minds clear, but when someone lost it, it took a toll on everyone. Ham felt edgy and agitated. The grunts now huddled silently. Graham had pushed them to the breaking point.

Ham picked up Graham's helmet and sat beside Roark and Latimere, and this small act had a calming effect on the others.

Roark looked at Ham and saw ugly welts on the side of his face from the flak in the hut earlier that day. "You OK?"

Ham smirked to disguise his feelings. "Trouble with you, Roark, is you make friends too easy."

"Mind your own business."

A gap-toothed grin crossed Hines' face. "Babysan, whadya think about being in shit as bad as this?"

"I don't have anything to compare, but if you say it's bad, that means it's going to get better."

Ham snorted. "All ops are bad—even rinky-dink patrols—for those who get hit. Even on the worst, some dudes can skate, but not on this fucker."

After a moment, Latimere asked, "Are you ever afraid?"

"We're all scared," Roark interjected.

"Fuckin' A we're scared." Ham thought for a moment. "Night's the worst. That's when you think about it. Only thing worse than thinking at night is a firefight at night. One op I was on, they came at us in waves, ran through the paddies like banshees. The nut was finding them the next morning propped up against the paddy dikes. They were dead and sheet-white, but every one was bandaged. That's when we knew they were so high on heroin they had stopped to treat their wounds before they came at us again.

"SMITTTTTTTTTTTY!"

Graham's scream drove a stake into the men's chests. They heard the grunts in the other room struggle to subdue him.

The men felt violated. Graham had worked on their fears and fatigue. The grunt in the corner was on the brink of snapping. His entire body trembled. "Goddamn Graham. Fuck Smitty and everybody's Smitty and all the Smittys."

The grunts' struggle to subdue Graham reverberated through the wall.

The Marine in the corner fought to keep from exploding. "One more time. Next time he opens his mouth, and I'll—." Then he whirled to his feet. "YOU HEAR ME, GRAHAM? YOU LISTENING IN THERE? I'LL DEEP-SIX YOUR ASS! SAY ONE MORE THING...ONE MORE THING, AND I'LL BAG-AND-FUCKING-TAG YOU!"

Ault and his A-gunner were among five Marines in the tower. Ault threw a fit when Gunny Jerardi picked him for watch. He didn't mind pulling watch, but he hated lugging the heavy pig up the mountain of rubble to reach the tower. When another grunt relieved him, he wedged into a corner of the bunker to get some shuteye. It was 0200. At most, Ault would get four hours sleep. He shut his eyes.

"Psssst." At 0300, the grunt on watch stooped low and woke the others. Something had caught his eye and he swung Ault's machine gun to the right. Then, he heard a noise on his left flank and whipped around but saw nothing. "Pssst, pssst," he whispered again. "Get up. Somebody's out there." He heard another noise and popped back up behind the pig. Movement along the wall to his right. The Marines' eyes bugged. "GOOKS!" He opened up with the pig, when the others in the bunker bolted as two ChiCom grenades bounced in. Two grunts scrambled for them, grasping frantically in the dark. For an instant, the machine gunner panicked and froze. He was going to jump out, but there were gooks to his left, and he swung the pig around and cut loose. Two NVA bucked and pitched off the parapet. The other grunts were still down groping for the ChiComs as enemy troops on the right sprayed the tower. The machine gunner crouched and fired above his head. He stiffened and waited for the ChiComs to blow

"DUDS." Ault grabbed one and hurled it out. Then, he popped up, took the gun and fired furiously at the swarming NVA.

Below, Marines poured out of the huts, scrambled across the road and clawed up the rubble heap. Fire from enemy positions along the top of the wall pinned them down until more grunts advanced to give cover.

In the tower, the men barely held on. Ault opened the breech and his A-gunner slapped in another linked belt. They were burning ammo at the weapon's maximum rate and the barrel of the pig glowed red in the early morning darkness. The NVA rushed them in groups of three and four. Two more ChiComs landed inside the bunker. The men instantly found them and flung them out. Both exploded. One took out an NVA fireteam right in front of them. Another grenade rattled inside the bunker and landed near Ault's leg. Ault grabbed it and it detonated. He took the brunt of it in his chest, but others were hit, and everyone was stunned by the concussion.

As the NVA closed in on the tower, more Marines spilled over the top of the wall. More clambered up the rubble behind them and poured fire down the wall in both directions.

Soon, the NVA fled down the back of the wall. Ham reached the top and popped blooper rounds. Ignoring the ladders, enemy soldiers leapt 20 feet to the ground below. Some broke legs and were riddled in place. Others scattered in retreat across the muddy courtyards, while Marines fired at their backs.

Roark made it to the tower. Doc Carson was working on Ault. Roark's watch read 0310. Terrifying and quick, the firefight was finally over. There was a lot more night ahead, but nobody would get any more sleep.

Gunny Jerardi climbed up and checked the tower. Roark watched him gasp at the carnage. Impossible to read his face in the darkness, but for the first time, Roark saw the Gunny's shoulders slump and his knees weaken. Gunny Jerardi looked down at the dead man. Ault.

Chapter Six

THE NEXT MORNING the men ate and worked on their gear. Those with extra T-shirts and socks dug them out of their packs. The monsoon had soaked through their packs, but anything was drier than the clothes they wore. Some men had immersion foot, deep cracks between their toes, from being constantly wet. Rubbing the toes tore skin and caused profuse bleeding, but some Marines found the pleasure of rubbing near orgasmic. Some perhaps secretly hoped they might be medevacked.

A dozen grunts were dispatched to the ARVN compound for ammo and water. Chow wasn't a priority. They packed enough to get through this day and most of the next. Several fireteams searched the courtyards on the other side of the tower. Gathering body counts, always a top priority, was Gunny Jerardi's personal favorite.

Now, Jerardi waited at the base of the wall when the fireteam returned.

"What's the count?"

Thirty-eight enemy KIAs and 60 blood trails. Jerardi figured most came from the day before. A few grunts overheard the news and scoffed. Everyone knew body counts were bullshit, though Hue was probably the one place where they could get a decent count. The enemy couldn't drag their dead away so easily here as they could in the jungle. Body counts were radioed from commanders in the field to regimental headquarters, where they would be inflated and passed up the chain. In lieu of occupying terrain, body counts provided one of the few measures of a unit's performance.

Satisfied, Gunny Jerardi walked back to the CP. Capt. Donlon was on the net confirming coordinates for another artillery strike. Face haggard and drawn, eyes bloodshot, he looked no better than his troops.

This morning, the rains had stopped, but the road remained a quagmire. The men sat on piles of rubble, ate their rations and grumbled. One grunt flung a can of ham-and-eggs-chopped into the mud, and spat. "How do they expect us to fight on this slop?"

"Beats shit-on-a-shingle."

"Shoulda joined the friggin' Army. The Army choppers in hot chow."

"Army's for pussies."

"Now, there's something I could eat."

Down the road, a score of replacements clattered out of the ARVN compound and headed toward Delta Company. Lieutenant Lidyard led the column. Their new utilities and boots clashed with their frayed and faded web-gear which had been taken from the latest casualties.

The salty grunts snorted and eagerly waited to wean the New Guys.

The boots shuffled through the ranks with faces flushed, quivering lips and shallow breaths. They were more frightened by what they saw as skulled-out vets than any immediate fear of Charlie.

The grunts howled and catcalled. To them, the cherries' rosy cheeks and milky complexions were side-splittingly funny. Their gullets jumped like pogo sticks and a few grunts gave them mock salutes.

"Tell me it's a fuck-up. They're joining the VC, not us."

"Be gentle with 'em now. Can't you see they're virgins."

"Old Victor Charlie's gonna be in deep shit now."

"Knock it off," Capt. Donlon said.

Lt. Lidyard led the new troops to the CP, and Gunny Jerardi chose where to place them. No matter that his platoon sergeants wanted as many new replacements as they could get, the men in the squads did not. Boots were dangerous in close quarters and bad luck at best.

"Put'em on point. At least there we can keep an eye on 'em."

"Yeah, and so can Charlie."

"That's enough," Donlon glared at his men.

Another man trailed the replacements. Despite Top Grover's orders, Grimm had left Alpha Company to head to the front. He left Hines as well. Badly decimated, Alpha Company would bring up the rear. Delta was lead company now, and Grimm had been determined to join them, join Roark. The final push of the offensive would provide enough stories for everyone. He entered Delta's CP as Gunny Jerardi reassigned the last of the new replacements and introduced himself.

"I'm looking for two other reporters I think are here."

"Head up the road. They're in one of those huts near the tower."

Soon, Grimm spotted Roark and Latimere sitting outside one of the huts.

"Sergeant Grimm," Latimere called.

"How you doing, Babysan?" He whisked them both inside. Ham followed. Grimm pulled out a flask of Jack Daniels.

"Gawd." Ham's eyes widened seeing the flask.

Roark motioned toward Ham. "He's OK. He's one of us. Grimm, meet Ham."

Ham raised his two M-79s. "And these here are the muthas."

Grimm gave the others a swig, and then passed it. Ham took a slug and sighed.

"What are you doing here?" Latimere asked.

"Just checking to see how you're doing."

"Where's Hines?"

"Left him back with Alpha Six." Good news to Latimere.

"You heard anything about Ehlo or Bayer?" Roark asked.

"Nah, they're OK, though. Would have heard something if they weren't."

"With this goat-screw going on?"

"You staying?" Latimere asked.

"Might as well. Word is they're gearing up for the big push. "Alpha was torn to shit and held back to reinforce the ARVN compound. That's where they think the gooks'll make their escape. G-2 says we got them bottled."

"I ain't seen no white flags," Ham said.

Grimm laughed. "And you won't. They intercepted an NVA radio transmission. Their ranks inside the Citadel are decimated and they've asked permission to withdraw."

"That true?" Ham asked.

"Yep, but their brass ordered them to stay put and fight it out."

"Fuck me," Ham moaned.

The men looked at each other in disbelief. Grimm acted as though he had just considered the consequences for the first time. "Deranged, ain't it?"

"I don't get it. Would the NVA actually do that?"

"That's what they said."

The men shook their heads dumbly at the thought of forced mass suicide.

Midmorning, Delta waited for the bombardment to commence. With Grimm's flask now empty, the correspondents' spirits had lifted somewhat, and though no one had anything approaching a buzz, their small attempt at disobedience had satisfied.

The grunts were edgy and volatile from all the stopping and starting. The process of hurry-up-and-wait was more draining than the exhaustion of constantly being pushed. When pushed, Marines pulled on adrenalin reserves to take them through the next battle. Now, their nerves betrayed them. Dark feelings lanced like shrapnel through their systems.

Roark cleaned his rifle while Latimere helped one of the new replacements. Suddenly, Hines stuck his head in the door. "Where's Grimm?"

"You lose your mother, Hines?"

"Fuck you, Roark. I seen enough shit without taking any of yours."

Latimere went back to work on the New Guy, pulling up and tightening his web gear. He opened the young Marine's magazine pouches and pulled out the mags. "These should go in with the rounds pointed down and toward your belt buckle. That way, you know where they are, and you can reload in one smooth action."

Hines stepped forward. "Ain't this a load of shit. I come from Alpha Company and the biggest battle of the war and walk in on a training session."

"Back off," Roark said.

"Where's Grimm?"

"He's around."

Hines' chest heaved. "What's he doing here?"

Grimm came up behind Hines. "What're *you* doing here?"

"Why'd you leave me like that?"

"Someone should stay back with Alpha."

"So you don't even tell me?"

"What's the matter, Hines?"

"Just don't like being left, that's all."

"Thought I'd give you a break." Eyes narrowed, Grimm scrutinized Hines. "What are you so hot about?"

"Nothing," Hines snapped. Hines' chest heaved beneath his flak jacket—from hurt as much as anger. Hurt from being deserted and dismissed, and anger because he was at the front again. Hines wondered why he trailed after Grimm, anyway. He balled a fist and held it close to his groin to steady himself then stiffened. Hines believed himself as good as any of them. "Just let me know what's going on, that's all." Lips quivering, Hines stood his ground.

Latimere could make no sense of it, but he didn't want to be around Hines that day.

An hour later, when the artillery strike ended, Delta Company moved. They climbed the mountain of stone and rubble then spread out along the wall and swept the courtyards. The courtyards were cordoned by thick, five-foot-high brick walls. Those in the open crouched and moved forward.

The squad leaders yelled, "FAN OUT."

Grimm had discouraged Hines from staying with them. There were three CCs as it was. Hines moped, flared up inside but finally relented and walked back to Delta Company's CP.

Roark and Grimm moved beside a pock-marked wall in a narrow, grassy alleyway. Ham and Latimere progressed along another. Roark trusted Ham but kept his eyes on Latimere.

The Marines tensed with every step crossing the vulnerable courtyards. Flanking units came up on line and halfway through the yards, a withering barrage of enemy fire erupted. One man caught a round in the navel that blew a golf ball-sized hole out of his spine. Two more grunts toppled in the next courtyard, and the men flattened on the ground. Squad leaders shouted for the men to move up as corpsmen crawled through the grass to the casualties. More grunts bunched behind the walls and popped up and fired into the yards in front of them. The enemy suddenly ceased fire before anyone could pinpoint them.

Shortly, the rest of the company moved up behind. The point squads filed through openings in the wall in groups of two and three. The squad leaders shouted them forward, and they bolted across the narrow alleyway and took cover behind the walls dividing the next row of courtyards. Before they entered the next yard, several grunts held their rifles over the wall and cut loose with semiautomatic fire. Then, enemy machine guns tacked across the wall and more grunts popped up firing.

The grunts waited behind the wall for a moment. "Weird," Ham said.

"What?" Latimere gulped air.

"How they fire and pull back."

"What do you think?"

"They're trying to draw us in to spring an ambush. We'd be stranded and couldn't pull back. They wants us to chase them so they can get us in a U and kick in with mortars."

"KEEP MOVING. MOVE IT UP!" the Gunny shouted from behind them.

Ham's heart pounded as Marines streamed through the openings in the walls into the next row of courtyards. The grass was taller there, rising above their knees. They duck-walked, kept low, and some moved cautiously, suddenly fearful of snakes.

"MOVEMENT," a grunt in another courtyard pointed. A machine gun chewed through a belt of ammo, but with no enemy response, the pig ceased firing.

Ham crouched near a wall and was suddenly startled to spot a spider hole. He froze and stared through the tall grass. He inched nearer and tried to look down the hole without offering a target. He booted mud inside it and a flurry of fire rang out and Ham reeled backwards. Latimere heard the click of a magazine being ejected, jumped in front of Ham and aimed into the hole.

In the dark shadows, Latimere saw an NVA soldier peer up at him. Both of them froze. He could make out the faint outline of an AK-47 lying across the man's chest and saw his hand grope for a mag.

"SPIDER HOLES. CHECK THE HOLES," Ham yelled from behind him. The other grunts scrambled and searched the yard for more spider holes.

Latimere didn't move. The enemy soldier's eyes looked waxy and glazed. To Latimere, he seemed to move in slow motion when he slipped in the fresh mag. Then, Latimere fired and saw the white of his eye burst crimson.

A grunt near the wall yelled, "FIRE IN THE HOLE." He threw a grenade and the explosion obliterated NVA screams. Marines backtracked and more cries rang out from other spider holes in the yards as grunts fired short bursts and threw more frags.

The enemy soldier Latimere had just killed had barely moved. Latimere wondered whether he had been suicidal or doped on something. Ham stood beside him and stared into the hole. Latimere gaped at the dead man, but Ham grinned. "Well-done, Babysan."

"He must have been drugged or something."

"Fuckin'-A, he was drugged. Fucker was geed up on heroin."

More firing now in the other courtyards. Squad leaders shouted to the men to double back and check the yards behind them for spider holes.

Ham dragged Latimere with him. "Babysan, why'd you run in front of me like that?"

"Because he fired at you."

"What made you think he wouldn't fire at you?"

"I heard his magazine release click."

"You're lucky, Babysan. Don't do that again. AK's are different from M-16's. The bolt don't stay back when you empty a magazine. Nine out of ten times a gook won't waste his full load. He jams a new mag in before he runs out so he's still got one in the chamber. Don't ever trust a gook."

Shaking, Latimere stood pat with Ham for a moment while the grunts reconnoitered the yards behind them.

Another rash of frag explosions into the spider holes, and then Delta company regrouped and advanced again. Squads filed down alleyways and poured into the courtyards.

Roark and Grimm were still in the alleyway behind a wall when a new firefight broke out. Like most battles, the skirmishes raged in fits and starts, but no matter how brief the volleys lasted, it was the kind of time no clock could track. With each new eruption, everything churned into motion, and the only thing that stopped completely was a man's heart or breath for an instant. Each time the fire let up, more men scrambled forward to the next wall.

Ham and Latimere crouched near an opening in a wall then bolted into the next yard. Rounds sang over their heads as they ran hunched down and flopped into the mud at the base of another wall. Picking themselves up, they heard the grunts beside them laugh. Two Marines had tied a small American flag to a strip of thatch and waved it above the wall and yelled insults. Enemy machine guns ripped into the flag and shattered the stick.

"Where'd you get that?" Latimere fumbled for his camera.

"Brought it with me from Phu Bai." The grunt waved the remnants again.

Latimere wanted the grunt's name, but a burst of machine gun fire sprayed their position and Latimere instinctively glanced at the opening ahead. For a moment, he feared being overrun.

Latimere crawled closer to snap pictures, and the grunts turned to the camera and smiled. Several men down the line fired over the wall. Enemy machine guns had pinned them down and chewed chunks out of the wall.

Ham crawled to the opening, which led to a narrow alleyway lined with another maze of courtyards. Latimere picked up his pack and slung his camera over his shoulder.

Ham popped his head round the corner and glanced through the opening. Twenty meters away, he saw movement in the yard. "GOOKS. GOOKS!"

"WHERE?"

"IN THE YARD, RIGHT IN FRONT OF US."

Ham's cries carried down the line to the grunts on their flanks. "GOOKS IN THE YARD! GOOKS ON TOP OF US!"

"HOW MANY?"

Ham inched an M-79 around the corner and saw them running across the yard.

"HOW MANY?" someone screamed.

"HOW THE HELL DO I KNOW?" Ham shouted.

Ham shouldered the blooper and aimed through the opening. Just then, an enemy soldier at the rear of the courtyard suddenly sprang half-crazed from his spider hole, and emptied his magazine at the Marines at the wall. Three men toppled before the other grunts splattered him with a furious salvo.

Panic swept the yards. Ham turned back to the opening but was driven back by fire. Enemy fire intensified even as the Marines burned through their loads, firing on full automatic.

More Marines spilled into the courtyards to reinforce them as enemy snipers fired down the alley on their flanks. The alley ran straight for two hundred meters, and NVA troops had a clear view from either flank. The men nearest the openings scrambled into the yards from both directions. A couple grunts popped smoke grenades as the other men crawled beside the walls on knees and elbows.

In the courtyards to their rear, Marines spat out volleys down the alleys until the snipers pulled back. Then, the men in the alley bolted forward through more openings.

Grimm and Roark were pinned down behind a wall in the yard beside Latimere. Roark cut back on his rate of fire. He had already burned through half his magazines. A moment later, he heard an engine in the alley to his rear and a mechanical mule rolled up. Martinez poked his head through the opening and called for wounded. Half a dozen casualties were already piled on the mule.

"You got any more wounded?" Martinez yelled.

Roark ran over to the mule. He grabbed magazines and from two dead Marines and refilled his bandolier. One of the wounded handed Roark another bandolier. "Give it to someone who can use it."

Roark shoved a fresh mag into his rifle. "How the hell did you get in here?"

Martinez grinned.

Grimm ran up and joined them. The fire eased as two corpsmen worked on the wounded. Doc Carson slid a plastic tube down a Marine's windpipe. The Marine bucked and went limp, and Carson headed to another man.

The CCs and Martinez rushed to other casualties and gave first aid. Grimm knelt over a man who had his abdomen blown open. He started mouth-to-mouth, but the dying man's vomit choked him.

Roark pulled another man against the wall. "Where're you hit?"

The man felt himself all over. "I don't know. Nowhere. Just stunned, I guess."

Roark shoved him backwards and ran to the next man.

"Doc," Martinez knelt over a wounded Marine. "Can this one be moved?"

"Yeah, but don't grab him under the shoulders, or he'll tear inside!"

Grimm and Roark helped Martinez haul him to the mule.

When back in the alley, Roark remembered Latimere. He wanted to peel off and find him, but Martinez needed help with a KIA.

"I'll help you with this one," Roark said. "Then I got to check on someone."

Suddenly, the ground erupted and blanketed them with mud. The concussion knocked them down as a barrage of enemy 82mm mortars CRUNCHED into the yards on both sides of the wall. More calls rang out for DOC and CORPSMAN UP.

Doc Carson reached an opening in the wall and called to the men in the courtyard in front of him, "You call a Doc?"

"Negative. Check the next courtyard over."

Carson rushed down the alleyway to the next opening. Mortars rained as Marines across the yard popped up and fired over the wall. They feared being overrun, and shrank inside their helmets to avoid the flak and shrapnel.

The mortars eased up, and more grunts packed near Carson.

Ham fired his bloopers, and whirled round to see Carson in the alleyway behind him. "Carson, got a couple wounded in the yard here."

"A guy named Trilling's down, too," someone shouted. "Over here Doc, he's with me."

Doc Carson shouted to Ham. "Cover me. I'm coming across."

Doc Carson took off with three Marines in trail. They scrambled across the yard through blinding mortar flashes, splays of mud and the tortured zing of whizzing metal. KEE-YOWWWWWWW! KEE-YOWWWWWW! Two Marines dove for cover, but one Marine and Doc Carson were caught in the open and gutted with shrapnel. Horrified, Ham turned to see Doc Carson toppled in mid stride. He staggered to all-fours, but another mortar hit in front of him.

"DOC!" Ham screamed, and leapt to his feet. Ham made a break for Doc Carson, but mortar rounds drove him back to the wall.

The Marines fired wildly, hurling grenades over the walls into the courtyards in front of them.

Grimm and Roark had maneuvered to an opening to the courtyard that Ham had crossed. Roark yelled. "Hold on, we'll cross and pick up Doc on the way!"

Grimm and Roark sprang from a crouch and tore into the yard. Grimm slipped and sprawled head-first into the grass as more mortars CRUMPED. Roark was blown into the air and landed on his back with a thud.

Chapter Seven

ROARK'S LEGS TWITCHED. He stared at the darkening sky, as if from a deep swirling well. His utilities shredded, blood streamed from cuts on his forehead. He felt the crunch of teeth in his mouth and was dully aware he still had a tongue. A large fragment of shrapnel was lodged in his arm, just below the shoulder, and his tibia protruded from his trouser leg.

He blinked, unable to move, a steel noose around his ribcage. He faintly felt the processes working, could faintly feel his pulse. Shock slowly oozed through him and dulled the stabbing pains burning through his body.

Roark's sky grew darker from the blur of black figures crowded over him. His limbs felt cold, and he shivered. Grimm ripped into the medical kit he had snatched off Doc Carson. Latimere picked at the smaller fragments embedded in Roark's legs.

So this was what it was like, Roark thought. Almost peaceful, it reminded him of the time he nearly drowned. He had accepted Death's verdict but splurted from his clutches and broke free of the waves.

Grimm administered a shot of morphine, but the needle broke off. Blood crusted at the corners of Roark's mouth.

A silent explosion flashed around them, and Roark's eyes rolled back.

Grimm grabbed Roark under his shoulders and Latimere took his feet. The popping of the fire grew vicious as they headed for the mule. Hunched over, they crossed the courtyard. Each time they heard a round coming, they flattened and covered Roark's body. After the explosion, they moved again.

They saw the mule in the alleyway. "There ain't no room. He'll have to wait for the next run," Martinez said.

"Your ass, we'll make room."

Martinez flared. "I already got too many onboard. No way I'm tossing them off to make room."

"It's Roark, goddammit," Grimm said. "He helped you, remember?"

"What do you want me to do?"

"Make room. He'll die if he waits until you get back. You got two dead on board taking up space."

The casualties on the mule moaned and winced in pain. Martinez glanced back and forth between Grimm and the mule. "OK, but do it quick."

Grimm and Latimere offloaded one KIA and lifted Roark onto the flatbed, muscling him between the others. Latimere hopped up beside him.

"Where do you think you're going?" Martinez said.

Latimere glared at Martinez. "I'm going."

"Get off there." Martinez's posture said he was serious.

Latimere climbed down. Roark clutched his forearm. "Wait. Take it."

Latimere leaned in closer to hear.

"Take the bandolier. B-Billy. Billy. Sorry..." he whispered.

Latimere carefully untied the bandolier and took it.

Martinez gripped the wheel. "You don't get the hell outta the way, your man's gonna croak before I get there."

"Come on," Grimm pulled Latimere back, "He'll get him there OK."

"No stops," Latimere shouted. "Go straight to the aid station."

Martinez wended through the maze of walls. He veered through a crumbling archway in the large wall, 200 meters to the right of the tower, and then raced through the streets to the ARVN compound. He sped through the gates and brought his mule to a stop.

Two Sea Knight helicopters circled overhead, and a grunt popped a canister of green smoke.

Martinez hopped off the mule. "Need some help over here."

Several corpsmen and grunts rushed to the mule and placed the casualties on stretchers. They took the KIA off last. A gunnery sergeant ran up behind them shouting to the corpsmen, "Get them over there. Wounded in one pile, KIAs in the other."

The corpsmen applied fresh bandages to the wounded to try to stop the bleeding. Two Marines carried away the dead man.

Near the mule, the corpsmen did what they could for the casualties and threw ponchos over them to keep them warm. Then, Marines hauled them to the parade deck.

Roark had been off loaded and placed on a stretcher. Martinez stayed with him while a corpsman stripped his gear.

"He's bad, isn't he, Doc?"

The corpsman loosened Roark's cartridge belt. Roark opened his eyes and struggled to speak. He stared at Martinez. "No...Pistol."

"Yeah, yeah," the corpsman said and flung the belt and pistol to Martinez.

It was an honor to receive another man's pistol.

"Don't talk, don't move," the corpsman said. He slashed away a swath of Roark's trouser leg and saw a piece of shrapnel the size of a silver dollar had wedged into the bone. The corpsman tied a tourniquet, slapped on a bandage and inserted an IV.

The small dose of morphine took hold and Roark lost consciousness again. The corpsman pulled a poncho over him and called the Marines to move him.

Two Marines lifted him and ran him to the helo-pad just as the choppers touched down. Their rotors blew dead fronds off the palms and whipped mud and green smoke in their faces. Half-blinded, they set Roark's stretcher down halfway between the rows of dead and wounded and shoved the plasma bottle under his poncho. The heavy prop wash from the helicopters beat against Roark's face, rousing him again, but his poncho flapped in the wind and covered his head.

The gunnery sergeant screamed into the prop wash. "PUT WOUNDED ON THE FIRST CHOPPER, DEAD ON THE SECOND."

Several Marines on the parade deck rushed to the stretchers and started carrying them to the helicopters.

Roark felt his stretcher being lifted off the deck. Sweat lathed his body. Through the fog of inertia, he strained to lift his arms. *Don't put me with the DEAD! I'm ALIVE, ALIVE!* Roark tried to call out, but he had no breath, and his words were lost in the din from the helicopters. Roark panicked. *NOT WITH THE DEAD. DON'T PUT ME WITH THE DEAD. I'M WOUNDED...I'M ALIVE!*

When they carried him past the helicopter for the wounded, Roark's poncho flapped under the prop wash. He felt a terror deep inside him. *GET IT OFF ME! BLOW IT OFF ME!* The poncho rose up and flapped again, but Roark couldn't raise his hands to pull it down.

The poncho flattened against his head again as they passed the first helicopter and carried him toward the second where they were loading the dead. Roark's lips turned purple. *THEY'RE PUTTING ME WITH THE DEAD! WITH THE DEAD!* His insides collapsed as he succumbed to horror. Roark thought to himself, this is what fear's like, what it's really like.

As they neared the second helicopter the prop wash whipped Roark's poncho yet again. This time it revealed the plasma bottle. "Jesus," the Marine gasped, and shouted to his buddy to pull up. "This one's alive! Get him on the other chopper."

Chapter Eight

IN THE DAYS THAT FOLLOWED, the battles blurred with a sameness. The week ending February 20 recorded the highest casualty count of the war, with 543 U.S. combat deaths. The Marines pushed through rows of courtyards and smoldering huts and tightened their stranglehold on the core of the Citadel. Much of the fighting was at bayonet range. The grunts used CS gas, and the NVA responded with their own mortar-delivered gas. It had been the first time in the war both sides fought wearing gas masks at the same time.

Eventually, tactical air restrictions were rescinded, and bombardments from the warships of the 7th Fleet, 14 miles off coast, pounded the north side with 200 shells a day. Marine A-4 Skyhawks and Navy F-8 Crusaders dropped bombs and napalm along the northeast wall of the Citadel. Light observation planes and Huey gunships dotted the sky during breaks in the weather.

Soon, the Citadel was reduced to a corpse-strewn rubble. A madness infected the men with each successive battle and every mounting casualty. Navy and Coastguard coxswains ferried many of the KIAs and WIAs to the south side of Hue, and fresh piles of body bags waited each time the boats returned to the Bao Vihn Quay.

Like every other grunt, Latimere was scared, exhausted and hungry all the time, but now when he looked at the grunts, it was like looking in a mirror. Like Hines had said, he now saw his own thousand-yard stare looking back at him. As with everyone, he simply wanted to survive, get through one more day, a day at a time. Survive, survive. Saddle up. Move out. Get down. Pull back. Move out again. Move it, MOVE IT, MOVE IT! Latimere would do whatever he had to—except think about it.

Day after day, the Marines pushed on. The decomposing bodies of enemy soldiers lay in every corridor and in every courtyard. Carcasses lay in the open, exposed and disemboweled. There was talk about the plague.

***

For days, Latimere was shaken about Roark, but the shock had an even more profound effect on Hines. If anyone had ever seemed invulnerable in Nam, it was Roark. Hines first heard the news from Gunny Jerardi. His first reaction was predictable, and he smothered a glow of satisfaction. Hines hated Roark and had secretly hoped he would buy it. He had thought about it, yet a wash of paralysis hit him seconds later and left him with a dead, hollow feeling. Not sorrow, exactly, but an irrational sense of injustice, that he was being punished. There was no anchor anymore, nothing he could count on, and it frightened him more than ever. If Roark wasn't immune, who was? Roark getting hit made Hines feel all the more vulnerable. A couple days later, Bayer and Hemmings linked up with him. Bayer told Hines about Ehlo. Now, all the remaining CC's were with Delta Company. Hines left the CP. Once again, he felt compelled to be with Grimm.

***

There were days the Marines advanced only a few meters. They attacked and were repelled, ending up at night the same place they had started that morning. The only respites were at night when they wrapped themselves in ponchos and sprawled below the walls in the courtyards and muddy corridors. The air was grainy and gritty, and a heavy layer of black ash and sulfur formed a shroud over the city.

Battles raged inside the Citadel. Elements of the 1st Battalion, 1st Marines and 2nd Battalion, 5th Marines commenced sweeping the surrounding areas on the south side of Hue and ferreted out pockets of NVA and VC near the Phu Cam Canal. Trying to coordinate their actions with the ARVN proved to be one more screw up in a long line of screw ups. The first Marines to lose their lives did so not because of enemy fire, but because the ARVN had failed to warn them about a minefield they just planted.

At the same time, four battalions from the Army's 1st Air Cavalry Division began sweeping through the NVA command and supply posts west of the city in the La Chu Woods. Using infantry, air strikes and helicopter gunships, they wiped out the last of the NVA support units. Meanwhile, naval gunfire sledgehammered the heart of the Citadel with increasing ferocity. More and more, Marines fell from "short rounds" as they tightened their noose around the Imperial Palace.

The men marched in a daze. Their bodies bruised and swollen, pus oozing from open sores and ulcers. They reeked, the stench of their own rotting flesh moving with the gait of men walking on broken feet.

Nights were the worst. Communication took on bizarre forms and the men scarcely looked at one another. During the day, they relied on instinct, but at night everything was magnified. They flinched at every new sound.

In the morning, jarred from their sleeplessness, they were on the move again. It was always a matter of what would rouse them first, enemy fire or the gunny shouting at them to SADDLE UP. STAND BY. MOVE IT OUT! Marines in Hue couldn't decide which was worse.

***

Grimm heard the loud crack of the round in his ear and knew what to expect. He tensed for the shock to hit him. He had been through it before and waited for the pain to flood through him. Even Latimere, wincing in the tall grass next to him, was certain Grimm was hit. Another volley of rounds hacked through the grass and smacked into the mud around them. "MOVE." Grimm rolled over to get away from the spot where the NVA had them pinned. They stopped several meters away and hoped the enemy hadn't followed their movement in the folding grass.

"You hit?" Latimere's face was inches from the mud.

"I don't think so," Grimm exhaled and felt his body for wounds, half-expecting the pain to come even now. "Fucking weird, man."

Several grunts were hunkered near a wall and called for help with their casualties. Grimm got to his feet and ran, Latimere in tow. They helped pull the casualties into the alleyway while an NVA machine gun lashed at them from a bunker down the corridor. Latimere and another grunt fired in spurts as Grimm and the other grunts dragged the men into the courtyard behind them. Three grunts scrambled to the wall and poured out cover fire while the rest loaded the wounded in ponchos and carried them across the yard and laid them in the next alleyway.

Grimm looked around for help. Where the hell were the reinforcements who were supposed to push up behind them? No one in the courtyards, Grimm looked down the alley and saw it. He'd been drawn to the alley as if pulled by a magnet, praying he was somehow wrong. At the bend in the road he saw the mechanical mule crashed into a wall. The driver slumped over the wheel, Grimm headed to him and pulled back his head. Martinez had been shot full of holes, and it looked as if the NVA had continued to use him for target practice. Martinez's smile was frozen on his face.

***

Nighttime, and Latimere sat in a corner of one of the huts. The openings had been covered, and grunts heated their rations. A few had found candles in the vacated huts, as did Latimere. The young CC couldn't keep his eyes open and couldn't stop thinking. He blinked into the semi-darkness and wondered whether the fighting would ever end. He had lost ten pounds in seven days, his stomach ached, but like all the men, he forced himself to eat, too tired or superstitious to let his energy waste away. Mud packed thick on his utilities cracked off in lumps whenever he stood up or sat down.

Cold inside, he shivered and held his hands over the back of his neck—a trick Roark had taught him—and his whole body gradually felt warmer. He remembered other things Roark said—like taking Lan back to Danang with them, and how Roark shook his head when he caught him doe-eyed and smitten. Roark had once said, "War ain't so bad, it's love that's hell." Latimere thought about Lan, but it hurt more than gladdened him. There was no place for her here, and yet it was *her* world, not his. Everything was upside down.

Latimere reached into his bandolier for a C-ration chocolate bar. He still didn't believe he couldn't look up and see Roark standing there. It was Roark's spare bandolier and in one of the pouches, a folded wad of paper was squeezed tight against a magazine. He pulled it out. A letter.

My dearest Billy,

Honey, how are you? We are fine, except that you're not here. Are you safe and well? Every morning and night before I go to bed I think of you, Billy. And so does your father. We think of your smiling face and how confident and proud you looked when you told us you were going over there. I'm sorry, Billy, for making such a fuss the way mothers do. You know I never meant the things I said to you, and only said them because I was so frightened and hurt and had so many hopes for you, I couldn't bear to see you go. I should have known you would make your own decision because you were always such a headstrong boy and always had a mind of your own. I am so very proud of you, Billy, don't forget that. More than anything in the world, I want you to know I'm behind you in whatever you do. Please understand, Billy, it's just so hard on a mother when it's her only child. If I have any regret in my life, it's that I couldn't have more children who would turn out just like you. I have always believed in you, Billy. All the love in the world, Mother.

p.s. By the way, Arthur's heading over!

Latimere sat numb and trembling. He carefully folded the letter and put it back in the envelope as if it would crack if he held it too tightly. He scraped dried blood off the envelope with his thumbnail. A few scraps fluttered to the floor. It was Billy. All there was left of him. He gently put the letter back in his bandolier, when Billy's face, laughing and fearless, reared up inside him. He saw

Billy running through the desert boxing the stars, saw Billy at his side, always there, protecting him.

Latimere remembered when they were sophomores in high school, and after a late night date, Billy raced him across the desert to their private sanctuary.

Visibly excited, Billy's words flew out. "Artie, you won't believe it. Guess what?"

"What?"

"Remember I told you I wanted to see a girl pee? Well, last night I did! At first, when I asked her, she thought I was kidding, but I talked her into it. She was naked and had to pee and I followed her into the bathroom, and she did it. She peed right into the toilet, standing up, like a guy. I mean it was a stream, like a horse. She spread herself down there and let it go in a rush. I never knew girls could pee so hard. I thought it would come out more delicate, you know?"

Billy always came up with something new about girls.

Latimere remembered their senior year in high school, and the one girl—the only girl—Billy ever lost. At first she was dreamy over Billy, like all the rest. Even Billy was smitten. Billy had seen her a couple times, and on Valentine's Day, Latimere and Billy were walking to a party when along the way they saw Billy's girl with her girlfriends. Billy's face lit up and they walked up to them.

"Speak of the devil," she laughed.

"Kiss off," Billy said and grabbed Latimere and left.

Billy was upset and didn't understand. He thought it an insult. *"Speak of the devil,"* she had said, as though Billy was stalking or harassing her. Later, Billy found out what it actually meant, that it was a compliment, an admission that she was talking and thinking about him.

But that was after Billy graduated. The last few weeks of school she ignored him. The damage had been done.

Suddenly, a distant explosion jarred Latimere, and his smile gave way to hurt again, the reality of the moment and where he was. Latimere thought about Gladys, Billy's mother, and shuddered. He wondered whether she knew, though it was probably too soon. But mothers always know, and it frightened him. He wondered at the instant Billy died whether Gladys had felt anything, a slight tug or tiny wince when she was drying the dishes or sitting on the bed in his room.

Latimere's nerves were mangled, his insides tossed, and it was an effort just to blow out the candle. He backed himself into a corner to make himself small and sat in the dark where he couldn't be seen and couldn't be reached, and he couldn't be touched.

***

The offensive in the Citadel continued unceasingly. The engagements grew bloodier as Marines took more and more ground and drove the enemy into the Palace of Perfect Peace. As more Marine units pushed up from behind them, herds of civilian journalists and camera crews crossed the Perfume and headed for the front lines. They hunkered behind walls to film the grunts popping up and firing. And during lulls in the fighting, the camera crews mauled each other vying to shoot the bloodiest wound or to interview the most wretched and shell-shocked Marine. That morning, a cameraman shoved his camera into a grunt's face. His eyes bulged from fatigue. Skinny and pale, he winced as a corpsman applied a bandage to his leg.

"Can you talk?" the interviewer asked.

The grunt looked dumbly at him. "I guess."

The camera whirred and as the reporter popped questions. "Can you tell us what you're fighting for?"

"Huh?"

"Do you know what you're fighting for?"

The grunt's mouth hung open. He stammered nervously. "To stay alive," he said.

"Of course, but beyond that. What do you think you guys are fighting for? Do you know?"

"...Guess so," the grunt whispered under his breath.

"Well, what then? What are you fighting for?"

"For their freedom, I guess. At least, that's what I think."

"Speak up a little if you can, OK? This is for the folks back home."

"Sure," he hesitated.

"Just tell us what you think," the reporter said.

"What I think?"

"Yeah."

"I dunno. Right now?"

The reporter turned away, perturbed. "What about any of you other guys?"

A burst of AK-fire raked the wall. The cameraman dropped into the mud, and turned his camera on several grunts who returned fire. Then, he swung back to the grunt he was interviewing.

The grunt cringed at the sound of another volley. "Man, I just wanna go home and go to school. I just wanna go home," he said.

***

Late afternoon on February 27, Delta Company tried to pull back and regroup. During the worst fighting they had encountered with a desperate enemy, the Marines pursued them through rows of huts and houses, prepping them with grenades and then made fireteam rushes inside. They tossed frags into the houses, and the NVA hurled Chi-Com grenades as they ran outside and fled into the courtyards. Delta's CO had ordered his men back, but it was too noisy and chaotic to be heard. All the misery, pain, fatigue and hatred was now turned on the enemy with a vengeance. Like rats trapped in a maze, everyone scrambled and fired and ran like hell.

A machine gunner climbed on top of one of the huts and raked the courtyards. Ham left Latimere and ran outside, a grenade in each hand. He raced across the alleyway and hunkered behind a wall. A blur of automatic fire streamed overhead, and Ham heard voices beyond the wall jabbering in Vietnamese. He pulled the pin on a grenade and let the spoon fly, waited a couple seconds, and lobbed it over the wall. When it exploded, Ham heard screams and then saw two Marines rush through an opening, and he moved farther down the wall, pulling the pin on his other grenade and clasping the spoon.

The grunts behind him shouted, but Ham was oblivious. He inched closer to the opening, his throat hot when he swallowed, his eyes burning with sweat. He wanted to toss the grenade but was afraid he would hit his own men. Fire cracked in the courtyard and a grunt screamed. Ham tore through the opening and swung his blooper from side to side. He saw NVA soldiers flee across the yard and hurled the grenade, then fired his blooper. The explosions blew the enemy troops to the ground. Ham crunched down and stared through the tall grass, looking for any sign of movement. He couldn't tell whether they'd all been hit or were just lying low in the grass. All his senses concentrated in the quivering blooper in his hands.

Behind the wall, the grunts screamed. "Ham, god-dammit. Come on. We're pulling back." Ham started back, but the grunt who screamed earlier was in the tall grass at his feet, writhing in pain. Ham dug into his first-aid pouch and ripped open the bandage packet. One grunt was dead and the man he worked on had been hit in the hip. Goo oozed from his intestines, and there were white flecks of spleen in a puddle on the ground.

Ham scooted to his knees, but an NVA soldier sprang up in the yard behind him. Ham whirled and fired. The round hit the man in the chest and blew him against the wall. Other enemy soldiers lying in the grass popped up and started firing now. Ham hugged the ground as a volley of fire cracked over his head. Then, he rolled through the grass as more fire came from another direction. Automatic fire sprayed the opening and blocked his escape. Rounds spattered around him, hitting the wounded Marine in the neck. Ham rolled in the grass, stopped, then rolled several more times before lying still. He was able to get another round in the chamber without moving too much, but he froze on his belly when he heard rustling in front of him. Not looking behind him, he slid back prone. He eased back farther until there was nothing under the toes of his boots. Then, he inched sideways and looked behind him. A spider hole at his feet.

Every muscle in Ham's body tightened. Immobilized, he stared down the hole in horror. His heart pounded at his throat, and he listened for movement inside the hole.

It was growing dark, and that frightened him. Ham heard the Vietnamese calling around him, and behind him he heard the clamor of the Marines' withdrawal. Keep still, he told himself. He felt the cold charge of fear that he was now alone. Wouldn't anyone come looking? Did they know he was missing? Keep still, he told himself again. They'll come, he said.

Ham fought to clear his head. Shrill Vietnamese voices became louder, grew closer. He felt his body shrivel, and he slinked closer to the spider hole and looked in. Ham turned and saw someone move toward him through tall shafts of grass. He slipped his legs down the spider hole and braced for the shock of finding someone there. Small and cramped, Ham struggled to back in. In a moment, his feet hit bottom, and he tucked his head down. It was so tight and claustrophobic, he could barely move and could only manage sharp, little breaths. The walls were a vise around his chest.

Ham inched his head up and saw them clearly through the tall grass. Three NVA soldiers. The short one probed the grass with the muzzle of his rifle. They headed right for him and stopped two meters away. Ham heard his breath whoosh out in a rush. Now, he begged for darkness. If they spotted him, it was over. He wouldn't have a chance of getting his blooper free, not that he could use it at that close range, anyway.

Ham watched them, but he didn't focus too long or hard because he believed if he looked at something too long or hard it would look back at him. The hole was slimy and wet and smelled like a stagnant sewer. He could not believe how heavy and humid his own breath was. He saw worms inches in front of him moving in the muddy walls of the hole. God only knew what slithered down at his feet.

One of the NVA walked closer. Ham's insides curdled. He felt his thigh cramp and bit through his lip to keep from crying out. Writhing in pain, he rubbed his leg violently then saw the soldier squinting. Ham froze. Then, for no apparent reason, the NVA soldier turned and walked away.

Suddenly, 60mm mortars screamed down on the courtyard, and the enemy soldiers scrambled in all directions. Ham exploded with vicious glee! He winced as the mortars fell, but felt safe if he stayed in the hole. He heard the screams as the NVA fled the yard. *GET SOME*, he cried to himself. *GET SOME!*

Ham stayed low until the mortars ceased. Almost dark. A few minutes more, and he could make his move back to the unit. You're home free, man, he told himself.

At dark, Ham tried to rise up. His leg still pained him, and he paused. He would wait a few minutes more and give the men a chance to settle in the lines and not be so jumpy when he tried to slip back. He stretched and his foot slipped backward. He suddenly realized the hole turned into a tunnel behind him. Then, he heard something rustle. The small of his back constricted and he froze. Someone was down there. Suddenly, something sharp thrust into him and sucked the air out. His whole body jolted, and there was another, harder thrust as the bayonet pierced his liver. Ham's last view of this world was an inky night sky suddenly and intermittently punctuated by the flash of mortars.

***

At the ISO duty hut in Phu Bai, Capt. Pell bent over his desk and stared numbly at the latest casualty reports. He felt sick and impotent. Four men had been hit, at least four that he knew of, Sullivan, Wilson, Ehlo and finally Roark. God, he wished this stinking war was over.

In the outer office, MSgt. Grover was every bit as burdened as Pell, but it wasn't over the troops or casualty reports. He had already dealt with that. If his show of grief over Roark being hit seemed counterfeit, Grover admitted to no trace of pleasure, either. For the umpteenth time, he read the latest letter his son had written him. Four pages chastising everything he stood for. Grover could tolerate the preaching, he had heard it all before, but the last few lines in the letter sickened him.

"...Dad, I hope you don't think I'm just saying these things and going out and getting drunk and forgetting all about it, but you have to know what they're saying back here, and I feel it's my responsibility to tell you. Everybody wants to be part of the revolution in creating a new world. They're heroes, Dad. These people are really courageous, you've got to know that. They put everything on the line. One girl I met is a really free spirit. That's what she calls herself, Free Spirit. Everybody's choosing their own names for themselves, names that actually suit them. It's neat, don't you think? She really cares, Dad, about what's going on over there. It really upsets her. Anyway, I'll write again soon. Good luck, Freedom (my new name!)"

Chapter Nine

ELEMENTS OF THE 5th Marines had secured the final sector running the length of the Citadel's southeast wall. Only the Imperial Palace and inner gardens in the Citadel's core, and 200 meters of open ground between the Marines and the palace wall remained under Communist control.

Everyone knew the Imperial Palace was the final objective in the mopping-up stage, but nobody knew what to make of it. There were reports that the last surviving elements of six NVA battalions, despite orders to fight and die in place, made their escape to the west. For two days there had been rumors about a crack company of Black Panther ARVN being rushed into position to make the final assault on the Imperial Palace.

Despite the rumors, nobody from Delta had seen the Black Panthers. The Marines of Delta Company saddled up, resigned that they would lead the final assault. There were a lot of mixed emotions and sentiments. Some men prepared for the worst. Everybody had the jitters and expected one last bloodbath—not inside the Imperial Palace itself, but in traversing the 200 open meters of ground to get there. Others simply set their teeth and sucked it up one last time to finish what they started. There was a hardcore minority of men who welcomed the sadistic pleasure and looked forward to routing the last pockets of NVA trapped within the Citadel's hub, but in fact, they really didn't expect much contact.

Latimere, who had felt doped for days, sat on a barrel where the troops were mustered near one of the Citadel's interior walls. Roark's departure had sucked most of the life out of him, and Ham and Billy Huff had sapped the rest. Marines found Ham the next morning when they swept through the courtyard. Balled up and stiff, his head lay face down in the mud at the top of the spider hole. There was a trickle of blood at the corner of his mouth, his eyes yellow and locked open. Ham's death drained any reserve Latimere thought he had left.

Latimere hiked his pack higher on his shoulders and checked magazine pouches. He had the same expression of weariness and battle-hardness as men who had been in Vietnam much longer. Three weeks in Hue had proven the equivalent of what some grunts saw in an entire tour.

Grimm walked up and tapped one of the frag grenades that Latimere had attached to his cartridge belt. "Where's your camera?"

"I lost it."

"Come on," said Grimm, "let's check the CO, find out what's happening."

They headed for the CP. Lt. Lidyard, who had taken command of Delta Company when Capt. Donlon was hit, was talking on the net. When they got within earshot, the lieutenant moved off, his radioman shuffling behind him. Grimm and Latimere couldn't hear what he said, but his body language suggested both shock and bewilderment. The lieutenant bit his lip. "Copy. This is six-acting, out."

Lt. Lidyard shoved the handset at his radioman and walked back to the CP. He was about to brief his Gunny to pass the word, then decided against it. Better fucking well do it himself, he thought.

"ALL RIGHT. YOU PEOPLE LISTEN UP. WE JUST GOT A CHANGE IN ORDERS. WE'RE PULLING BACK. BE READY TO MOVE IN ONE-ZERO MIKES."

The grunts stared at him.

"PASS IT ON," the gunny shouted.

At first, the grunts were elated, but then they suspected there probably wouldn't be any contact anyway and wondered why they were being yanked out.

"How d'ya like that shit," someone said.

"Good enough for me."

"What the fuck is this?"

"Screw it. There's no gooks left here anyways."

"Yeah? So suddenly we're turds again."

"So what."

"So maybe I don't like it."

"You're brain-dead. You don't like it, you go ahead and stay. Me, I can't make my hat quick enough."

"STAND BY," the lieutenant shouted.

Across the 200 meters of open ground, near the large wall surrounding the Imperial Palace, a neatly dressed company of ARVN soldiers advanced through the clearing, firing sporadically. Some carried ladders to scale the wall, while others vaulted through the holes already blasted in it. There was no enemy fire. Behind the point squads, a South Vietnamese camera crew carried tape recorders and movie cameras.

Confused, Latimere broke away from Grimm and headed for Lt. Lidyard. Grimm followed.

"LET'S MOVE," Lidyard called.

"YOU HEARD THE LIEUTENANT," Gunny Jerardi echoed. "LET'S GO. ON THE DOUBLE. MOVE OUT."

Latimere stopped before the lieutenant. "Excuse me, sir."

"What is it, Marine."

"Just wondering what's going on."

"Who are you?"

"Marine correspondents, sir," Latimere said.

"Well, here's one flag-raising ceremony you won't be covering."

"Why not?"

"Because there's not going to be one."

Troops shuffled past them and slowed to overhear.

"GET A MOVE ON," the lieutenant barked. "Gunny, keep these men moving."

Gunny Jerardi rode the men. "PICK UP YOUR FEET. KEEP MOVING."

"Why *aren't* we raising the flag?" Latimere asked.

Lidyard whirled on him hard. "What's in a flag-raising?"

"Maybe nothing, but we came this far."

"Regulations state no American flag can be flown in Vietnam unless accompanied by a South Vietnamese flag. You should know that, Marine. Orders are that no Americans are to set foot inside the Imperial Palace. It's an ARVN show now."

Latimere reeled. "We spill our guts and they raise their flag?"

"That's the size of it. I don't like it any better than you, but there it ends. There's a little factor of South Vietnamese morale to be figured in. They need their own heroes to look up to. If that's what will make the difference, then that's what we'll do. Wars aren't won by firepower anymore, but by politics."

It was too much to think about after everything Latimere had been through. Most of the company had filed past them, and Lt. Lidyard started forward. "You, too. Let's go," he said to the correspondents.

Latimere's face turned blue as if he'd stopped breathing. "Negative. No, sir."

"What's that?" Lidyard said.

"No sir. I'm not going anywhere, except in there."
He pointed to the palace.

"That's a negative, Marine."

"Oh, no it ain't."

Latimere ripped through his utility pockets for his press pass. He held it up. "See this? Means I can go anywhere to get a story. No disrespect sir, but..."

"I'M GIVING YOU AN ORDER."

"YES SIR, YOU CAN, BUT I'M A GODDAMN CORRESPONDENT, AND I HAVE A PASS WHICH SAYS I CAN GO ANYWHERE, AND I'VE GOT MY OWN ORDERS."

"GET BACK HERE, GODDAMMIT."

Latimere headed across the clearing. Several quick bursts of M-16 fire erupted from the palace grounds.

"MARINE!" Lt. Lidyard shouted.

"I'll get him," Grimm said.

"DRAG HIS ASS BACK HERE!"

Grimm charged after him. Latimere reached the wall. Scores of ARVN were already inside the palace but the heavy firing suddenly stopped. More ARVN climbed the ladders and sat laughing on the wall. There was a huge hole in the wall from an artillery shell, and a platoon of ARVN were crammed outside it.

Latimere heard a string of commands shouted through a megaphone, and the ARVN poured through the hole into the palace grounds.

Latimere pushed through their ranks. Grimm reached the back of the platoon and bulled ahead after him. They got as far as the hole when they heard another string of commands, and the ARVN turned around and stampeded back out the hole. Latimere and Grimm flattened against the side walls and let the ARVN swarm past them. When he could budge, Latimere squeezed forward again. It took Grimm longer, but he maneuvered through the hole and joined Latimere inside.

So much confusion and staging went on that nobody noticed Latimere. Surreal, the mock battle only registered in waves.

A South Vietnamese director garbed in black beret and civilian khakis, shouted through a megaphone. On cue, the ARVN streamed through the hole again, charging across the grounds and firing in the air. A yellow and red striped South Vietnamese flag was hoisted up the flagpole.

The director shouted and waved his arms ordering the troops back. They pulled down the flag and scrambled back out the hole again.

Abruptly, another assault began. The director screamed through the megaphone and a handful of troops fell to the ground faking bullet-wounds. Overacting, one soldier clutched his chest, sank to his knees and writhed in foolish agony. Latimere's chest sank, and the black hole that was his mouth became a frozen scream when the young ARVN soldier keeled over and sprawled softly on the ground. The ARVN raised his head up and caught Latimere's eyes. The hint of a smile crossed his delicate face.

Part Four

FLIPSIDE

All of that seems so long ago now. In two weeks it will be November and the weather is turning cold again. They still call me Babysan, but only in jest, and only the guys who have been here awhile and imagine that they are close to me. The rain beats down hard and it is a crazy time. It is the first time in months I have needed to talk.

The war is not going well. Everybody is much more negative these days. Aside from everything else that didn't go exactly as planned, you probably already know that Tet didn't end the war. Or maybe it did, insofar as it was the turning point, but even though we won every major battle in the offensive, we've been hearing for months how public opinion back home has turned against us.

It's funny I guess. Talk about funny, since we're talking about Hue, here's another funny thing I'm not clear on. In the months following Tet we discovered the North Vietnamese troops had slaughtered or buried alive more than 3,000 civilians whose bodies were uncovered in numerous mass graves around the city. Only the executions barely made the headlines, at least nothing like the revelation of the My Lai massacre of more than a hundred civilians by one U.S. asshole Army infantry platoon. My Lai got the big ink, while Hue and her victims dropped out of sight. I guess it's understandable when you know everybody's slant on the war.

Just one more funny thing and I'll drop it. It also has to do with Tet—not in Hue, but in Saigon. I just found out about it myself and I wonder if you think it's as funny as I do. You know that famous photo by Eddie Adams? You know the one, where all of a sudden this South Vietnamese General pulls out his pistol and shoots this hand-

cuffed VC point blank in the head and the blood comes spurting out? The famous photo that made all the news? Which drove one more nail in the coffin of our involvement over here because it was so graphic? But here's the funny part: All the newspapers printed the photo but not the story behind it. It turned out that the VC had just killed the general's best friend's family, a major's wife and his six children. Nobody had much interest in running the story though, considering everybody's attitude these days. But maybe you don't think that's as funny as I do?

But a lot has happened since then as you can imagine. One thing is I'm on my second six-month extension over here. Only because I have more time left on my enlistment and, like a lot of the guys who broke me in, I've come around to thinking it's probably better over here than pulling duty in the States.

I guess I needed to talk more than I realized. I never intended to go into this stuff. What I really want is just to fill you in on some of the guys, what little I've heard about them, since I'm the only one left that you know anymore.

Hue was pretty heavy, though. Even though it was the biggest battle of the war, I still remember the good times, and especially all the guys, and how absolutely green I was! But except for getting all that experience I was so hungry for, I don't think I've changed much. Maybe you can tell, but I don't think so.

Everything lumped together, things aren't that bad over here. I've been lucky. Only a couple pieces of shrapnel, which everybody in the field gets and sometimes doesn't even know it until the slivers work their way to the surface, months later.

Most of the time I just do my job by rote, and when I get back to write my stories in the rear, there's always a few good nights with the newer CCs getting polluted at the

Thunderbird Club and telling sea stories, or telling them stories about Hines which never gets dull. If anything, I wish there were more characters among the CCs now, like it used to be. Everyone was such a renegade back then! Remember those guys? But it's like everything else in life, it's cyclical. All in all, it's as good as you make it. It's only one or two times when my chest starts beating violently that I imagine it to be the effect of some unsuspecting drug I have been slipped that won't let go of me.

What else? You might wonder if I have written anything lately? Well, I haven't, no. Except pieces for the Marine Corps rag, The Sea Tiger. *But not any poetry or stuff. Not one single poem. I think it's pretty much a thing of the past. Which is one way I've changed, I admit.*

As for the new guys, there's not much worth telling. I'm the one with the most time in-country now and some of the cherries can be pretty much of a pain. What the hell do you talk to them about? So you just keep silent. You feel like a goddamn grandfather bouncing a grandkid on his knee and telling sea stories. So you don't.

I still get letters from a few of the guys though, although not very often anymore. In fact the last letter I got was practically two months ago, from Bayer. He's doing fine. Surfing and working on his tan at the beach. He's got a night job as an assistant editor for a newspaper in Santa Monica. He says his skin is chapped and orangish ever since he got back from Nam, for some reason or other. But his number one complaint is that he's going prematurely bald and can't get his hair to grow and it's futile trying to get a piece of ass back there if you don't have long hair!

So that's from Bayer.

I checked the records on my old best friend Billy Huff, just to be sure, but sure enough he was dead. It's funny how your childhood passes before you, like when they say your life passes before you when you're near death. I just never thought it would happen when you were only twenty.

I've never heard from some of the guys. Hines, for instance. Grimm has been pretty good about filling me in when he writes. He says Hines is going to school in San Diego, studying under Herbert Marcuse. He says Hines has these phony medals on top of his mantle, even though he's now passionately against the war. Which only goes to prove that a fanatic can change his mind, but never his fanaticism.

Roark, from everything Grimm says, acts the same as always, just like you knew he would. Like the world is his oyster. He's still the only one I knew that Nam never really changed. He's doing OK though, and just walks with a slight limp. Apparently it's pretty well knocked him out of the acting business, so he's spending most of his time writing instead. He's been trying to peddle a screenplay about Tet, but nobody's interested in anything that doesn't show a vet going berserk or something.

Well, that's about it, I guess. I just wanted to fill you in on some of the guys.

Oh, yeah, I almost forgot: Lan. You remember her, the girl I met in Hue—the first girl I ever did it with? Well, after Tet was over, after they started pulling us out, I tried to find her. Of course I checked the yellow house again and a lot of other places too, like the university. But I never found her. Well, after a lot of time passed, I figured it wasn't in the cards for us to see each other again, when a month ago I was walking in downtown Danang, and I was sure I saw her walking on the other side of the street. She had her back to me and I ran after her, calling her name, and caught up with her. I'm not even ashamed to say my heart skipped a beat. But when she turned around it wasn't her. It was someone else. But she was like her in some ways though, because she had beautiful almond eyes and she was a whore. And in one way she was even better, because we had a helluva night together. A helluva good night.

-30-

About the Author

 As a Marine Noncommissioned Officer, Mike Stokey volunteered for three consecutive tours in Vietnam during which he was involved in some of that conflict's most brutal fighting, including the Tet Offensive at Hue and the siege at Khe Sanh. He is highly decorated as a result of line combat and was wounded in action.

During these tours of duty he forged a close and lasting relationship with Dale Dye (Capt., USMC, Ret.) and volunteered to help Dye in the formation and functioning of Warriors, Inc. Over the years with Warriors he has served in virtually every advisory capacity and has been the principal advisor and/or assistant for Warriors in all military entertainment endeavors from major motion pictures to video games.

In civilian pursuits, he has worked as an Associate Producer for "STUMP THE STARS" (aka "PANTOMIME QUIZ"), and has written more than 60 half-hour animated television shows for children including *He-Man* and *Gulliver's Travels*.

Printed in Great Britain
by Amazon.co.uk, Ltd.,
Marston Gate.